Manhattan Dinner Club
Volume 2

Jean C. Joachim

Moonlight Books

SEDUCING HIS HEART

(Manhattan Dinner Club, 2)

Second Edition

Jean C. Joachim

A Moonlight Books Novel
Second Edition
Seducing His Heart

Cover design by Dawné Dominique
Edited by Sherri Good
Proofread by Renee Waring

PUBLISHER
Moonlight Books

Dedication

THIS BOOK IS DEDICATED to rescued pugs everywhere, and pugs awaiting rescue...and to the people who rescue them, pug angels all.

Acknowledgment

Many thanks for your help and support in the creation of this book: Larry Joachim, Marilyn Lee, Kathleen Ball, Sandy Sullivan, my Tuesday Tales friends, JJ's Book Buddies, my editor, Tabitha Bower, my proofreader, Renee Waring, Sandy Sullivan, and to my readers.

SEDUCING HIS HEART

Jean C. Joachim

Chapter One

THE ELEVATOR DOORS opened, revealing a man and woman in a heated clinch, kissing as if the end of the world had arrived. Bess Cooper cleared her throat. The man cracked an eyelid open and turned his head slightly. He eased the woman away and cast a sardonic eye at Bess.

"Who the hell are you? If you've come to see the apartment, it's been sold," he said, straightening up.

"I live here. Who the hell are you?" Bess rested her fists on her hips.

"I live here, too." The man pulled his tie loose and unbuttoned the top button of his shirt.

"So, you're the new owner of fifteen B?" *Tall, lean, gorgeous black hair. Familiar face.*

"They told me a little, old lady lived in fifteen A." He pulled a handkerchief from his pocket and wiped his mouth.

"'They' is a real estate agent?"

He nodded.

"Big surprise. An agent who lies," she sniffed, shifting her weight. "You're my new neighbor?"

"Guilty. And you're the little, old lady?" His cool gaze traveled her length and back in a heartbeat. A slow grin curled his perfect lips. "Remarkably well-preserved."

Bess chuckled in spite of herself, covering her mouth.

"Hey, Whit..." The brunette in the elevator tugged on his lapel.

"Whit? Now I remember where I've seen you. Whitfield Bass. You do the news, right?"

He smiled and executed a half bow. "Again, guilty as charged." He placed his palm on the lower back of the woman with him, and they stepped out. "This is Candy Wayne. And you are?" At the mention of her name, the rail-thin woman with short, dark hair snaked her arm around Whit's waist, moving up against him.

"Bess Cooper." She extended her hand.

Whit shook it, but Candy remained glued to his side, treating Bess to a frosty stare.

"Nice to meet you both." Bess smiled.

"I've seen you before." Whit stroked his stubbly chin.

"I model. What do you do?" Candy shifted her weight.

"I cook."

"Oh, you're a housekeeper." The brunette raised her eyebrows.

"Got it!" Whit snapped his fingers. "Not a housekeeper, a baker. On TV. *Baking with Bess*, right?" His face lit up.

Bess blushed. "Guilty."

"Aren't you a little chubby for TV?" Candy raised thick, fake, black lashes to shoot a disapproving glance at Bess's hips.

"Not according to my producer." Bess entered the elevator and pushed the button for the lobby.

"You don't look chubby to me," Whit commented, resting his gaze on her chest. "Just right," he said, as the doors closed.

Bess chuckled as the car descended. When she reached the lobby, her favorite doorman, Crash, manned the desk.

"'Morning, miss." He tipped his hat.

"Got a new neighbor. What's your opinion, Crash?" She sidled up to the man in uniform.

"Not too friendly. Dates those fashion models. Just another celebrity to me, miss."

"Is he a serial dater?"

"This guy gets around." Crash blushed at his own words.

Bess cocked an eyebrow. "Doesn't surprise me. Famous newscaster. Handsome guy."

"Now, don't you go falling for him, Miss Bess. He's a player. You're a nice gal. Hate to see you get hurt by his type."

She patted his arm. "Thanks, Crash, that means a lot. I'm immune. Besides, I've got Terry, and I'm not a serial dater."

He chuckled. "No, ma'am. You stick to one guy. At least one guy at a time."

Now, it was Bess's turn to flush. "I try, Crash."

"This guy. The cop. He's okay. I like him."

"Glad you approve. See you later."

Crash smiled and tipped his hat again. Bess stepped out into the pleasant, mid-September, morning air.

Her brow furrowed as she wondered what it would be like sharing the hallway with a man who had hot and cold running women. While the image of his straight jaw, clear eyes that seemed to strip her naked, and great body swam through her brain, an alarm sounded. *He's a womanizer. Stay away.*

She straightened her shoulders as she proceeded up Central Park West to 81st Street then turned left, heading to Zabar's. Entering the gourmet food store, she headed for the coffee section. After buying small quantities of several brands, she picked up an assortment of teas. She had filled two grocery bags by the time she finished.

Bess picked them up, surprised at how light they were. *Tea weighs nothing.* She marched down the street, lost in thought about what to make with each beverage.

Crash opened the door to The Wellington. Bess nodded to him as she continued on her way upstairs. Her mind on her baking, she didn't see Candy Wayne barreling toward her. The skinny young woman plowed into Bess, knocking her bags to the ground. The contents scattered.

"Broken heel." Candy held up half of a four-inch spiked pump before she teetered onto the elevator. When Bess swore under her breath, her pug, Dumpling, barked.

The woman looked disheveled, top half-tucked in, skirt askew. "Sorry. Sorry," the model mumbled as the doors shut. The elevator descended, leaving Bess to clean up the mess. She heard scratching at her door and the squeaking of hinges as the one down the hall opened. Whit, wearing a fluffy white terry robe, and probably nothing else, stuck his head out.

"What the hell?"

"My dog. When she hears me, she barks." Bess, on her knees, swept boxes of tea and bags of coffee together.

"What have you got? A Rottweiler? A shepherd?"

Bess laughed. "A pug. She *thinks* she's a Rottweiler."

"A pug?" He chuckled. "Do you need a hand?"

"I'm fine."

"Did Candy do this?"

Bess clamped her lips together in a fine line and continued to scoop her purchases up and dump them in the bag. Dumpling kept barking.

Whit padded barefoot out of his apartment and knelt down next to Bess. He picked up several items and read the labels. "Chai tea, Kona coffee, Loganberry jam..."

Bess plucked each container out of his hand one-by-one and whisked it into the bag. "I'm doing some research on coffee and tea."

"How interesting. My research involves sifting through dry, boring article after dry, boring article on the Internet."

"You do what you do, and I do what I do."

As she stood up, he handed her a package of black licorice. "Bet we're the last two people in the city who like this stuff," he said.

"I doubt it." She stiffened.

As he leaned over, his robe parted, and she got a good view of his chest—totally touchable, firm, but not bodybuilder hard. Black chest hair in moderation made her fingertips tingle at the thought of running them up his pecs. With an effort, she ripped her gaze from his body and directed it to the cartons of food still on the floor.

"Thanks," she said, reluctant to be beholden to him, even for the retrieval of one item.

"It's the least I can do after Candy barged into you."

Bess gave a curt nod and headed for her apartment. The minute the door opened, the small pug raced out. She headed straight for Whit, barking her head off. He laughed but backed up.

"I hate clichés, but aren't you going to call off your dog?" he asked, his back to the wall.

"Dumpling! Dumpling, come, baby girl." Bess called. "She's a ferocious little beast. Especially when she sees a certain type of man."

"Oh?" He cocked an eyebrow. "And what type would that be?"

"Players."

Bess stifled a smile. After casting a suspicious eye at Whit, the dog retreated, panting, and obeyed orders. "She wouldn't hurt you." The pug closed her mouth and faced her mistress.

"Really? Are you sure?" The crease in his forehead eased. He bunched his robe together and tightened the sash.

"Your girlfriend needs a lesson in manners." Bess picked up a bag in each hand. Dumpling kept an eye on Whit as she accompanied Bess.

"Oh, she's not my girlfriend."

Bess raised her brow. "Could've fooled me."

"In fact, it was only our second date. A long one, perhaps, but only the second. I play the field." Again, under his sexy stare, she felt naked. Instinctively, her arm covered her chest.

"Good for you. Watch those STD's, they can be nasty."

"Speaking from experience?" He cocked an eyebrow.

Heat rose through her cheeks as her temper flared. She dropped both bags, causing Dumpling to start barking again. "You've got a lotta nerve."

"You're the one who brought it up. Not me. I'm a great believer in safe sex. Are you?"

"None of your business." Bess gathered her belongings and whistled for Dumpling, who quieted down immediately and followed along.

"Will I need to use hand sanitizer every time I pass your door?" He smirked.

"Hilarious! Can't understand why you didn't go into stand-up comedy instead of news. Let's see...maybe because you're *not* funny?" She stepped back into her apartment and slammed the door. His laugh was loud enough to hear through her door.

Frowning and muttering to herself, she lugged the food into the kitchen with Dumpling trotting behind. The dog curled up on her small, fluffy bed and was snoring before Bess got everything unpacked. She brewed a pot of coffee and sat down with a pad and pen.

The buzzer broke into her thoughts. She picked up the intercom and okayed the visitor with Crash. Her assistant, Ned Lester, walked in. She never kept the door locked, figuring, with such vigilant doormen, she'd never need to.

"Where have you been? I've left ten messages. Did you need me to pick up anything on my way over?"

"Got everything myself. I was in the hall. Damn new neighbor. His snotty girlfriend plowed right into me. Then, he came out to help pick things up."

Ned's eyes lit up. "Was he cute?"

"Aren't you taken?"

"You didn't answer my question. Not for me. For you."

"I guess you could say he's good looking enough. If you like his type."

"What type?" Ned perched on a bar stool at the counter, his pad ready, pen in hand, and his blue eyes gazing at Bess.

"I mean, black hair, gray eyes, good bod."

"Wow. Better than Serge?"

"He was annoying." Bess returned to the coffeemaker and poured a cup for Ned.

"Now, you're lying. I can always tell. You get a little twitch under your left eye. Only for a second. But it's there."

"Okay. He's gorgeous. But he's a womanizer. Besides, I have Terry."

"Do you? Is it still once a week and no overnights?"

"So?" Bess sipped her brew.

"Seems you two are kinda stuck."

"I like him. He's a cop. Makes me feel safe. I'm happy."

"Are you?" Ned stared, but Bess avoided his eyes.

"Let's get to work. How to frame this? Best desserts for coffee and best for tea?"

"Maybe we can get two shows out of this idea instead of only one." He scribbled away.

"Good thinking. Hmm, what does go best with coffee? Anything chocolate."

"Oh, God. Chocolate. Here I go. And, by the way, you're not fooling me. I'm letting you change the subject...for now." Ned grinned.

Short with brown hair and blue eyes, Her assistant, Ned, was attractive, but out of Bess's reach, as he was gay. He took good care of her, kept her secrets, and shared her love of food. Ned was more family than her real family.

Bucking to become her sous chef, Ned would have been the perfect choice. While she was dying for him to be promoted, she dreaded it, too. She relied on his support, and he never questioned her judgment. They were the perfect team. Bess hated the idea of breaking in a new assistant.

Ned perused row after row of cookbooks on her shelves, seeking one specializing in desserts. Within half an hour, they tossed ideas and recipes back and forth. Slowly, the episode took shape, pushing all thoughts about the attractive, obnoxious Whitfield Bass from her mind.

Once they had decided on dishes and recipes, they made a shopping list. Ned headed for the store while Bess took a break. She strolled to the window with her mug. Dumpling pushed to her feet, stretched, then padded over to join Bess. Her choices of possible desserts were numerous enough to make her confident they'd find a few outstanding ones to suit the show.

Her mind turned back to her new neighbor. *He's trouble for any single woman. What about Terry? I don't even have him twice a week.* She chewed a nail then stopped, horrified.

"How many times have I told you to stop this disgusting habit?" Ned entered, carrying two bags.

"I know, I know. I'm sorry. I wasn't thinking."

"Your hands and nails show. You can't be ripping at them with your teeth." He gently slapped her hand then raised it to kiss.

"You're right. I forget. Worrying about how I look on camera is the worst part of this job. When will I be able to bite the hell out of my nails and no one'll care?"

"When you're unemployed." He retrieved the package he'd dropped at the door and carried it into the kitchen. As he unpacked, he chattered away. "What were you so wrapped up in?"

"Nothing. Thinking. About life."

"Your life?"

"Butt out, Ned. Now, let's melt this chocolate with the European butter and see how they blend. We'll need some salt, because the butter is sweet. Only a whisper," she said, sliding her apron over her head and tying it behind her back.

GRINNING, WHIT CLOSED his front door. *What a spitfire across the hall. Little old lady, yeah, right. Bet she's great in bed, once she gets over her bad attitude. Great body, too. Supermodels are okay, but bony as hell. No meat. Nothing to squeeze.*

Sexually satisfied from his morning romp with Candy and freshly showered, Whit dressed for work. Before his mind became tangled up with news stories and a book he was working on in his spare time, he stopped to check his calendar to see who'd be decorating his arm.

Hmm. Katarina. Italian movie star. She's got a temper. Dinner. Dancing? Then sex? He smiled to himself. Having a stable of available women was perfect. He never had to dine or sleep alone. The one thing he swore he'd never have on his bucket list was marriage and kids. *Never. Not gonna put some poor kid through the same hell I had. No way.*

Supermodels fit the bill. They were so absorbed in their ambition and their careers marriage was not on their radar. The thought of ruining their shape with a pregnancy made his bed partners nauseous. So, he had to forego permanent companionship, devotion, and friendship, so what? His life was regulated. He did what he wanted, when he wanted, and with whom he wanted. Still, an empty feeling lingered. His perfect life wasn't quite enough, and Whit didn't have a clue.

Katarina had been difficult the last time they'd gone out. She had been demanding, criticizing the five star restaurant he had taken her to, and a chilly partner in bed. *Time to trade her in. No, not for Bess. Too close. Never start something with someone who lives on the same floor. All I need is a stalker across the hall.* He grinned. *She doesn't seem like the type to stalk me. Slap me, maybe. Stalk me? Doubt it.*

He'd started down the hall when a heavenly aroma assaulted his nose. *Chocolate? Fresh coffee?* His stomach rumbled. *Yum.* A vision of spreading warm chocolate with his fingers on certain parts of Bess's body then licking it off made his groin twitch. *I'll bet she knows everything there is to know about sweets. And I know lots of ways to consume them she probably hasn't even tried.*

The ding of the elevator brought him out of his reverie. He sighed and traveled to the ground floor. Raising his hand in a half-wave to the doorman, Whit directed his feet down Central Park West to the television studios of Eagle Broadcasting.

While he walked, he wondered about Bess. *Will great smells always be coming out of her place? Will she invite me in to try some of her stuff?* A salacious chuckle escaped his mouth as he imagined a tasting at her place where she was the dessert.

Once he was immersed in his work, he forgot about Bess and the chocolate. He worked hard, trying to nail down the details of a story from Asia. He'd applied to *New York News Review* for a job as a foreign correspondent, the perfect job. Being on the move, he couldn't have attachments. He was hoping for Hong Kong, far away from home.

He took particular care over stories from the Far East, figuring each one was like a job interview with *NY News Review*. When he finished his broadcast, he checked his watch, caught a taxi, and met Katarina on the East side.

Dinner was a long and tiresome affair. Whit tried to focus on her rantings about her manager and the director of a movie she wanted to do, but his mind kept wandering. Her screeching criticism hurt his ears. After an intense day, he longed for something softer and more soothing. A cup of exquisite hot chocolate or a piece of sinful devil's food cake—to nourish his body and soul – would do nicely.

The vibes from Katarina weren't good, turning him off. While her body wouldn't quit, he would. Over coffee, she shot him a salacious look.

"So, we go back to your place or mine?"

"Not tonight. I've got an early day tomorrow." An early day never stopped him before. Lying through his teeth, Whit signaled for the check.

Katarina stuck out her lower lip in a most unattractive way. Her pouty face confirmed his decision to get away.

"But I was counting on it." Her whiny voice grated on his nerves.

"Sorry. Another time."

He paid the bill, put her in a cab, and hopped in one himself. On the way to his apartment, Whit stopped and sniffed. The faint smell of chocolate and coffee lingered in the hallway. He took a deep breath, closing his eyes, and was practically knocked down when Bess barreled out of her place with Dumpling in tow. The baker bounced off his chest.

He grasped her arms, to keep her from falling. She looked up into his eyes. Her large, blue orbs drew him in. He froze, his fingers digging into her. Then, Dumpling barked before assaulting him, sinking her teeth into his leg and pulling, throwing her head from side-to-side rapidly.

"Dumpling!" Bess yelled, tearing her gaze from his. Her eyes widened as she watched her dog tear a hole in the bottom of his pants. "Oh my God! I'm so sorry." She jerked on the leash, and the pug dropped the cloth and backed up.

"It's nothing." He released Bess.

"She's ripped your pants. I'll replace the suit."

"Don't worry about it."

"She's my dog, and I'm responsible. Let me get my checkbook." She turned.

"Please." He placed his hand on her arm. "I can have it fixed or get a new one myself."

"I insist."

"It's an expensive suit."

"I never walk away from my responsibilities."

"Honestly." He waved at her. "Forget it."

"How much?" She narrowed her eyes and rested one hand on her hip.

He sighed. "Three thousand dollars."

"Three thousand dollars! Is it made of spun gold?" Her eyebrow shot up.

"The price of a good Italian suit. I told you, don't worry about it."

"You think I don't have money to burn? I can afford it. No sweat."

"No reason for you to shell out three grand for a tiny hole made by...what's the dog's name?"

"Dumpling."

"Dumpling?" Whit doubled over with laughter.

"It's not funny," Bess huffed.

"Oh, yes it is! She *is* a little dumpling, too."

"She can be pretty ferocious. Don't underestimate her. Look what she did to your pants." Bess pointed.

"World's tiniest hole made by world's smallest dog." He gasped for breath.

Whit knelt down and held out his hand. Dumpling eyed him suspiciously before she inched closer to sniff. He stayed still, waiting for the okay from the pug before he petted her.

"She's adorable." He gave her a gentle scratch behind the ears.

"I think so." Bess smiled. Dumpling licked Whit's hand, officially declaring him a friend.

"I'll take these to the tailor, and, if you want, you can pay to have them re-woven. Okay?"

"Fine."

"What were you cooking before? I swear I smelled chocolate and coffee."

"Good sniffer. I made both."

"Making chocolate?"

"Making some chocolate desserts, and coffee—combining them. Mocha. But you're not interested in the experiments of a lowly baker when you have world affairs on your mind." She turned toward the elevator. "And I still have to walk my dog."

He grabbed her arm. "But I am interested. I find dessert a lot more fascinating than world politics. Do you ever have tastings, or samplings, or whatever at your house?"

She cocked an eyebrow at him. "Are you wangling an invitation?"

"Any time you need a guinea pig, I'm here."

She chuckled. "I'll remember your offer. See ya." She stepped into the elevator with Dumpling. Whit went inside and removed his pants to examine the small tear. He smirked. *Gives me another reason to see her. Ring her doorbell. Maybe I'll get some of those desserts she's preparing.*

The next morning, he donned running gear. As he was about to go for a spin in Central Park, his phone rang. It was Elsa.

"Friday, Whit?"

"Absolutely." He leaned against the wall and envisioned the tall, cool blonde naked. His mouth watered.

"Vunderful. See you then."

Whit put his cell away and made a face. *Another vegan meal. Ugh. What's so wrong with steak, anyway? Hell, a date's a date.* He shrugged his shoulders and hit the street. After his run, he headed for the tailor's before stopping at the drugstore to refill his supply of condoms. While he didn't expect much stimulating conversation from Elsa, he did expect to get laid.

I wonder if Bess ever cooks steak. How about the best dessert with steak? How about inviting me over for a taste? How about tasting together, naked? He shook his head. *Stop thinking about her. She probably wants to find some nice, quiet guy and settle down. Have two point five kids. House in the 'burbs. Picket fence.* He shuddered.

His taste buds cried out for steak. Whit stopped at the deli for the best Philly cheesesteak in Manhattan. "Hey, Mike. Got any bones back there?"

The man behind the counter stopped slicing meat. "Bones?"

"Yeah, like for a dog? A small dog?"

Chapter Two

"WHAT DO YOU MEAN, SICK? No one gets sick in September," Bess paced.

"Well, I am." Ned sneezed into the phone.

"Hey, keep it to yourself."

"Thanks for the ton of sympathy."

"I'm sorry. I'll make chicken soup and have it delivered."

"Thank you." He sniffled.

"I'm making the mocha pie, the pudding, and the cake. I need you to taste it."

"Even if I was well enough to come over, I can't taste shit, babe."

"Damn."

"I'm sorry, Bess. You'll have to rely on your own taste buds."

"I hate to do it. I'm prejudiced. I always prefer cake to pudding."

"Then find someone else. How about Terry? Or your sexy neighbor?"

"Terry! What a good idea. He loves my baking."

"Oh, I'll bet he does." Ned snickered.

Bess felt herself blush. "Thanks for the suggestion. Feel better. Call me if you need anything."

"Serge is in Italy. You wouldn't happen to have a gorgeous hunk in your back pocket you could send over?"

"Ned! Unfaithful thoughts. Naughty boy. Stand in the corner for ten minutes."

"I'm going back to bed. Alone." He sighed.

“Take care.” Bess slumped down on the sofa. Dumpling jumped up to snuggle into her. She petted the dog and opened her cell. “Terry? What are you doing today?”

An hour later, cake was cooling on a rack by the window, mocha pie was in the oven, and Bess was stirring pudding on the stove. The air was rich with the scent of chocolate laced with coffee. Bess opened her windows and the front door to remove the fragrance.

She hummed one of her favorite tunes, Phillip Philips’s “Gone, Gone, Gone,” as she gently stirred, adjusting the burner temperature every minute or two.

“Does your invitation still stand?” Whit’s voice jolted her out of her reverie. Dumpling leaped up from her bed, barking furiously. She ran over to the door and sniffed Whit then returned to the living room sofa, making herself comfortable, before drifting off to sleep.

“Oh my God! You scared me to death!”

“Sorry. But you had the door open, and the aroma lured me in.”

“I’m airing the place out.”

“I’d give a fortune to have my apartment smell like this for even one day.” He walked into the kitchen. His gaze flitted from counter to counter, cabinet to cabinet. “This makes NASA look like kindergarten. Is there any gadget you don’t have?”

She shook her head. “Only what I need for my work.”

He wandered through the large space, picking up an odd utensil here, a tiny bowl there, looking them over and clucking his tongue. “A man would have a tough time outfitting an expensive kitchen like this for his wife. What does all this stuff cost?” He looked at her.

“I didn’t need a man to buy this for me. I bought it myself. Over time. You accumulate stuff. Kitchen tools don’t wear out. Besides, it’s tax deductible. Most of it.”

“Still, this kitchen is worth a fortune.”

"I don't see how it's any of your business." She straightened her shoulders. "Did you come in here to criticize my spending habits? What are you doing here, anyway?" She rested one hand on her hip.

"Your door was open, and the smell, divine. I thought maybe you meant you'd offer me a taste of whatever it is you're cooking up."

"Don't you wait for an invitation?"

"I doubt one would be coming from you."

"Exactly."

"Take pity on a poor man who hasn't tasted dessert for more than twenty-four hours."

"Tasted? Damn. I do need a taster. Are you experienced?" She cocked an eyebrow at him.

Whit burst out laughing. "Honey, I've been eating for thirty-five years."

"Not exactly what I meant. I need a professional taster. Not some schmuck who wants free food. I need someone to tell me what the recipe needs, what's too much or too little." She shifted her weight.

"Oh, sorry."

"Hey, it's okay. Lots of people don't consider what I do for work. They think I'm fooling around, for fun. Crap. This is work. And perfecting a recipe is not something everyone can do."

"I apologize. You're right. This is work. And you must be very good at what you do to have your own TV show. I didn't mean any disrespect. I've never had anyone ask me before. The way you put it, guess I don't have any." He frowned and dropped his gaze to his hands.

"Hell, any port in a storm. My taster, Ned, is out sick. I need someone to try these. Someone besides me. After a few dishes with similar flavors, sometimes my taste buds get confused."

"Maybe you need a fine wine to cleanse your palate between tastes. I have just the ticket. It's my favorite Cabernet—"

"Perfect! You're a genius." Bess clapped her hands together, waking her pug, then ripped open the door to her industrial-sized freezer and bent over, pawing through frozen packages on the bottom shelf. She sensed Whit's eyes on her rear, but she didn't care. She grabbed the icy container and stood up. "Lemon sorbet!"

"What?"

"A light, fruity sorbet is a perfect palate cleanser."

"How about my wine?"

"You can bring it, too, but this sorbet is better."

"Be right back." Whit returned quickly with a fresh bottle of Cabernet Sauvignon. Bess handed him a corkscrew, and he went to work. She poured the thickened pudding into small, white ramekins and placed them carefully on the rack by the window to cool.

"Wine glasses?"

"Third cabinet from the left, top," Bess answered as she handled the hot cups.

Whit opened several before he found them. "I'm impressed with this kitchen. And it's so well organized. I don't know many women who have perfect kitchens like this."

"Guess you don't know many women who cook," she said, under her breath.

"I heard you."

"This isn't a kitchen for family cooking. It's my office."

Whit poured a glass and handed one to her. "I can't seem to say anything right, can I?"

"Nope. But you're gonna get to taste the mocha magic dishes, anyway."

"Mocha magic?"

"Yeah. Kinda like the sound of it."

"So do I. And so does my stomach."

He stood near enough for a spark to leap between them. Bess stepped away, breaking the feeling. He wore a white, button-down shirt, sleeves rolled up to his elbows, and navy blue pants. She stared at his forearms, the muscles lean and powerful, covered lightly with dark hair. His hands were slightly square with long, tapering fingers. He had no beer gut, and the scruff on his face was perfect. A shiver shot up her spine.

Eyes cool at their first meeting were still a clear gray, almost translucent, but now they stared at her with unexpected heat. His gaze traveled slowly over her body, leaving the sensation of a caress from a warm hand.

He raised his glass. "To the queen of mocha magic."

Bess clinked hers with his before taking a healthy sip. "This is excellent."

He smiled. "I prefer the best."

"The best in wine, the best in women...what else do you prefer the best in?"

"Nothing I can discuss with a lady present," he snickered, turning Bess bright red.

She took more of her drink then fished a handful of forks out of the drawer. She handed one to Whit. "Let's get started," she said. He followed her to the cake. She uncovered a small bowl and spread chocolate frosting over half. "We taste with and without frosting."

"Interesting," he said, nodding his head.

"The frosting is only chocolate." She doubled back and scooped out two small portions of sorbet in little cups. Then, she held out a piece of cake on a fork.

He closed his lips over the moist confection and pulled it off the utensil. With closed eyes, he savored the morsel then gave his verdict. "This is the best cake I've ever eaten in my life."

"Fine, but does it have too much coffee? Not enough? Is the flavor balanced?"

He raised his eyebrows. "Balanced?"

She sighed. "This is why I need a professional. Balanced—exactly the right amount of coffee and the right amount of chocolate to give you the perfect mix of flavors."

"I think I need another piece to be certain." He reached for the fork, but Bess snatched it away.

"Oh, no. I'll give you another sample. You have to have a certain amount. You can't shove half the cake in your mouth then give me accurate feedback. You can take some home later." Again, she fed him. Eyes closed again, he chewed then licked crumbs off his lips. Bess's heart kicked up for a second. *Focus. Concentrate. Take your eyes off his mouth.*

"I'd say the balance between the flavors is perfect. I wouldn't want even a tad more coffee or a tad less." He grinned. "What am I supposed to say?"

"You're supposed to tell the truth." *Not butter me up to get me into bed.*

His eyes widened, and he frowned. "It *is* the truth!"

She cocked her head slightly.

"Absolutely. Why would I lie? Believe me, I can be enough of an asshole to be completely honest. I wouldn't spare your feelings for a minute."

"You're being blunt."

"Which do you want? Tactful and dishonest or blunt and honest?"

"Can't we do tactful and honest?"

He laughed. "You're a handful." He shook his head.

"Okay. So, the cake is good. Onto the pie."

She handed him the small dish of sorbet and a tiny spoon. He took some and followed her to the next confection. Bess placed the food in his mouth and waited anxiously for the verdict.

"It's good, but it needs something," he said, running his tongue over his lips.

Bess smiled and went to the refrigerator. She returned with a little bowl of hand-whipped cream. "How about this?"

His eyes lit up. "I can think of many uses for t."

She slapped his shoulder. "Focus." She applied a dollop to the pie then fed him again.

He savored, eyes shut. "Perfect. Exactly what it needed."

"Yes, the pie is denser than the cake. It needs the whipped cream to lighten it."

"Well put."

"You're catching on pretty quick." She took a healthy sip of wine.

"Thanks. Now the pudding?"

Bess handed him the sorbet dish, and Whit cleansed his palate.

"Wait! Let me add the whipped cream first this time."

She scooped up some pudding and the right amount of cream. He opened, and she spooned it in. He took the creamy dessert off the utensil. She watched his mouth. Heat gathered inside Bess, making her damp. She fanned herself.

"This one is a teeny, tiny bit heavier on the coffee," he said, directing his gaze to hers.

Bess opened the window wider then tasted the pudding. "I agree."

"Warm?" he asked.

She nodded. *I could jump him right now. Smear him with pudding and whipped cream and—*

"How'd I do?"

"Fine. For a first timer, excellent." She moved to a cabinet and pulled out two plastic storage containers. She loaded a healthy piece of cake with frosting into one and a giant slice of pie in the other. "You can take a couple of ramekins with the pudding, if you like. I'm going to be tweaking the recipe, though," she said as she placed everything on the counter.

Whit took a big swig of his Cabernet and leaned back against the cabinet. "I can take these home?"

"Your payment for helping me." She finished her second glass. The combination of the wine, the desserts, and the closeness of his tempting body ratcheted up her heat, sweat gathered on her upper lip. She turned away from him and wiped it off.

Bess covered up the pie and took it to the refrigerator. She stayed longer than necessary, cooling her face and body. Then, she packed up the cake.

Whit stood only a breath away. He touched her hand, making her shiver as she wiped a smidgeon of food from his chin with her thumb. He rested his arm around her shoulders and eased her against him.

Reason flew out the window. As she swayed toward him, her voice grew softer, causing him to bend down to hear. "We shouldn't."

The wine had reduced her inhibitions to ashes. His breath fanned over her cheek, his mouth only a kiss away. She lifted her glass to keep from touching his lips with hers before she realized it was empty. The front door opened, saving her.

Terry stood, filling the frame with his wide shoulders. "I heard there was a tasting here. I had no idea you'd be tasting my girlfriend, buddy." He rested his hand on his weapon.

Bess's eyes widened. She jerked away from Whit. He dropped his arm and stepped back, raising his palms to Terry.

"No harm, no foul, man. Tasting some new stuff for her show."

"Looks more like you were about to taste her. Bess?" Terry walked into the living room and turned his gaze from Whit to Bess.

"What he said, Terry. Ned is sick. I needed someone to taste my mocha magic desserts. You were busy."

"Well, I'm not busy now. Run along, buddy."

"First, I'm not your buddy. Second, this is Bess's call. I was only helping."

"It looked like it. Gonna help her into bed, too?"

"Terry, you're jumping to conclusions. Whit lives down the hall. He's a neighbor..."

"I smelled the stuff, the door was open...hey, you'da walked in here, too, if you'da smelled the chocolate and coffee stuff. Wow, it's amazing. This lady can cook."

"Yeah, I know. But the only man she's cookin' with is me. You can leave now."

"You'd better go," Bess said in a low voice, handing him the containers.

"Okay, okay." Whit moved toward the door.

"Thanks for helping me. Here, take this," Bess said, holding out the wine bottle.

"Keep it. Share some with Mr. Neanderthal here. Thanks for the food," Whit said, tucking the desserts under his arm.

"Weren't you leaving?" Terry asked.

"Yeah, yeah. I'm going. You're a lucky guy." Whit closed the door on his way out.

"I know." Terry fastened his stare on Bess. He approached her, pulling her by the waist up against him. Then, he kissed her hard.

Bess pushed on his chest, and he let her go.

"What?" Terry's eyebrows rose.

"You were very rude to my neighbor." She carried the dirty forks into the kitchen.

"Neighbor? I can spot a guy moving in for the kill a mile away, babe. This guy was all over you."

"We were tasting everything. He was very helpful. Now I know what I need to do."

"If he'd been any more helpful, you'd be on the floor with him grinding into you right now. Couldn't you wait until I got off?

"You said you didn't know when you'd be free. I did wait. He wandered in."

"Maybe, next time, you should keep your door closed...and your legs, too." Bess stepped forward to slap him, but he grabbed her wrist. "Don't. Don't ever hit me. You don't know what I might do. I'm trained to defend, and I'd hate like hell to hurt you."

"Don't talk to me like that. It's degrading," she said, water filling her eyes.

Terry pulled her hand to him and kissed it. "I'm sorry, honey." Tears flowed down her cheeks. Terry caught them with his thumb. "Come here." She inched closer, and he circled his arms around her, gently. "You know I'm crazy about you. I got jealous. I'm sorry."

"You come in with your gun on and scare everyone to death."

He removed his weapon and sat it on the front hall table. "I'm sorry. I forget."

Bess wiped her face and nose with a tissue. Terry moved behind her and massaged her shoulders. He leaned down to kiss her neck. "Now about the tasting..." he whispered.

"There's plenty left," she said, closing her eyes and resting back against his chest.

"I was hoping there would be."

"Let me get a fork."

"I had something else in mind," he slipped his fingers under her T-shirt and caressed her waist then moved them up.

"Oh?"

"I want you, babe. Now." He turned her around and kissed her. She opened for him, and he demanded her total surrender. Before she could take a breath, he had her shirt off and her bra unsnapped.

Bess broke from him and led him to her bedroom. Suddenly, she was hot, hotter than a blazing fire, and she needed him. He was down to his boxers before she could unzip her jeans.

Terry slid her pants down and off then hooked his thumbs in her panties. "Love you in red," he said, practically panting.

"Yeah?"

"Yeah. Let's take 'em off." Terry picked her up and tossed her onto the bed. He pulled out a condom and covered himself. One swipe of his fingers across her burning flesh, and she was ready.

"Second time, we go for foreplay," he said, pushing up on his knees. He plunged into her, eliciting a groan from both of them. Bess raised her legs higher, and he buried himself all the way in. Her fingers gripped his shoulders as he moved in and out, increasing the pace as he went.

When she closed her eyes, a vision of Whit, stripped to the waist and bending down to kiss her, flashed through her brain. Bess opened to see Terry above her. The heat inside her coiled up and burst forth like firecrackers. She grunted loudly as pleasure filled her veins.

Her hands slid down his back, which was covered in a fine layer of sweat, to rest on his rump. He continued to thrust in and pull out, moaning louder with each movement. Finally, he called her name and stopped.

Heavy breathing almost drowned out the *click click click* of tiny toenails on the wood floor. Dumpling entered the room and flopped down on the dog pillow next to the bed.

"Thanks, Dumpling, for not crowding us." Terry grinned. He pushed up on his hands and placed a sweet kiss on Bess's lips. "You're the best, babe," he said, pulling out and making his way to the bathroom.

Bess lay back and closed her eyes. *Who did I make love to? Terry? Or Whit?* Dumpling climbed up the doggie stairs and curled up on the mattress beside her. With her brow creased, Bess stroked the dog absently.

"I've got to shove off. I'm sorry."

"What?"

"Yeah. It's this undercover shit." He checked his phone. "Meeting my partner in twenty minutes."

Bess sighed. *I'm confused. Need to think.* She pushed to her feet and wrapped a pink, silk robe around her frame.

"Next Friday, as usual?" He donned his clothes quickly.

She nodded, following him to the door.

Terry fastened his gun belt at his waist and faced her. "You're a sweetheart," he said then planted a kiss on her lips.

"Yeah, yeah. See you Friday." She needed to be alone.

Dumpling followed, barking. As he headed into the hall, Whit's door opened. The broadcaster stood still, staring with narrowed eyes at Bess in her robe. When she felt heat from him, she tightened the sash. Neither smiled. His gaze traveled her length before he offered a curt nod. The ding of the elevator diverted their attention. He joined Terry.

Bess shut her door. Tears pricked at her eyes. *What am I doing?* She sank down on the sofa after swiping a ramekin of pudding from the counter. As she ate, she considered her options.

She glanced at the calendar on her fridge. *Only three days until the Dinner Club meets.* She smiled. *They'll tell me what to do.* She padded into the kitchen and prepared Dumpling's food. Then, she microwaved some leftovers for herself.

She turned on the television and lounged on the couch. After wolfing down her dinner in a few gulps, Dumpling settled in next to Bess, rested her head on Bess's leg, and fell asleep.

Chapter Three

BESS TURNED DOWN THE heat on her special spaghetti sauce. The water for the pasta was almost at a boil when the buzzer from the lobby sounded. *The girls are here!* She grinned as she gave Crash the okay to let them up.

"Your friends are here, Dumpling. Are you going to greet them?" She opened the door, and the pug raced into the hall, her tongue lolling. The little dog looked around, then trotted over to Whit's door. She sniffed and barked. He opened it and bent down to pet the tiny animal.

"Dumpling, come to say hello, eh?" He straightened his tie and closed the door behind him. When he looked up, his gaze met Bess's.

"Hot date?" She cocked an eyebrow and watched him blush.

The elevator interrupted them. The doors opened. Rory unhooked Baxter as Miranda unleashed her pugs, Romeo and Juliet. The dogs barked, sniffed, and raced around each other in the hall. Whit hugged the wall to avoid being trampled. Dumpling led the crowd away from him as she took off into her apartment. The others followed. Rory and Miranda glanced at Whit as he passed them.

He pressed the button for the lobby. "Good night, ladies," he murmured. Bess waved the women in.

"Who the hell was that?" Rory asked. Miranda simply gave a low whistle.

"My new neighbor." Bess closed the door.

The sound of the buzzer alerted her to Brooke's arrival with her pugs, Freddie and Ginger. Once the women were assembled, Miranda opened a bottle of pinot noir.

"Did you see the gorgeous hunk coming out of the building, Brooke?" Rory asked.

"Hunk? There was a guy walking in the other direction. Couldn't see his face."

"He looked familiar," Miranda said.

"Whitfield Bass, the news guy." Bess sipped her wine.

"He lives here?"

"Yeah. Just moved in."

"Hell, a hunk across the hall? How...how...convenient." Brooke snickered.

"Terry didn't think so."

The women glanced at each other. Rory spoke up. "Terry?"

"Let's eat, and I'll tell you what happened." Bess added the fresh pasta to the water then handed plates to Miranda, silverware to Brooke, and napkins to Rory.

"Yum, spaghetti and meatballs," Miranda said, peeking into the pot of tomato sauce.

"And green salad with fennel and hearts of palm."

"I love this club. I'm starved," Rory said.

Bess served steaming dishes of her special meatballs and sauce. Brooke tossed the salad. Miranda manned the wine. While they ate, Bess explained what had happened during her tasting.

"So, who do you like best, Terry or Whit?" Rory took a forkful of spaghetti.

"I thought, Terry. But Whit is...something about him is so...so appealing. Something beyond his being such a hunk. There's something in him reaching out to me."

"Uh oh, be careful A certain something is safely covered." Miranda wiggled her eyebrows.

Brooke burst out laughing. “Shame on you. She’s serious.”

“Oops, sorry.” Miranda blushed.

“It’s confusing.” Bess put down her fork, tears blinding her eyes.

Brooke reached over and rubbed her back. “Why are you so upset? If you prefer Whit, then Terry’ll have to accept it.”

“Whit’s not interested in me. He dates supermodels. He’s off to meet one tonight. Flavor of the week, the night, whatever. I’m definitely not his type.”

“But what you said about the tasting?” Rory asked.

“Attraction. Sex. Nothing more. I doubt he’d ever consider me for more than a roll in the hay. It’s not enough for me.”

The women ate without conversation.

“This is the best spaghetti and meatballs I’ve ever eaten.” Rory broke the silence.

“Thanks. I have a great treat for you.”

Miranda’s eyes lit up. “What?”

“Mocha Magic. Three desserts.”

“The stuff you made for Whit?” Brooke asked.

“I didn’t actually make it for him...but, yeah, I guess.”

“Does this have some magic in it? Is it an aphrodisiac? Should I call Hack and tell him to be naked and ready when I get home?”

Bess giggled. “Must be it. The chocolate and coffee together.”

“I’ll let you know if your magic works.”

“You and Hack? From what you’ve said, no aphrodisiac needed,” snickered Brooke.

When the women finished, they cleared the dishes.

“Let’s take a break before the sweet stuff.” Bess plopped down on the sofa and was immediately joined by Dumpling, who snuggled against her.

“I think you ought to get to know this Whit guy better before you label him a player,” Miranda said, dipping a dirty dish into soapy water. The ladies never let Bess clean up. Rory finished clearing, and Brooke picked up a clean towel. Miranda placed the plates in the dishwasher then tackled the pot.

"What's with Terry, anyway? How come he let this guy move in on you?" Rory asked.

"Terry's only available on Friday nights."

Brooke raised her eyebrows. "How come?"

"He's undercover on Saturdays and some other days, too."

"That sucks." Brooke dried the pot.

"I feel like I'm treading water. Not moving forward." Bess set the three desserts out plus small plates, forks, and spoons.

The pugs raced through the living room, legs scurrying and sliding on the wood floor. Baxter was in the lead. They ran in a circle two or three times then headed back to the bedroom.

Miranda put a forkful of cake in her mouth. "Oh my God! This is incredible!"

The other women dug in and raved about each one.

"I don't know how Whit resisted ripping off your clothes and making love to you on the counter after eating this." Brooke licked her lips.

"Hack is definitely going to benefit from this. A true aphrodisiac."

"You think so?" Bess asked. The women nodded. "Hmm. I hadn't thought about it. Maybe I should mention it on the show?"

"You'll boost chocolate sales all over the city," Rory said.

"All over the country," Miranda said.

"I'll check with my producer."

The women finished cleaning up. Bess called Dumpling. The dogs trotted into the living room. Each received a treat from one of the women then scouted out his or her special spot on the sofa, curling up to snooze. A few cuddled up on top of each other into one mound of snoring pugs.

"What should I do?" Bess twirled a lock of her hair.

"Go with your heart. Many a player has reformed. Get what you want." Miranda gave her hostess a hug.

"Make some demands on Terry. Pin him down. Make him commit." Brooke found her coat.

"Or focus on your career and keep it light. Don't commit yourself."

Bess blew out a breath. The camaraderie and support of the Dinner Club made her smile. "Thanks, guys. I feel better. I've got plenty to think about."

Rory pushed to her feet and stretched. "Time to go, Baxter."

Bess and Dumpling walked their guests to the elevator. After her friends were gone, Bess cradled her dog and stood by the window, watching the New York City lights come on as the sky turned from teal blue to black. *Terry O'Neill, you have some explaining to do. Be prepared to be on the witness stand when you show up on Friday.*

FRIDAY AT SIX A TEXT arrived from Terry for Bess. He was on his way. Dinner was ready. She planned to try out a new recipe for lamb stew. The aroma made her mouth water. She refreshed her wine and sat back on the sofa.

Bess moved toward the door when she heard the bell from the elevator ding. Terry had spruced up. His hair was combed, and he'd shaved. He looked more handsome than ever as he removed his holster and pistol and carefully placed them on the table. *I hate having a gun in my house.* He had Cabernet under his arm and a bunch of red roses in his hand. Bess put the flowers in water and handed him a corkscrew.

When he finished opening the bottle, he took her in his arms for an amazing kiss. He cupped her cheek and brushed it with his lips. "Something smells good. Besides you." He settled on the couch while Bess retrieved a beer from the fridge and handed it to him.

"Lamb stew. It's chilly today. Good stew day."

"It's my favorite. How did you know?" His blue eyes lit up as he grinned. Pushing to his feet, he joined Bess in the spacious kitchen. She peeked in the pot, scooping up a little bit on a spoon. She blew on the morsel before feeding it to him. He snapped it up like a dog being spoiled by his master.

A bark from the floor grabbed Bess's attention. Dumpling sat attentively.

"Someone else wants a taste, too." Bess spooned up another little bit of the meaty dish, blew on it to cool it, and then placed the tidbit in the dog's bowl.

Terry chuckled, watching the small creature clean the dish quickly. "Looks like her favorite too." He turned his attention to Bess. "Like to get a taste of you, too," he said, wrapping his arms around her and burying his face in her neck. She turned toward him to accept his kiss. He held her to him. "You're cuddly," he whispered.

"So are you." She closed her eyes, drinking in his scent mixed with a touch of lime aftershave and a little sweat. *He's all man.*

"Can I have you for dessert?" he asked, raising his eyebrows and shooting her a lustful stare.

The blue-eyed blonde sensed the heat rising to her cheeks as she directed her gaze to the floor. "Maybe."

"But you're my girl."

She raised her head. "Am I? Am I your girl?"

"Of course."

"Then why do I only see you on Fridays?" Bess stared into his eyes.

"I thought I'd explained this. Saturday nights I go undercover."

"Undercover or under the covers? And with who?"

"I can't tell you. Too dangerous."

"For you or me?" She cocked an eyebrow and rested her hand on her ample hip.

"Both of us. You have to trust me, babe."

"You don't make it easy."

He sidled up to her and raised his hand to stroke her hair. "You're beautiful."

A timer went off. Bess moved away from him. "Dinner's ready."

She was full after only a few bites. Unanswered questions about their relationship sent her appetite south. While toying with her food, she watched him chow down. He ate two large portions of stew, noodles, and steamed asparagus.

She smiled at his obvious enjoyment.

"I don't know what you did different in this stew, but it's amazing."

"It's a secret. I had to sign a paper saying I wouldn't reveal any of my new recipes. The station has first claim to them."

"Wow, you're something." He grinned and shook his head.

"Are you making fun of me?" She raised her brow.

"Not at all. Never. You're the most incredible woman. Commere." He took her into his embrace. "You're an original, Bess. Never known a chick like you."

"You're an original too," she said, burying her face in his chest.

Before Bess could serve dessert, Terry's phone dinged. He opened it to read a text.

"Gotta go, babe."

"Already?"

"It's my life. You know the drill."

"I suppose. Don't have to like it, though." She stared at the floor.

"It's hard to love a cop." When he headed for the door, Dumpling jumped up and barked.

"I'm not the only one who wants you to stay."

He laughed. "You two are a great pair." He stepped into the hall. Bess joined him. He kissed her passionately.

When she came up for air, her gaze met with Whit's as he stepped off the elevator. A tall, thin blonde hung on his arm. He nodded at Bess. She shot a small smile back.

Terry slapped her rear gently and brushed her lips with his one more time. "Next week?"

She nodded.

"Goodnight, gorgeous," he whispered then turned. When he saw Whit fumbling with the lock, he frowned and pointed. "Stay away from my girl."

"Blow it out your ass, buddy," Whit said. "Bess and I are friends. Nothing more. I've got better things to do than explain my life to you." He scowled at Terry, ignored Bess, and turned his key. When the door popped open, he grabbed the blonde, disappeared into his apartment, and slammed it shut behind them.

"Fuck off, jerk-off," Terry called out.

"Way to go, Terry. Way to make nice with my new neighbor." Bess shot him an angry look.

"Sorry, sorry. At least he'll stay away from you." He stepped into the elevator and the doors shut as Dumpling approached, barking.

Whit popped his head out. "Shut your mutt up!" he yelled, slamming the door a second time.

Bess stepped back as if she had been slapped. She picked up her pug, who was still carrying on, and went inside. Tears pricked, then filled, her eyes. She returned to the window to gaze out across the park at the lights of Fifth Avenue. "Bess and I are friends. Nothing more."

Pain gathered in her chest. Dumpling turned soulful eyes to her mistress. She replied. "Why am I crying? Isn't this what I wanted? Now, I don't have to choose. Now, I know. Only friends. Be grateful, not sad. Still, he didn't have to slam the door in my face."

Dumpling woofed.

No matter the logic, her heart hurt. *Guess our chemistry was more for me than him. Best I find out now.* She dried her eyes and cleaned up the kitchen. Afterward, she went into the den, turned on the television, and patted the sofa. Dumpling jumped up and snuggled into her lap. At eleven, she yawned, stretched, and pushed to her feet. "Time for your walk, little girl."

After attaching the dog's harness and leash, they headed for the elevator. The sound of Whit's door opening drew her attention. The blonde draped herself over him like an expensive fur. They smooched. The heat of embarrassment spread up Bess's chest into her neck. She heard whispering but couldn't make out words. The woman giggled. They joined Bess at the elevator.

Her expression turned stony as she attempted to ignore them. The woman tugged on her.

"Guess I should thank you. You gave Whit some great ideas about what to do with chocolate." She giggled again.

Anger choked in Bess's chest. "Happy to oblige," she said through clenched teeth. The elevator arrived. The blonde pushed her way in first. Bess hung back. "Oh, did he show you what to do with the whipped cream, too?" At the sound of a gasp, she went on, "I guess not. Too bad." Dumpling trotted in with Bess following, turning her back to the stunned pair.

"Whipped cream?" She heard the blonde's voice, followed by the sound of a soft thud, like a hand hitting a clothed body. Bess smiled as they descended to the lobby.

She exited first and turned right to head down

West, hoping Whit would be heading uptown with his girl. Instead, she spied him raise his hand to flag down a taxi. She blew out a breath. *Good, leave, quickly.* As she relaxed into a comfortable stride, a smooth, deep voice spoke from behind.

"What was your crack about whipped cream?"

She whirled around to see Whit standing with his hands firmly planted on his hips.

"I'm busy. Walking my dog. Can't you see? Why don't you," she made a gesture of sweeping with her hand, "vanish somewhere, like smoke. Yeah, disappear." She turned on her heel and continued downtown.

But he wasn't to be brushed off so easily. Whit grabbed her arm. "What the hell was the crack about whipped cream?"

"What the hell was the crack about chocolate?"

"Elsa was being an idiot."

"You don't say?" She picked up her pace.

"Don't walk away when I'm talking to you." Whit raised his voice.

Bess turned abruptly to glare at him. "Who do you think you are? You can't talk to me like you own me. You're not my father. I'll walk away whenever I damn well please." She spun on her heel and huffed off. When she got to the curb, she noticed Whit wasn't behind her. *Don't turn and look. Don't look at him. Don't look. Don't!* She swiveled her head for only a second. He met her gaze with his. *Crap!*

He sauntered down the street, displaying a new confidence. "So..."

She cocked an eyebrow at him and resumed her walk, jerking the leash.

"You're dragging your dog."

"Am not." Bess clicked her tongue at Dumpling, urging her to move faster, but the dog was busy sniffing and didn't pay attention.

"Yes, you are."

"Am not."

"I'm calling the A.S.P.C.A." Whit whipped out his cell.

"Don't you dare!" She reached for his phone, but he yanked it away, barely beyond her reach.

"Touchy, aren't we?"

"You win the award for the most annoying human being...ever!" The heat of anger filled her cheeks.

"I can't hold a candle to you."

She lifted her hand and took a swing at his face, but Whit was too quick. He grabbed her wrist and twisted it behind his back. Bess fell into his chest. Dumpling pulled to go the other way, trapping Bess. Whit closed his free arm around her waist and held her, her breasts crushed against him.

"You're a fire cracker. Sexy as hell." He brought his mouth down on hers.

Bess clamped her lips shut, but Whit ran the tip of his tongue over them so gently she opened for him. Her senses took over as her mind shut off. She leaned, unresisting, as he stroked her back and explored her mouth. Warmth rose inside her, and she responded. Her body melted into him, and her tongue danced with his. The heat generated was almost unbearable.

Bess fogged over until the voice of a stranger snapped her back to reality. "Get a room."

She jerked her head back, disengaging from Whit. Shame at her lack of control colored her cheeks. "Let me go."

Whit dropped his arm and released her wrist. "Sorry. I didn't mean to...I got carried away. You were so...so and I—I'd never hurt you, take a woman by force or anything. I'm so sorry."

Bess fussed with her clothes, tugging at her shirt, and straightening jeans. "It's nothing. Forget it. I have."

"What? You've forgotten it?"

The little muscle under her left eye twitched. "No biggie."

"Monumental." He ran his fingers through his hair and blushed.

"I'm sure Elsa, Candy, or any of a dozen...no, a hundred, supermodels can pucker up better than I do. And who'd know more about it than you?" She looked up, her eyes daring him to respond.

His voice oozed soft and seductive. "None of them kiss like you." He paused. "Trust me. I know."

"I'll bet you do."

A bark from Dumpling brought Bess back to the reason she was outside. The pug pulled toward the front door, and Bess increased her pace to keep up. Whit followed. The only sound in the elevator was a snort or two from the little dog. Whit stood a respectful distance. She kept her eyes looking straight ahead.

"I know you're with the cop. I promise not to do it again."

"Good. After all," she said, as the elevator opened, and she stepped out, turning to face him. "we're only friends, right?" A pained expression swept over his face. "Goodnight." She grasped the doorknob. Dumpling barked her farewell and followed Bess inside.

"Goodnight." he lingered in the hall.

Tears stung as Bess removed Dumpling's harness and padded to the kitchen for a dog treat. *What's wrong with me? I have Terry. Do I? Whit isn't interested in me. He's a seducer and took a chance. Why am I making this complicated? Leave him alone.*

As much as she reprimanded herself, something about him touched her heart. There was something sad about the man. She had no idea what it could be and wasn't sure she wanted to find out. She stood at the window, looking out at the lights. Dumpling barked once then trotted to the doorway.

"I'm coming, girl," Bess said, switching off the lamp and heading to the bedroom. As she leaned over from her bed to shut off the light, a text from Terry came in.

Need to meet tomorrow night. Seven. Can do?

Chapter Four

IT WAS WEDNESDAY. SHE'D be taping her Mocha Magic show on Thursday, so she had the day off. As she often did when stressed, Bess baked. After a morning walk with Dumpling, Bess dumped flour, butter, and sugar, on the kitchen counter. Since Terry loved her apple pie, she decided she'd tinker with the recipe. She added cinnamon.

She had expected a follow-up text, but none came. She chewed her lip as she peeled apples and dropped a few slivers of the fresh fruit into the pug's bowl. She arranged slices uniformly on the fresh pie dough.

Two variations came to mind. First, a crumb-topping not overly sweet. The second was an open-faced one with sharp cheddar scattered over the apples.

As the pies cooked, she paced, checking her watch every five minutes. When the timer sounded, she pulled out the crumb-topping one and put it on the cooling rack. She sprinkled freshly grated cheddar on top of the second, turned the oven off, and let it sit for fifteen minutes. When she opened the door, the cheese had melted nicely into the fruit. She put it with the other to cool.

"I can't take this. Come on, Dumpling, we're going for a walk."

As soon as she uttered the word "walk," the little dog jumped up and went to the door. Bess tossed on a fleece jacket to protect against the crisp, October wind, harnessed her pooch, and headed for the elevator.

Dumpling pulled her owner toward the park. The leaves were changing, displaying a variety of shades, from gold to brilliant red. They strolled along, stopping to let the dog sniff at the occasional tree and lamppost. What could Terry have planned?

Then her thoughts turned to Whit. How would she handle a friendship-only relationship with Whitfield Bass? She bought a coffee from a vendor and sat on a bench talking to Dumpling, who perched next to her.

Time slowed when she wished it would rush by. They continued their walk south of the Great Lawn and to the East Side. Grassy fields were still green. Bess broke the rules by letting the pug loose in a field for a short romp.

Her mind flipped back to the day she had met Terry at pug hill in Central Park. She smiled as she recalled their flirtation and his allowing her friends to get out of expensive, off-leash tickets. She chuckled at the memory as she headed back to Central Park West.

A long, hot bath soothed her nerves. She dressed in velour pants and top in deep purple, which emphasized the blue of her eyes. A drop of blush to her flawless, peachy skin, mascara, a dab of perfume between her breasts, and she was ready.

After throwing together a salad and feeding the dog, Bess cut two pieces of each pie and put them on plates. She munched on the greens while waiting for Terry. He was prompt, for a change. He knocked, causing Dumpling to jump up and race to the door, barking.

"Like I didn't hear him?" she said to the pooch.

"Hi, baby," he greeted, kissing her. His gun handle pressed against her. He scratched the dog behind the ears, stepped inside, and closed the door. Bess sank down on the sofa and patted the cushion next to her.

Terry joined her. "I can't stay long."

"Long enough for pie?"

"Apple?"

"Is there any other kind for you?" She pushed to her feet and headed for the kitchen, Terry following. Dumpling wandered over to her bed. She circled a few times, curled up, and closed her eyes. "I tried a couple of new things. Tell me what you think."

"Sure."

Bess placed the plates on the counter. "Which do you like better? Or are both bad?"

"Bad? Your pie? Ridiculous." They tucked into the crumb one first, eating in silence for a while.

"So? What's the verdict?" Her gaze met his.

"Both. Love both. They're different. Apples and oranges—pun intended," he said, chuckling.

"No preference?"

"Can't say. Maybe the cheesy one is a little better. But they're both great." He stood up and placed his hands on her upper arms. "We need to talk."

Her pulse kicked up, and her heart raced.

"What's up?" She tried to keep her tone casual, but the light of concern in his eyes showed he wasn't buying it.

"You know my work is...difficult. Dangerous. Right?"

"Yeah. I assume you're careful."

"Things have gotten...out-of-hand on this assignment." He rubbed his eyes.

"What do you mean?"

"It means I have to stop seeing you."

"What?" She rose from the stool.

"I hate like hell to give you up. I have no choice."

"What do you mean, 'you have no choice'? Everybody has choices...all the time." A spark of anger mixed with the adrenaline flowing through her veins.

"It's not safe. I'm putting you in danger. This is our last time together."

"You're breaking up with me?" Her mouth fell open.

"No, no. Not breaking up. Only taking a break. A long break. Trying to keep you safe, Bess. I don't want to do this, but I have to."

"You don't want to, then don't."

"Baby, it's a done deal. We're through until things are safe. If you still want me then..."

Emotion crawled up her chest. "If I still want you?"

"By the time it's safe again...who knows when it'll be."

"So, this is the end of us?"

He nodded. "I'm afraid so. Bess, you're great. The best."

"You're not in love with me. Never have been."

"You're not in love with me, either," he responded.

But almost. Emotion tightened around her heart and speaking became difficult. His eyes were hooded and unreadable. She'd seen the look before whenever she had questioned him about his work. She'd disliked it then and hated it now. "We're heading there."

"With a little more time, who knows?" He stroked her hair. "But we're out of time. We have to call it quits."

Bess burst into tears. Terry pulled her into his embrace. "Don't cry, baby. You're the best. We had good times."

She clutched his navy shirt as her tears wet the fabric. Terry kissed her forehead and ran his hands down her back. She pushed away from him, hunting for a tissue. After cleaning her face, she stared at him. "I almost think you're sorry to leave."

"What does a guy have to do? Cut off his left nut to convince you I didn't want to do this?"

Silence followed. Terry checked his watch. His cell dinged. When he glanced at it then shoved it in his back pocket, his gaze connected with hers. She saw regret. Emotion flared up, bringing fresh tears to be blinked back.

"Gotta go." He headed for the door. She followed, with Dumpling third in line.

"Terry, I..." But the words stuck in her throat.

"I know, babe. This is a terrible way to end things. I get it. At least you'll be safe."

He kissed her at the elevator then was gone. The sudden draft of cool air replaced the heat of his body against hers and brought his departure home. She stood frozen.

Whit's door opened. He was tying his tie as he joined her. "Hi. How are you?" He bent down to pet Dumpling, who sniffed his leg.

Bess faced him. His cool, gray eyes set her off. Tears flooded forth, gushing down her cheeks. She raised her hand to her mouth as she ran to her apartment. Whit was right behind her, but she slammed the door in his face. Bess threw herself down on her bed and cried until she fell asleep with her pug curled up next to her.

A WRONG NUMBER ON HER landline woke Bess at two in the morning. After sleeping in her clothes, she was uncomfortable and disoriented. She tugged at her shirt, which was twisted around, and jammed her pants leg down. Bess padded into the kitchen and checked her cell. No message from Terry. Did she dream the break-up?

Totally awake, she put the kettle on to boil for tea. Dumpling yawned, shooting an annoyed look at Bess for interrupting her sleep. The pug promptly curled up in her kitchen bed and was snoring almost immediately.

There was a message from Ned.

> *Am well enough to work. Will be at taping tomorrow. Hope you have something new for next week. What are you working on?*

Bess smiled. *The pies. Perfect for next week's show. Damn. I have to be on camera. Look at me. Crying. I'm a mess.* She pulled out cucumbers, lay down on the sofa, and put a slice on each eye to reduce the puffiness. Classical music played on her laptop. She tried not to think about Terry. "The Nutcracker Suite" came on. The music calmed her nerves.

There was a knock on her door. Startled, she jumped, and Dumpling barked. She opened to find Whit, tie hanging loose, shirt open, eyes a touch bloodshot. The faint aroma of rum swirled around him.

"You're a little loud. Some people are trying to sleep."

"Fully dressed?"

When she attempted to close the door, he jammed his foot in front, keeping it open. "I'm asking nicely."

"Don't you like classical music?"

"The Nutcracker? Makes me want to put on my tutu and prance around the living room. Yes, I like classical. Not in the middle of the night."

As she was about to agree to turn it down, a feminine voice piped up. "Come to bed, Whit," the whiny woman pleaded.

Bess's eyes widened. She peeked around him to see Candy standing in her skimpy bra and panties in his doorway. "I'd guess sleep is not on your agenda for the next few minutes." She pushed the door hard, but his foot still blocked it.

"How the hell do you know what's on my agenda?" His eyes clouded. "A few minutes? You insult me. Making love? At least an hour, maybe two."

"Go away." Color heated her cheeks.

"How much time do you spend in the sack with your cop?"

At the mention of Terry, fresh tears threatened. Words stuck in her throat.

His cocky expression melted into one of concern. "What happened?"

"None of your business. None of your business how much time I spend in the sack with anyone. Go to bed. Go to sleep. I don't care. Leave me alone!" Her barrage of words forced him back. She seized the opportunity to slam and lock the door. Bess leaned her forehead against it. Dumpling whined. She quieted down and heard steps in the hall. Whit's door closed gently. She let out a breath. *Do I have to face him and the women he's screwing every day? Damn.*

Her cell rang. It was Ned.

"Are you okay?"

"Why do you ask?" She tried to control the shake in her voice.

"Because I sent you a text, and you didn't respond. You always answer. Often with something snide. It's the highlight of my day. So, what's up?"

"Nothing."

"Bullshit. Then why are you up in the middle of the night?"

"How do you know I'm up?"

"You answered on the first ring, and you don't sound sleepy. Unless you're doing something naughty with your hot cop and I interrupted?"

"Nope. I'll be ready for the taping tomorrow. And I do have something new. Can you come tomorrow to taste?"

"Dinner thrown in?"

"Of course."

"I'll be there."

"Good."

As she was about to hang up, he spoke up. "And whatever it is, I hope it gets better. I hope you'll be okay."

"I will. Thanks, Ned."

"Love you, lady."

"Love you, too."

She sighed and put down the phone. After washing up, she shed her clothes and climbed back between the sheets. Dumpling joined her. She slept deeply until eight o'clock, when the alarm woke them.

She dragged herself out of bed. Exhaustion made every step a chore. *Taping day.*

After a shower, Bess threw on jeans, harnessed Dumpling, and headed to the studio. The show provided her wardrobe for the show. While they were taping, the pug curled up in her back-room bed and snored away.

Bess focused on baking. Ned's presence helped. He kissed her cheek and their gazes locked. But she couldn't shake the heaviness in her chest. It stayed with her throughout the day. The mocha magic recipes, products, and program brought raves. The tasters from the audience went on and on about each one, then were stumped to pick one they liked best. Bess was able to toss in a line about the aphrodisiac properties of the chocolate and coffee mixture then laugh it off.

After the audience left, her producer, Woody Bledsoe, approached her. "The mocha stuff rocks. The show was great. A big winner. We're gonna re-run it when you go on vacay. Brilliant, Bess. Great job."

Ned tugged on her arm. "Let's go." He turned to the producer. "She's got some fabulous new take on apple pie."

"Go, go. Don't let me get in the way. You're amazing, Bess. Very creative. Ratings are through the roof. Corporate is overjoyed."

"Thanks, Woody." She slipped her hand through Dumpling's leash loop and walked out with Ned and the pug. Once they were on the street, Ned narrowed his eyes. "Okay. Out with it. I want the truth. What the hell's going on?"

The story tumbled out, in words so fast she couldn't stop, then in fits and starts. She took a breath, then swallowed. Terry's absence hadn't sunk in yet. But tomorrow was Friday and the truth would come clattering down. Ned took her hand as they walked up the avenue. When the late afternoon breeze chilled, she shivered.

Crash tipped his hat and bent to greet the dog, who gave him her paw in exchange for a treat. Once inside the apartment, Bess fed Dumpling then offered Ned the sample pies, explaining what she had done and why. It wasn't long before they were immersed in discussion about the recipe, cinnamon quantities, directions, and cooking times.

Relieved Ned had curtailed his usual sarcastic humor, Bess's nerves were raw and her patience gone. Focusing on the cheesy apple pie helped.

"Dessert first, now dinner? This is whack."

"You were sick. You missed my spaghetti and meatballs."

"The meal you made to go with cannoli?"

"I've got some leftover in the freezer. How about I heat it up?"

"Sounds great."

While Bess worked in the kitchen, Ned regaled her with the trials and tribulations of his relationship with Serge, his boyfriend of six months. She laughed, made sympathetic noises when appropriate, and was grateful for the diversion.

Ned complimented her over her Italian cuisine and kept her up until ten. After he left, she slipped on her jacket and took Dumpling out for her late night walk. They strolled down Central Park West, not in a hurry, with no particular place to go.

On the way back, a taxi pulled up. Whitfield Bass got out. He smiled and stood aside to let her enter the building first.

"Are you feeling better today?" he asked as they rode the elevator.

"I'm fine, thank you. Returning from a hot date?"

"Business dinner."

"Really?" She cocked an eyebrow at him.

"I'm not out tomcatting *every* night. A man has to attend to business once in a while." He grinned.

"Goodnight." Fatigue and upset had worn her down. She fumbled with her key in the lock. "Damn. Forgot." She turned the knob, and the door opened. "I never lock it." She gave a mirthless laugh.

"Obviously, you're not fine. Is there something I can do?" Whit stood poised on his own threshold.

"Nothing anybody can do. 'Night." She slipped into her apartment and closed the door.

FRIDAY MORNING BESS slept in, not rising until eight o'clock. She dressed quickly and took Dumpling out for their morning walk. Once back in the apartment, she paced like a caged animal.

"I can't stay here all day, Dumpling. I'll go nuts. I'm sorry, girl." Bess threw on her fleece jacket over jeans and a light cotton sweater and hit the street. First, window shopping, then brunch in a local eatery, followed by a movie.

She returned refreshed. She unpacked two new dresses and a pair of heels.

"Nothing like new clothes to make a girl feel better, baby girl." She faced Dumpling. The dog flopped down on the bed and curled up. Bess put her clothes away before she tackled the mail. A movie she'd rented had arrived. It was a romantic one called *Holiday* she'd intended to watch with Terry. She sighed and tossed it on the couch.

She plucked the ingredients out of the fridge for a salad and went to work. When it was done, she plopped down in front of the television and put in the DVD.

"Oops. Sorry, girl." She pushed to her feet and padded into the kitchen to fill the pug's bowl with dinner and fresh water. Dumpling snarfed down the food in record time. The phone rang.

"Hey, Mom. How are you?"

"As well as can be expected. But I have good news."

"Yeah? Go ahead." Bess took a forkful of lettuce, knowing her mother would be going on for a bit.

"Remember the guy, Ronnie, your sister was dating?"

"The one with five car dealerships?"

"Yeah. The biggest account at the bank where she works."

"And?"

"He asked her to marry him last night. And she said yes!" Bess could hear the satisfaction in her mother's voice.

The news sliced through her heart like a well-honed knife. "Great, Mom. Give Janie my best, will you?"

"I will. I knew you'd be happy for her. Her life is coming together. Vice President at the bank. Soon a married woman. I hope you'll come home for the wedding."

"Of course, Mom. Wouldn't miss it."

"Are you all right? You sound funny. You're not sick are you?"

"I'm fine."

"Pregnant?"

"No!"

"When are you going to give up the little cable TV thing and come home? When Janie moves out, what am I gonna do?"

"You'll figure out something. I'm not leaving the show. I'd love to talk, but I've got something in the oven," she lied.

"Maybe Janie can get you a teller job at the bank?"

Bess took a deep breath and blinked rapidly. "I'm fine. Doing well. I'm not sick. I don't want to burn my pie, Mom. Talk to you soon." Bess hung up and fell limp back against the sofa cushions. Dumpling barked then leaped up to lick her face.

Janie's thirty. She's getting married. I got dumped. I'm thirty-two with no prospects. What am I doing with my life? Not getting married, for sure. Maybe it's too late for me, anyway. Maybe I should concentrate on my career and forget about guys.

Bess poured herself a glass of wine and went back to her movie. Wallowing in self-pity wasn't her style, but today, she made an exception. A double whammy, the first Friday without Terry, and then her mother treating her like a loser.

At ten, the film finished, Bess snapped the dog into her harness and headed outside. As soon as they returned, she slipped out of her clothes and into a silk robe. As she poured a mug of hot chocolate, her doorbell rang.

Bess peeked through the peephole. *Whit.* She opened the door.

He stood in all his masculine glory wearing nothing but a fluffy, white terrycloth robe. He was barefoot as well. "This is most embarrassing. I took a shower and remembered I'd left my newspaper on the mat. Like an idiot, I have my windows open, and when I came out, the wind blew the door shut. Now, I'm locked out. I was wondering if you could go down and get my key from the doorman. I can't go down like this."

Despite her life being in the toilet, Bess laughed aloud. The more she did, the brighter red he blushed.

"This isn't funny."

"It's hilarious." She tugged on his sleeve. "Come inside." He stepped in, and she closed the door, still chuckling. "Are you wearing anything under there?" she asked.

"What do you think?" He arched an eyebrow. "Last time I saw you, you were practically comatose."

"Thank you for cheering me up. I'm having some hazelnut cocoa, would you like to join me?"

"I have a date. Where's my phone? Shit! It's in the apartment." Bess launched into a new round of laughter. When her sides ached, she gripped them, but continued to guffaw.

"It's not funny. Honestly. I'm going to get dumped for this."

As soon as he uttered the words, her laughter turned to tears. Pain shot through her, and her cheeks wetted.

"Damn it, what'd I say?" He looked helpless. Dumpling ran over and barked at Whit. "I didn't do anything, little girl," he said to the dog, but she growled anyway.

"Dumpling, down. It's okay. It's not his fault." She took a deep, shuddering breath. Bess padded across the room to retrieve a tissue.

Whit followed. He came up behind and placed his hands on her upper arms. "What happened? What's wrong? Won't you tell me?" he asked in a soft voice.

She blew out a breath. "Dumped. You said dumped."

"Did you break up with the cop?"

She nodded.

"Did he leave you?"

Again, she nodded.

"I'm so sorry. What a stupid man."

Bess turned around and raised her gaze to his. He was but a whisper away. A tiny shiver ran through her. "He's not stupid. He's protecting me."

"Protecting you?" Whit raised his eyebrows.

"It's about his work. He said it was too dangerous for us to continue seeing each other."

Whit snorted. "I thought I'd heard 'em all, but this a new one."

"You don't believe him?"

"Do you?"

"I do. Why would he lie?"

"Oh, a million reasons."

"You're saying he doesn't want me?" Like salt in a wound, the sting of fresh pain was sharp.

"No, of course not. He'd be a fool to walk out on a chick like you."

She stepped back. "What do you mean, a chick like me?"

"Well, I...uh..." He reddened anew.

"I'm listening."

"A very desirable chick...beautiful, smart, funny, can cook like nobody's business..."

"But not sexy."

"Did I miss something? We're only supposed to be friends, but yeah, hot as hell."

A small grin tugged at the corners of her mouth. "I do believe him. He does undercover work, and he looked so sad to break up." Tension in her shoulders eased.

"Go ahead. Believe him. But guys lie. Trust me. Guys lie...big time."

"Duh. I've been around for a while. I'm not a twenty-one-year-old, wide-eyed newbie."

"You don't look like a seasoned vet." He grinned.

"Terry was telling the truth. And now, he's gone. And I miss him." Her eyes watered again.

"Don't cry. I can't stand it. Please." He stepped toward her and took her in his arms. She laid her cheek against his bare chest, the dark hair there tickling her nose. He stroked her back with one hand and held her tight with the other. "You don't deserve to have your heart broken."

She closed her eyes, drinking in the scent of him fresh from the bath, smelling like soap and spicy aftershave. He smelled good, damn good. She rested her hand on his pecs. His chest was like iron. He kissed her hair and folded his arm around her shoulders. The heat from him warmed her. When she realized they were both naked under their robes, a thrill shot through her.

Tilting her head back, she looked into his eyes. The clear gray, so cool before, had turned hotter. He stared at her, his gaze traveling down to settle on her lips. Her throat was dry, and her mouth parched. When she licked her bottom lip, his mouth came down and brushed hers. When she didn't resist, he pressed harder.

The thin silk of her garment didn't provide much of a barrier. His hands on her hips felt like they were resting directly on her bare flesh. His fingers pressed in, giving her goose bumps. She opened, and his tongue possessed her mouth. She eased the lapels of his robe aside and flattened her palms against his skin.

He glided his hands down over her An ache grew inside her. While his mouth worked its magic, she slid her hands up his chest, giving him easy access.

Then, as quickly as mutual need had skirted on the edge of control, it stopped. Whit lifted his head, hair flopping over his forehead, his eyes filled with lust. Her gaze connected with his. She licked her swollen bottom lip and pulled her hands away. He fastened his firmly on her waist, then set her back a few inches.

"I'm sorry. I keep apologizing, but I shouldn't have done it."

"I don't belong to Terry anymore."

"You're the kind of girl...the kind who...I can't date."

"Why?"

"You're the kind of girl who wants forever. A girl who wants—and deserves—more than I can give. You want it all—a husband, a home, kids..."

"How do you know?"

"Come on, Bess. You can't fool me. Your place is warm, inviting –like a home. Your cooking...damn. It's like a family kitchen. Are you saying you don't want those things?" He shifted his weight.

"I'm not. I mean, I do. I do want to be married some day. Do I have 'Wanted—husband, kids, and home' tattooed on my forehead?"

He chuckled. "There's something about you. Something nice—warm. Like the way you treat your dog, your friends. Everyone gathers here."

"That's bad?"

"It's wonderful. But it's not for me. I'm never going to get married."

"How can you predict the future?"

"I have my reasons."

Bess was stunned. She knew he was a player but had never suspected he couldn't form an attachment. After all, even players get married –many of them do, eventually. He moved quickly to the intercom, buzzed the doorman, and explained his plight.

"Crash is coming up in ten minutes with my keys."

Bess sank down on a stool. Her mind swirled with feelings, emotion warred with reason. He'd left her wanting him, aching. But the idea of another broken heart scared the crap out of her. "You're a 'love 'em and leave 'em' type, aren't you?"

"I don't hurt anyone. I date girls who aren't interested in forever."

"Those skinny models?"

"Yeah. They sure don't have what you've got," he snickered, glancing at her chest. Bess pulled her robe tighter. "They're career women. The thought of their bodies distended by pregnancy scares them shitless.

They aren't looking for anything more than a couple of nights or a couple of months of fun, dancing, sex, and a famous man on their arm. I help them get publicity—their favorite food."

Bess sat with her mouth slightly open.

"Hey, it's a perfect arrangement. They get what they want, and I get what I want."

"And what is it you want?"

"A little attractive companionship. Someone to have dinner with. I hate to eat alone. Sex. It works—for both of us."

"And me?"

"You'd never fit into the equation. I don't want to hurt you. I like you, Bess. Like you too much."

The doorbell interrupted them. Crash was there with the keys. Whit mooched a ten from Bess for a tip. Before returning to his apartment, he stopped in her doorway.

"Can I take you to dinner tomorrow night?"

"I thought we were only friends."

"Can't friends have dinner?"

"I suppose."

"I know you're upset about the cop. Let me buy you a nice dinner. You pick the restaurant. Okay?"

"Sure. Why not."

"Pick you up at seven." With those words, he was gone.

She heard his door open and close. The ding of the elevator, followed by a shrieking female voice, drew her attention.

"You bastard! You son-of-a-bitch! You think you can get away with standing me up?"

Banging drew Bess to her peephole. It was Candy beating on Whit's door. Bess leaned back against hers and smiled. "One less model in the life of Whitfield Bass, I think, Dumpling."

Chapter Five

BESS WRAPPED THE TOWEL around her chest after her bath. She opened her closet door and chewed on a nail. The shimmering, midnight blue silk dress brought out the blue in her eyes and made her blonde hair glow. It had a low-cut neckline and a slim fit, though it didn't hug her curves too tightly. And she had the right shoes, too – silver pumps.

She looked at Dumpling, who watched Bess take special care with her hair, pinning it up on top of her head with some loose, frond-like curls trailing down her neck. The dog gave her a stern look. A dozen questions ran through her mind. She stopped when she didn't like the truth staring her in the face. She must not forget Whit was Mr. No-Commit.

The bell rang at seven on the nose. She swept the door open to find a handsome man, wearing a charcoal gray suit, white shirt, and gold tie. His gray eyes widened when he saw her.

"Wow! You always dress like this for dinner?"

"It's a new dress I bought to cheer myself up. Is it too much?"

"It's amazing. You look...gorgeous."

She watched his gaze light on her breasts and stay for a heartbeat too long. She smiled. *I've got something those skinny models don't have. Breasts! The poor man is breast-deprived.* She chuckled.

"What's so funny?" His gaze shot up to lock with hers.

She sensed color in her cheeks. "Nothing, nothing."

"Let's go. Maybe after two glasses of wine, you'll tell me what made you laugh."

"Don't count on it."

"A mysterious woman? A challenge." He took her hand and headed for the elevator.

Crash flagged down a taxi, and they rode through Central Park to Limoges. The Maître d' showed them to a table for two tucked into a windowed space, overlooking the park. The table, covered in a soft, pink cloth, was lit by a solo candle.

"Why did you choose this place?"

"Jean Louis, the chef, is always trying to worm recipes out of me. But I love his cooking. He's great. The food is superb."

"I've been here before. You're right, the food is fantastic." Whit signaled for the waiter and ordered a bottle of wine. When their glasses were full, he raised his for a toast. "To a happier winter for Bess."

She smiled and sipped. "The wine is excellent." She buttered a piece of French bread. Before taking a bite, she spoke. "Can we continue where we left off when Crash interrupted us?"

"Do I have to take my clothes off?" His eyes sparkled.

"If you want to, but you might get arrested."

"Okay. Shoot."

"You said you like me, too much. You were going to tell me why you don't want to get married."

"Was I?" He cocked an eyebrow. "I don't remember."

"Come on, Whit. You think I need a friend? Well, I think you need one, too. So, open up. Tell me."

The waiter brought menus, and they both ordered Coquilles Saint Jacques.

Whit sat back and took a big sip of his wine. "Where to begin..."

"At the beginning." She sat back, her gaze connecting with his. "I'm a good listener."

"Here goes. Shortly after I was born, my mother left the family. She deserted me, my dad, and my three brothers."

"How awful."

Whit raised his hand. "My oldest brother, Jeff, said it was chaos. Dad was a journalist and traveled extensively. We were foisted off on relatives and babysitters when he had to be out of town...which was most of the time."

"Who raised you?"

"A variety of people, but mostly Jeff. He was eleven at the time."

Bess slid her hand over his and squeezed.

"Robbie, closest to me in age, was five when our mom took off. He was devastated and blamed me for her desertion. He was convinced if I hadn't been born, our mom would have stayed. He hated me from then on, beating me up every chance he got."

"He's over it now, right?" She wrapped her fingers around his palm.

"We haven't spoken in—five years. Maybe more?"

"Oh, God. Whit. I'm so sorry."

His stare locked on the candle. "I tried everything to win Robbie over. I finally gave up."

"His loss," she mumbled.

His lips twisted into a rueful grin. "Thanks."

The waiter arrived with their food. The scallops were perfect, but Whit only toyed with his food. Telling his tale seemed to rob Whit of his appetite.

"I'm so sorry. I had no idea this story was so...so...sad."

"Not your fault. Am I sorry things are the way they are with Robbie? You've no idea." He took a forkful of food.

"I'd think this would make you want to have a family more than most."

"After years of pressing my nose against the glass, watching other families celebrate holidays and birthdays, being happy, I finally realized it wasn't going to happen for me."

There was a moment of silence as they ate.

"So, you gave up?"

"It's reality. I turned my energies elsewhere. I excelled at school. Got a full scholarship to Kensington State."

"Impressive, for sure. But it doesn't mean you can't have what you've missed."

"I'll be damned if I'm going to let a woman walk out on me...destroying my life and leaving me with a house full of broken kids who can't be fixed." His face reddened.

Bess ate quietly, gazing at Whit. He avoided her stare. The waiter returned to ask about the meal. Whit nodded and ate slowly.

"Do you keep in touch with your other brothers? Your dad?"

"Jeff and I are still close, though he lives in Baltimore now. Dad is in a senior apartment. I visit him when I can."

"And your other brother?"

"Mal? He died in Iraq."

Emotion closed Bess's throat. She blinked to keep her tears at bay. *Don't start crying. He won't like it.* "You've had a helluva life," she said, wiping her mouth with her napkin.

"On the other side, I'm a television journalist with Eagle Broadcasting. I've traveled all over the world doing news stories. I had a great job reporting for The New York Globe before I went into TV news."

"You've been very successful."

"I rarely get turned down for dates, no matter how famous or glamorous the lady. I have a healthy nest egg. I'm living the good life."

"You are."

"So, why ruin it with marriage?"

"Why take a chance on one woman when you can keep loneliness away with so many, right?"

"Wow, a woman who gets it." He grinned. "I knew there was a reason why I liked you."

Pathetic. But I should talk? Like I have a great life outside of my work? I'm no better off than he is.

"What about your family?" He took a sip of wine, his gaze steady, focused.

"Nothing to speak of. I'm the black sheep. My little sister stayed home, got a great job, a wealthy fiancé and takes care of my mom. At least, they live in the same house."

"Don't they acknowledge your success?"

She shrugged. "A cable TV cooking show isn't as impressive as bank vice president. My sister is engaged to an important man in town."

He nodded. "So, you're in second place."

"It isn't a race. I'm happy for Janie. She has what she wants. Problem is, so do I, or almost. But I'm the only one who thinks it's worth much."

"Does it matter what they think? Aren't you proud of your own accomplishments?"

"I am. But sometimes, it hurts."

He took her hand and kissed it. She slipped it away.

"Oops. Friends don't do kiss hands, do they?"

She shook her head.

"You can't control the feelings or perceptions of others. Don't waste time trying."

"You're right."

"I got it. And I gave up on Robbie."

At the sound of a throat clearing, Bess looked up. Jean Louis stood next to their table, dressed in all his chef's finery, including the proud, stiff, white hat.

"Ah, Mademoiselle Cooper, enchanté, toujours. How lovely you are here again." He kissed her hand and bowed.

"Jean Louis, this is Whitfield Bass. Whit, Jean Louis."

The chef gave a curt nod to Whit and turned his attention back to Bess. "I will gladly pick up your bill if you will only share your recipe for the Mocha Magic cake with me," he said, his eyes glowing with mischief.

Bess wagged a finger at him. "Uh, uh, Jean. You know I can't."

"But it looks so wonderful! I need the formula. I want to serve it here. I promise to call it Bess Cooper's Mocha Magic Cake."

"Nope. Sorry," she said, shaking her head.

"Perhaps, Monsieur Bass, you can reason with her?"

"This lady has a mind of her own, I'm afraid."

Frowning, Jean Louis bowed again and was gone. Whit chuckled. "You sure have him around your little finger." The busboy cleared their empty plates away.

"He's always asking for my recipes."

"Ever date him?"

"Jean Louis? He's probably married with five kids."

"Not all desirable men are married." He opened the dessert menu.

"Right. Some are only interested in friendship," she quipped, raising an eyebrow.

"Or friends with benefits."

"A concept invented by men like you."

"Men like me? What am I like?"

"Want the milk and never, ever plan to buy the cow...uncommitted for life."

"Got me there. How about dessert?"

The waiter appeared, pen in hand.

"I'm full. But you go ahead."

"How could I enjoy something sweet without you joining me?" His stare burned her skin.

"Not tonight. I've eaten enough."

"Watching your weight?"

"Trying not to overdo it."

"You look fine to me. Great, in fact." His gaze traveled over her torso and back, making her feel naked.

"Only coffee, if you don't mind." She hoped the dim lighting would cover her blush.

"Coffee for the lady, and Espresso for me." Whit closed the dessert menu.

Conversation over hot drinks turned to lighter topics. Whit discussed his problems with his producer, and Bess bemoaned the rigorous demands of hers. They traveled home and parted in the hall after Whit planted a kiss on her cheek. *This feels stupid after our hot time together.* Dumpling barked as Bess entered the apartment. She leashed the small dog and immediately took her for her nighttime walk.

WHIT CLOSED THE DOOR and yanked at his tie. He pulled it off and unbuttoned his shirt. *Can't believe I'm getting undressed alone after a fancy dinner? She's so hot, but off limits. She wants it all. Marriage.* He pictured a messy house with screaming infants, toddlers running wild, pots boiling over on the stove, and Bess long gone. A shiver ran through him.

He took off his clothes and sat in T-shirt and boxers in his living room with the newspaper and a glass of brandy. After skimming the headlines for anything new and finding nothing, he put it down.

An image of a beautiful, buxom Bess in an immaculate house, holding a gorgeous, golden-haired infant danced through his head. She beamed, her blonde hair shining. He entered to a big welcome from her and the baby, who cooed and smiled at him. Bess gave him a sexy kiss and put the child to bed. He envisioned a romantic dinner for two in their cozy home and an amazing strip tease by her afterward before he jerked back to reality. He laughed at himself.

Do I want the family I never had? If I could get a guarantee. If a wife could swear she'd never leave or die before her time. It might be different. Never happen.

He snorted once and grinned. After washing up, he stretched out on his king-sized bed, folded his arms behind his head, and stared out his floor-to-ceiling windows. The moon was full. The lights of Manhattan twinkled, mocking him, shining out from hundreds of thousands of homes, many with families. His mind wandered to the apartment across the hall.

Is she in bed? What does she sleep in? What color was her underwear tonight? Was it lace? Did she wear a thong? Is she naked and alone right now? He couldn't stop thinking about her and fell asleep wondering how it would feel to make love to Bess.

In the morning, Whit arose at six, showered, dressed, and grabbed a bowl of cereal with his coffee before heading to work early. Though he wasn't expected until noon, he often showed up before then to work on his book or write a few freelance stories for publication in magazines. His producer didn't object, and he had all the services of the station at his disposal. He was all business, listening to the news on the radio to get a jumpstart on his day.

At seven thirty, he opened the door. *Bess doesn't take Dumpling out until eight.* He glanced at her door and smiled. He had enjoyed talking to her at dinner. She was a better listener than any other women he had dated. *Models, always so full of themselves. Steer the conversation around to them, their next job, who stole the cover of* Cosmo *from under their nose, and what clothes they've bought. Damn boring.*

When he entered the studio, the place was buzzing. Seemed as if there had been a big fire in Brooklyn, a shooting in Newark, and the whisper of a scandal in the police department. Whit greeted his fellow workers and settled down at his desk. As an on-air person, he had a small office with a door instead of a cubicle. His phone rang.

"Pickford Williams, here," came the introduction when he answered.

"Hey, Pick. What's up?"

"Hey, Whit. How many women d'you fuck this week?"

"We're not at the fraternity house, Pick. I never kiss and tell."

"Who's talking about kissing?"

Whit laughed. "What's up? Any news on the job?"

"How'd you guess?"

"Oh. Thought you were interested in my sex life."

"I'm interested in having a sex life like yours myself. Never happen. I'm only the editor-in-chief of *New York News Review*, not a hot broadcaster, like you."

"Cut the pity party."

"Okay, okay. Charlie, our guy in Asia, is retiring. The job opens up in a few months. I'd like to send you there a couple weeks early so he can introduce you to his contacts. You have to move slowly in Asia. Protocol, manners, who you know, and all the bullshit. Will you be ready in a few weeks?"

"Damn straight. Perfect timing." *Get out of New York before I fall for Bess.*

"Okay. I'm writing your name in pen. I'll get you a letter when I have a firm date. Okay?'

"Dream come true. Thanks, Pick."

"Don't thank me. Do a fucking great job."

Whit had applied for the position six months earlier. After his disappointment with Gemma, he'd known he'd have to leave New York. *Too many temptations here.* He'd been waiting for this call, biding his time, keeping the opposite sex at arm's length—not always an easy task. Lately, it had become almost impossible, with the luscious Bess on the same floor. Why wasn't he more elated?

I'll pop the champagne when I get the letter. Until then, anything can happen. Pick can go down in a plane. Best not to celebrate until I have the offer in writing. He pushed the feeling of disappointment out of his mind and heart to confer with his producer, Samantha Jones.

"Usual bullshit, Whit, protestors at the mayor's office—parents up in arms with the School's Chancellor. The fire in Brooklyn netted a couple of local heroes, at least one in the fire department. Two firemen hospitalized. Police are investigating the shooting of a kid robbing a bodega in Newark. Some tip about police corruption. Same old, same old," she fired off.

"You're jaded," he said.

"Been doing this too long, I guess. Everything's covered except this."

"Police corruption?"

"Here's the tip." She shoved a piece of scrap paper at him. "Doesn't look like much."

"I'll follow up anyway." Whit took it back to his desk.

He got nowhere with the informer and shelved the task as other, more urgent stories poured in. It was November first, and he couldn't believe how many newsworthy things were happening in New York City. As fast as people dropped printed copies of emails and Associated Press wires in his inbox, he organized each into a thirty-second story and typed it up. Copyboys picked up his printed stories and delivered them to Sam.

Whit and Sam had bumped heads right from the start. At first, he wasn't sure if it was a flirtation thing. He wasn't at all attracted to her and worried it might hurt him on the job. But then, as he had observed the nasty way she treated others, he had discovered she was plain mean. He tried to avoid her to make his day more pleasant, but before each broadcast, they had to come together and –fireworks!

Whit wanted to do human interest angles, and Sam couldn't care less about people. She was all for splashing scandals across the screen, and not above embellishing a few, if necessary. "Scandals bring viewers, Bass, not the bullshit, crap you write," she had once announced at the top of her lungs. She didn't give a damn who was humiliated, as long as she got her way.

The ratings were pretty steady, tending to back up her theory. But Whit's stories drew letters and phone calls, convincing him people were watching. He cringed every time he walked into Sam's office. *Not for much longer, Ms. Number One Bitch. Soon, I'll be overseas, and you'll only be an unpleasant memory.*

After his broadcast, Whit loosened his tie and closed his office door. Once again, he dialed the tipster with the info about police corruption. This time he made a connection and quietly scribbled down the information while the person on the other end of the wire talked. He placed his hand-written notes in the top drawer of his desk and locked it. Then, he grabbed his jacket and headed home.

A Philly cheesesteak and a beer from the deli made his mouth water as he went up in the elevator. The smell of something buttery baking tempted his nose, switching his taste buds from meaty to sweet. *Wonder what she's making. Will I get to taste it?*

He plopped down at the small, round table in his spacious kitchen and unwrapped his food. Sifting through the mail while he ate, he saw a postcard from a real estate agent in Rye, New York. *Damn! The stone cottage.* He flipped it over to read the other side. It suggested he put the place on the market.

He smiled ruefully as his mind drifted back to the day he had bought the place. It was exactly what he'd always wanted—quaint, old, sturdy, and located near the water in Rye, a small, charming town on the Long Island Sound. It was near enough to the city, so he could be at the studio in less than an hour in an emergency. It was perfect.

The house had two stories, three bedrooms—plenty of room for a wife and children. A half-smile stretched his lips. Gemma Timmons, top model. They'd been dating for a year. Had it been love? He wasn't sure, though he had spent a ton of time with her. She had catered to him. Anything he had wanted was okay with her, in the bedroom or the kitchen. Yeah, a model who could cook. And she had said she wanted marriage.

Whit had decided to ignore the warning bells in his head, the doubts in his heart, and proposed to her. He'd hoped to escape the past and create the family he craved. She'd accepted. Then he found the house. Sure, he'd been wrong to buy it without her. But he had fallen in love with it. The stone fireplace. The view of the Sound. And it was old. French doors to a small patio in the back added charm he couldn't resist. The large, sunny bedroom had made it perfect. He had been sure she'd love it too. He'd sprung the place on her as a pre-wedding surprise.

But Gemma didn't love it. She wanted something larger, grander. She called it "cramped," "musty," and "ancient." She craved something modern, like Whit's apartment, with a black leather sofa and stark, white walls. He was sick of the coldness of his digs. For a family, he'd envisioned something warmer, cozy, and told her so. Something exactly like the stone house. He and Gemma'd had their first serious fight over it. Then, the idea had come to him.

He had wondered all along if she'd been more interested in his salary than him. So, he had contrived a test. He lied and told her he'd been fired. He had wanted to see what she'd do. She had been sympathetic for the first day or two. When he had said he might take a newspaper job for a lot less money, she had drifted away. She had booked more modeling dates out of town.

It became clear if he wasn't going to make big bucks and be famous, she didn't want him. He had broken their engagement, with no complaints from her. In the media, she had said it was friendly. It was anything but for Whit. His bubble had burst. His intended wife had bugged out, deserting him even before the wedding. Nervous enough as a fiancé, once he saw her true colors, he ended it. He had vowed marriage was off the table. He'd never make the same mistake again. He hardened his heart.

He'd gotten used to the idea he was going to cheat Fate, turn back the clock, and have the warm, loving family of his dreams. A new happiness had invaded his well-worn heart. But when it all crumbled like month-old bread, he had been crushed. Once again, he was left with his nose pressed against the glass. He watched other happy families, other men, have wives and children who loved them, while, once again, he'd been denied. He'd been depressed for weeks.

He had become bitter and stopped dating then turned philosophical, deciding not everyone was meant to have everything. He had a successful career and financial security, what more could he want? He stuffed away his desires for a family, resigned to his fate as a single man, and closed his heart off to commitment.

But he'd never stopped loving the stone house. Decorating had only gotten as far as buying a couch and a bed before his engagement died. Broken-hearted, Whit had never finished furnishing the place. Never went to see it. Though he'd ditched the dream, he couldn't bear to sell the place.

He'd reconsidered two months earlier, but never notified the agent. Now, he made a note to call her in the morning. *Time to unload it, since I'll be leaving for Asia.*

Even though his heart hung heavy in his chest, he refused to own up to the real reason. Whit lost himself in a Nero Wolfe mystery until sleep claimed him.

The most God-awful noise he'd ever heard woke him up at four o'clock. A cross between a squeal, a bark, and a scream, the sound pierced his ears, jerking him awake.

What the hell? Is someone getting murdered? Bess! He leaped out of bed, grabbed his terry robe, and raced to the hall. When he flung open the door, his mouth dropped.

Chapter Six

WHIT RUBBED HIS EYES. The skinniest, mangiest pug he'd ever seen screeched while Dumpling had him cornered. She growled at the other dog with a ferocity incongruous to her size. *What the hell? Such a little pipsqueak? Aggressive?*

The scrawny pug dropped the rawhide chew from his mouth and cowered. Bess was talking to Dumpling, but the little female wouldn't back down. Finally, her mistress picked her up and hauled her inside. When the door closed behind them, Whit stepped into the hall. The other pooch made eye contact with him then quickly looked away.

"Poor thing," he mumbled, crouching down and extending his hand.

Shivering, the pug took a step toward him.

"Don't be afraid. I won't hurt you," he whispered. But the big-eyed canine didn't move.

The door across the hall opened. Bess stopped abruptly, sucking in air. "Oh my God. I'm so sorry, Whit. I didn't mean to wake you."

"What's going on? Who's this?"

"My friend, Rory, does pug rescue. Hers was aggressive with this little guy, so she brought him here. I thought he and Dumpling were getting along, but then he went for her rawhide, and it's been World War Three ever since."

"He looks pathetic."

"He's been mistreated, starved. He needs help."

"Good luck. I hope you find him a good home."

"I'm in a tight spot here. I need a place for him to stay for a few days. Would you...could you?"

"Me?" He pointed at his own chest, his eyes wide.

"You don't have a dog, and you've got plenty of room. The little guy could get acclimated to a calmer environment. Only for a few days."

"Why I couldn't...I don't know anything..."

"It's wonderful of you to say 'yes.' I didn't know anything about dogs, either, until I got Dumpling. Not much to learn. You'll be great."

"Hey, wait! I didn't say...I didn't agree..." Before he could finish his sentence, Bess picked up the quivering pup, came over, and kissed Whit on the cheek. One lick from the dog and Whit was hooked. Bess transferred the pug to Whit's embrace. "What's his name?"

"Homer. But you can change it, if you like."

"Homer?" He chuckled. "Perfect. Like the poet, eh?"

"Or Homer Simpson. Take your pick."

"I don't have any..."

Bess held up her hand, interrupting him. "I have everything. Wait here."

"Where would I go?"

She disappeared into her apartment, which started Dumpling barking again. When Bess returned, her arms were full. Whit stood back to let her into his place.

"Here you go," she said, padding into his kitchen. On the counter, she set down several cans of food, a plastic container of kibble, a harness, leash, a chew toy, and a small rawhide bone. She picked up the last item and shook it at Homer. "This was the 'bone of contention.' Dumpling decided she had to have it, and Homer wasn't about to let go."

Bess found a small bowl in the cabinet, filled it with water, and placed it on the floor. Homer lapped it up.

"He's kind of a mess. Stinky, too." Whit wrinkled his nose.

"I'll be right back." While Dumpling barked in the background, Bess returned, carrying a plastic bottle. "Here. Use Dumpling's doggie shampoo." She glanced around. "He's small enough to fit in your kitchen sink. Give him a bath, and he'll be sweet-smelling again."

"At four in the morning?"

"Your decision."

"Where'll he sleep?"

"Dumpling has several beds around the house, but she spends the night in mine."

"Men must love her," he murmured, staring at her flimsy robe.

"I've had no complaints," she said, blushing as she crossed her arms over her chest.

"I'll bet," he chuckled.

Her blush deepened. "Thank you again for taking Homer. I'm sure Rory'll have a new home for him soon."

"I hope so. My hours are irregular."

"Crash walks Dumpling sometimes, if I can't be home. Don't worry. I'm sure everything'll be fine."

Whit petted the dog. Homer licked his hand. "He's stopped shaking."

"He must trust you."

She's buttering me up, but what the hell. Having a dog for a few days might be fun.

"Homer's only a year old, so he's probably going to be active. But he's house-trained, so he shouldn't relieve himself inside. You'll have to pick up after him outside. It's the law."

"Got it."

Bess covered a yawn with her hand. "It's late." She headed for the door.

Whit put Homer down and took hold of the knob.

"Thank you so much," she said, kissing him on the mouth.

Before he could react, she was at her doorway and gone. He touched his lips. *Nice.* "Come on, Homer. Let's get you cleaned up. You got me a kiss from the hot chick across the hall. Guess you're good luck." He picked up the shampoo and turned on the water.

Whit dried himself and Homer as best he could after the dog's bath. Homer shook off all over Whit, who dumped his robe in the laundry. Then, he placed the damp little pooch on a towel on the bed. Homer curled up and was snoring before long. Whit chuckled and fell asleep.

Homer woke him at seven, crying at the door. Whit threw on sweats, fastened on the harness, and out they went. The dog stopped at the nearest post and lifted his leg. After ten minutes outside, the animal returned home. Whit took down another bowl and filled it with food. Homer uttered a small squeal before he demolished it in the blink of an eye. Whit watched, astonished.

Shortly after eating, the dog threw up. Whit cleaned it up, muttering, "What the hell? God damn dog. You threw up perfectly good food. Now I suppose you're hungry and want to eat?"

Whit marched across the hall and rapped on the door. Bess answered.

"He threw up." Whit frowned.

"How much did you feed him?"

"He's starving. I filled the bowl, and he polished it off in about two seconds."

"No. Too much, too fast. Give him a smaller portion to start. When he keeps it down, you can give him a little more. Get him used to a normal amount, slowly."

"Why didn't you say so before?"

"It was four o'clock, Whit. I'm sorry. I wasn't thinking straight."

He returned to his apartment and feding the dog again, adding a small portion to the food bowl. The pug gobbled it down in two seconds. Whit waited five minutes for him to throw up, but he didn't.

"Cooking and dogs, now too. Bess is sharp."

Whit showered, dressed, then headed to the station. He stopped in the lobby to give Crash instructions and payment. He planned a trip to the pet supply store during his lunch hour. Walking to the studio, Whit whistled as he trotted briskly down the avenue.

Later, he returned home laden down with bags containing dog food, beds, treats, and toys. The dog barked as soon as Whit came to the door. *Good little watchdog.* Once he was inside, the pug went wild, jumping up on him, trying to lick his face, running in circles, and dashing into the living room and back. Whit dropped his bags as he watched the silly animal race from room to room.

"I sure don't get such a greeting from anyone else," he said, laughing.

He leashed the wiggling pup and took him for a walk. When Homer pulled toward the street, Whit tightened his grip on the leather strap. Back in his apartment, he fed Homer, poured a shot of good scotch over some ice, and sat on the sofa. The dog wolfed down his food and leaped up on the sofa, rested his chin on Whit's leg, and closed his eyes.

After reading his mail, Whit looked down at the sleeping dog and smiled. *Almost like having a family.*

A ruckus outside his door with loud barking and laughter drew him to the peephole. He saw several women and what appeared to be a herd of pugs go into Bess's place. He combed through all the things he'd bought at the pet store and pulled out the ones he had questions about. After tucking Homer under one arm, he marched across the hall and knocked on the door.

BESS HELD A GLASS OF wine in one hand and the front door knob in the other. Whit stood in the entryway, legs akimbo with Homer tucked into his embrace.

"Sorry to bother you, but I've got this stuff says it's for ticks, and I'm not sure how to use it or when."

"Come in."

The minute he entered the apartment, the women stopped talking. They checked him out. Watching, Bess chuckled behind her hand, then made introductions. The dogs ran in from the back, barking. Homer squirmed in Whit's arms, anxious to join the others.

"Is it safe to put him down? Is Dumpling going to attack him?"

"I think it's okay. As long as he doesn't take her chew toys." Bess bent down, scooping up a couple of rawhides.

"I didn't mean to interrupt anything." He lowered Homer gently to the floor.

"You're the neighbor, Whit? I'm the pug rescue person. Thank you so much for taking Homer." Rory extended her hand.

"He's great. We're having a good time."

"Glad to hear it. We're working to find him a forever home."

"No rush." Whit raised his palm. "I like having him around."

Rory shot a glance and a smile at Bess. "You might be able to keep him, if you're interested."

"I am."

The other women approached slowly, their gazes traveling his length. A conversation about rescues started. *I'm going to hear from them when he leaves.*

"Let me show you how to put it on Homer," Brooke said, reaching for the packet of tick prevention medicine.

Miranda joined her, explaining how and why it was necessary. Whit hung on every word. When the dogs came racing back into the living room, Whit nabbed Homer, on the run, and held him still. After the liquid was applied, the pooch broke out of Whit's grasp and raced into the bedroom.

"You don't think anyone's going to attack him, do you?" His brow knitted.

Look at him. Already the worried dad. He's going to be a great dog owner.

The women buzzed around, pouring him a glass of wine, offering him some guacamole. Whit smiled, rested against the granite counter, and appeared to be at ease. *Surrounded by beautiful women, of course he's not nervous. He's in his element.*

"I've seen you before .What are you all doing here?"

Bess explained how the club worked.

"No male members?"

"Women only." Bess answered then returned to the *boeuf bourguignonne.*

"Something smells delicious." Whit changed the subject.

"I'll bet a whole lot of delicious smells come out of this place," Miranda quipped.

"I get hungry walking from the elevator to my door." He chuckled. "Since you eat here regularly, what's Bess's best dish?" Whit refilled two wine glasses beside his own.

"Chicken piccata," said Miranda.

"For me it's her veal stew," Rory said.

"I love her meat balls and spaghetti," Brooke added. "Why don't we let him stay?" Brooke turned big eyes on Bess.

"It's not our usual...but if y'all say he can stay, then he can stay. There's enough food."

"We never made a 'no men' rule," Rory said, taking a sip from her glass.

"I've got some great red wine. Be right back."

The minute he left the apartment, the women clustered together.

"Oh my God, you didn't say he was *this* gorgeous." Rory looked at Bess.

"He's much better looking in person than on television," Miranda piped up.

They buzzed about his hair, the width of his shoulders, and the incredible clear gray of his eyes until the door opened. Conversation ground to an abrupt halt.

Whit's gaze traveled from face to face. "Was it something I said?" His eyes sparkled with mischief. As Bess pulled him in and shut the door, the timer buzzed. Amid a flurry of activity, Bess took out the stew, Miranda drained the noodles, and Brooke tossed the salad while Rory finished setting the table and lighting candles. Whit uncorked the two bottles of wine he'd brought.

As they sat down, the dogs raced into the living room. Their nose-radar alerted them to the serving of dinner. Each approached its owner and sat, begging. Bess passed out treats to each to offer her dog. She stopped at Whit. "Don't hold it in your fingers, you might get nipped."

"He wouldn't bite me, would he?"

"He's new, so I don't know. Not on purpose, but if he has a hard mouth, maybe."

"Hard mouth?"

"Trust me." Bess grabbed his hand. She laid the treat on his palm then held his hand down close to Homer's face. The dog scooped the tidbit up without drawing blood. "I think he has a soft mouth," she said, dropping Whit's hand.

"Hard, soft. So many things to learn." He shook his head.

"You'll get it. We were in your shoes once." She squeezed his shoulder and smiled before giving Dumpling her treat. The pug kept her eye on Homer.

Bess served plates piled high with fragrant stew. They were passed from person to person and bottles of wine made the rounds. And then, silence.

"What dessert did you make to go with this?" Whit asked before putting a spoonful of stew in his mouth.

"Pear and apricot compote. And a plum torte."

"I thought I smelled something wonderful. It was like butter baking."

"Plum torte. My mom used to make that in the fall."

"Any leftover?" She detected the note of hope in his voice.

"Of course."

"Ah, my lucky day. I meet three charming, beautiful women and am fed like a king. This must be a dream."

"Oh, brother. Some malarkey." Rory rolled her eyes.

"Flowery talk doesn't go over well with this group." Bess glanced at Whit.

"I meant every word!"

Bess shot him a look.

"Perhaps I'd better eat and shut up." He picked up his fork.

The ladies laughed. The dogs settled down, each finding a place on the sofa, a chair, or the rug. Some cuddled together with another pug, while others rested alone. Homer inched closer to Dumpling, who issued a low, warning growl. The young male cowered. The female lay back and closed her eyes, allowing him to move toward her. Homer curled up back-to-back and closed his eyes.

"I see our dogs have made their peace," Whit said.

Bess blew out a breath. "Thank God. What insanity, having dogs who live across the hall hate each other."

As soon as they finished eating, Miranda, Brooke, and Rory cleaned up. Whit cleared the table. They created a spotless kitchen in no time.

Miranda looked at Brooke and raised her eyebrows. Rory checked her watch. "I think it's time to go. Baxter!" She called for her pug.

"But it's only eight thirty," Bess said. Before she could offer take-home leftovers, the three women had packed up their pooches and hit the elevator. Whit tilted the wine bottle over her glass and raised his eyebrows.

"Why not?" She took her drink to the sofa, sank down next to Dumpling, and put her feet up on the coffee table.

Whit followed. Bess's gaze roved over the city as the teal sky darkened, melding into night highlighting the twinkling lights, like tiny sparks, dotting the darkness. She lifted her glass. "I'm lucky to have such good friends."

"I think they're sizing me up for you."

Bess faced him. "I've told them we're only friends."

He inched closer. "Are we only friends? Are we sort of related now, through our dogs?"

She laughed. "You've got quite a line, Whit."

"Hey, I tried." He sat back and gave her a long look. "You've heard my life story, what about yours?"

"Me? Too boring for words."

He ignored her attempt to shut down the conversation. "How'd you get into cooking?"

She shifted around, trying to get comfortable.

"Give."

"Okay, okay! I started a long time ago."

"Why?"

"Patience! I'm getting there. I was a regular, boring kid when I was little. My favorite things were raking leaves with my dad, reading, and taking pictures. I'd take long nature walks with my father. He taught me about plants and animals, and I took pictures."

"Doesn't sound boring to me."

"Wait. My sister, Jane, is two years younger. She was the smart one, always getting the best marks in school. I was a daydreamer."

"Creative, maybe?"

"Shhh! Do you want to listen or not?"

"Okay, okay. Sorry." He held up his palm and took a sip of wine.

"Jane and my mom were inseparable. Mom drove Janie to be number one in her class. She wouldn't let her come on walks with Dad. Jane was always studying and practicing to become a cheerleader."

"Not you?"

"I had no interest. She succeeded, too. Still, Mom and Dad would get into awful fights about us. Dad wanted Mom to stop pushing, and Mom wanted Dad to push me more." She took a breath to steady herself. "Here comes the hard part."

Whit took her hand.

She smiled. "One day, spring, I think. They had a huge fight. It was right before dinner. Dad had had a few. I don't remember what they said, but Dad grabbed the car keys and left the house. Mom stood at the door, screaming after him. I blocked it out as simply one more fight. But it wasn't."

Whit raised his eyebrows.

Bess's eyes watered. She breathed in, shuddered, and then pushed the heels of her hands into her eyes. "It was their last fight," she whispered. Whit handed her his handkerchief. "Dad got into an accident, a DUI, and was killed. Fortunately, he didn't hurt anyone else. Wrapped his car around a tree."

He squeezed her hand then pulled her into an embrace. For a moment, Bess hid her face in his shoulder. "It was a long time ago. I was fourteen." She sighed and wiped away her tears.

"It's pretty young to lose your dad."

"Not as young as you losing your mom." Bess took a sip of wine.

"My situation was different." He shifted in his seat. "Go on."

"The shock affected us all. There was no more fighting allowed in the house. Mom went to work. I bought the groceries and cooked. Janie did the laundry. We all cleaned together."

"A team?"

"Yeah. All bad feelings were forgotten. Janie and I did babysitting on Friday and Saturday nights. We contributed to the food bill."

"And?"

"So, I learned to cook, by trial and error. I took out lots of cookbooks from the library. I learned. Janie became the top math kid in school. She won a full scholarship to college."

"What about you?"

"I couldn't go. Within a year of Dad's death, I took over running the house. Mom worked lots of hours selling real estate. Sometimes she'd do well, and some months we were overdue on everything."

"Life must have been tough."

"It was. Survival. At sixteen, I was making pies and selling them to local restaurants. I could make and sell six on a Saturday. Sold 'em for ten bucks. We needed the money. I didn't even think about college. I knew I couldn't go."

"What did your mom say?"

"We never discussed it. The guidance counselor tried to change my mind, but I knew what Dad would have wanted me to do. So I stayed and helped out."

"And your photography?"

She laughed. "I made a couple of scrapbooks, but the stuff was pretty pathetic. I put my camera away after Dad died."

"Terrible." Whit shook his head.

"What's terrible were my pictures. I didn't have any talent."

"Continue."

"Nothing more to say. Janie graduated with honors. And I got my freedom. After winning a couple of cooking contests, I had an offer for a cable cooking show in Baltimore. I took it. Janie landed a job at the bank, supported Mom, and I was free."

"How old were you?"

"Twenty-four. I worked in Baltimore for four years on the show before I got this deal."

"Still in touch with your mom and Janie?"

"Sort of. Janie's pretty busy. We were never close. Mom is happier with her. As vice president of the local bank, she gets a lot of attention. Mom loves it."

"But you have your own television show?"

"I know. But it's cooking. She says anyone can cook, but not everyone is gifted in math. She has a point."

"Not everyone can cook like you do."

Bess shrugged her shoulders. "I've been with this program for four years. I'm happy. I love what I do, even if it isn't unique."

"I think it's unique. I've never eaten food as good as you make. And I've been to some top restaurants."

The heat of a blush warmed her cheeks. "Thanks."

"You sell yourself short."

"I'm good at what I do..."

"The *best* at what you do."

She patted his hand, which was still holding hers.

Whit leaned over and kissed her. It was a slow, probing kiss. Bess lifted her chin as he slipped his arm around her waist. He pulled her closer and increased the pressure on her mouth, warming her. He raised his head, and his clear eyes stared into hers. The intensity startled her. Hers widened. Something flickered in his then disappeared.

He brought his lips to hers again, but more demanding this time. His hand cupped her cheek while his arm moved her flush up against his hard chest. A soft moan escaped as she opened for him. He angled his head to deepen the kiss, creating enough heat to melt her insides. She softened against him, like chocolate in the sun. She steadied herself, bringing her arms up to join around his neck. He tasted delicious, and she wanted him.

As quickly as he kissed her, he retreated, burying his face in her neck, kissing his way down to the neckline of her sweater. His hand closed around her breast. His touch sent flames all the way to her toes. When his thumb found her peak, pressure grew between her legs.

Bess slid her hands down his pecs, digging her fingertips into his muscles as she unbuttoned his shirt. He groaned when she came into contact with his bare skin. Her hand brushed through the dark hair on his chest. He slipped the shoulder of her sweater down, exposing her breast, resting in a white lace bra.

"Beautiful," he murmured, reaching into the cup and raising her flesh to his lips. He nibbled on her then flattened his tongue and circled it. She gasped as her sex pulsed with desire, making her squirm.

When he raised his head, lust shone through his eyes and a slight sex flush colored his cheeks. "Can we go somewhere more...comfortable?"

Bess could hardly breathe.

"I want you," he whispered. Then, he stood and offered her his hand. "Come, Bess."

She rose silently, took his hand, and led him to her bedroom.

Chapter Seven

WHIT HAD FILLED HER mind and her senses, morning, noon, and night. From wondering what he was eating, to whom he was sleeping with, she'd allowed him to creep into her thoughts day after day. Her skin tingled at his touch. The taste of him never left her.

Curiosity had grown into obsession which had morphed into passion. She wanted him with every fiber of her being. Now, she was going to fulfill her desire, and her body hummed in anticipation.

On the bed, the dogs snored softly. When the would-be lovers entered, she reached for the hem of her sweater.

He stopped her. "Wait. Let me. I've wanted to for a long time."

"Make love?"

"Undress you. It's my fantasy."

A blush of pleasure warmed her. Facing him, she dropped her hands. Whit lifted her top over her head slowly, then folded it and put it on a chair. He reached around and unsnapped her bra with one hand. She let it slip to the floor. His eyes feasted on her breasts as he raised his hands to them. She finished unbuttoning his shirt and pushed it off his shoulders.

"You're beautiful," he murmured, lost in exploration of her chest. She lost her fingers in his thick hair and kissed his head, bent in front of her. She reached for the snap on her jeans, and he undid his belt buckle. They removed their pants and faced each other.

"Wait! Let me," he said, as she hooked her thumbs in the sides of her white, lace panties. Whit slipped his hands under the sides and eased them down, his gaze following their descent. When she was naked, he dropped his boxers.

Her gaze skimmed down his abs to his erection. Her eyes widened. "Wow."

He blushed and chuckled. His gaze traveled up and down her bare frame. "Great body," he said, stepping closer and resting his hands on her hips. He pulled her up against him and ravaged her mouth while he traced her curves. Wrapping her arms around him, she crushed her breasts to his chest. His hands seemed to be everywhere at once, coaxing, caressing, and exciting her.

An ache grew inside. She wanted him, now. Bess ripped the covers down on her bed. Whit kissed her as he lowered her gently. "I'm going to take my time..."

"But you're..."

"Not rushing this." He moved to nibble on her neck, and then returned to her breasts. She sighed, closing her eyes. Her mind shut off. Every touch acted like a tiny electric shock, going straight to her core. His expert fingers glided over her soft skin, stopping to lightly pinch a sensitive area, and to roll her nipples until they were hard. He devoured her breasts with his lips.

"Models tend to be kinda flat chested, aren't they?"

"They've got nothing like these. God, they're gorgeous." His breathing was ragged.

She gripped his shoulders, enjoying the feel of strong muscle. The smattering of hair on his chest tickled her abdomen. Try as she might, she couldn't stifle a giggle. He raised his head.

"What's so funny?"

"You're tickling me."

"Where?"

She ran her hand through his fur. "There."

He smiled. "Let me fix it." He arched up, massaging her belly with his thumbs, then gave a lick or two. He opened his fingers and skimmed them down to her hipbones. Sitting back on his calves, he stared at her.

She squirmed slightly, embarrassed.

"Feeling shy?" He raised his gaze to hers.

She nodded.

"Don't. Please. Let me look at you. I've wanted to for the longest time. Just for a moment."

"But..."

"Oh, honey, don't stop me now," he whispered. He parted her thighs. Bess sensed heat in her face—then he massaged her with his thumbs.

If he'd thrown a can of gasoline on the fire building inside her, she couldn't feel any hotter. Could she explode. Fisting the sheets, she called his name. He chuckled softly, as he slid a finger inside her, then a second.

"Oh, God, Whit. Come on...please!"

"I'm not finished, and you're not ready."

"I am. I am. Oh God, I am!" She thrust her head back into the pillow and bit her lip. He eased his hands under her rear and raised her up. Before she could utter a word, his tongue made contact with her flesh, and she bucked.

"Hold still!"

"Are you kidding," she breathed, eyes closed. Again, she heard his soft laugh before he went back to tantalizing and teasing. Moans slipped through her lips. "If you don't—"

Before she could finish, an orgasm ripped through her body, making her shudder for a second, then contractions sent pure pleasure shooting through her. A loud groan shuddered in her chest as she tilted her hips. Reaching out, she wrapped her fingers around his erection and opened her eyes.

Bess shot him an evil stare and watched his smug expression fade. "Now, we'll see who holds the winning hand."

He laughed.

"Okay, okay, poor word choice. But I'm in control now," she said.

"Oh, yeah? We'll see who's in control."

She tightened her grip slightly as she pumped her hand, stopping him cold. His head bent over as he groaned out a few curses. Dislodging her hand long enough to grab his pants, he found a condom and unwrapped it quickly. She closed her fingers around his dick again. He faced her. "If you don't let go, this'll be over in a few seconds."

Bess laughed and dropped her hand. He covered himself. She opened her legs, and he mounted her, slipping inside. She gasped.

"You okay?" he asked, concern clouding his beautiful eyes.

"Oh, God. Yeah. Hell, yeah. Oh, my God." Her eyelids fluttered as he pushed up all the way. After closing his fingers around her thigh, he eased her leg up and thrust in harder, burying himself deep. She sucked in air. *It's so good. So good.*

"How are you?" he asked, his expression still concerned.

"Great! Oh, great." She stared back, smiling.

He kissed her and increased the pace. Her body heated again. Emotion bubbled up inside her, but she tamped it down. She moved her hips in tandem with his, fastening her fingers around his shoulders. He lowered his head to suck on her neck. She licked his earlobe then raised her hand, combing it through his hair. The scent of their passion mixed with his sexy aftershave and his own, unique fragrance worked like an aphrodisiac.

"I want you, oh God, how I want you," he muttered, pumping into her.

"You have me."

Pushing up on his hands, he stared down with lusty eyes. Thrust after thrust re-kindled her fire. Heat engulfed her and she came hard. Her hips undulated on their own as spasms shot warmth to every finger and toe. His expression of ecstasy followed a loud groan and her name. She studied his face as he climaxed. It was the most handsome she'd ever seen.

Sweat beaded on his forehead as he gazed down with loving eyes. "Wow! The most incredible—most awe-inspiring—"

He stopped. The warmth in his gaze made her smile. She ran her hand over his rough cheek and down over his chest before she brushed her lips across his. *His body is perfect.* "You were wonderful. Amazing," she whispered.

A loud yawn and the *click, click, click* of two sets of claws on the wood floor disturbed their peace. Bess glanced over to see Dumpling and Homer poised next to the bed. The female looked completely bored and licked her nose. The male panted, his tongue lolling. Bess leaned over to pet her dog. Satisfied she'd been given some attention, Dumpling marched over to the puppy bed and curled up with Homer close behind.

"When you have a pug, you're never alone," Bess said.

He rolled off her and stretched out. She cuddled up to him, resting her head on his chest. He closed his arm around her and stroked her hair.

"So, was it everything you thought it'd be?" *Begging for a compliment? What's the matter with me?* She chastised herself.

"More. Never imagined it'd be so intense."

She pushed up to make eye contact. "You imagined our sleeping together?"

"Didn't you?" He ran his finger down her cheek.

Bess burrowed her face into his furry chest to hide her embarrassment. *Only night after night after night.* "I plead the fifth," she squeaked.

He laughed. "Not admitting anything? Okay. I get it." They lay together in silence for a while, until Whit spoke up. "Don't you feel it?' His hand caressed her breast idly.

"What? I feel your hand."

"Come on. You know what I mean. The electricity. The chemistry."

"Between us?" She sat up.

"No, between me and Homer." He shrugged. "Of course, between us!"

"Okay, okay, I admit it."

He leaned over and kissed her. "Thank God. Thought I was losing my mind. Bess, honey, sweetheart. You and me."

"I don't want to have chemistry with a man who can't commit." She pushed away from him, swung her legs over the side of the mattress, and stood up.

"Commit? We've only been to bed once. Known each other a couple of weeks. And you want a commitment?" He scratched his head.

"I didn't say commitment. I said I don't want chemistry—"

"I heard, I heard. Chemistry happens. It isn't something you can will—or wish away."

She stared at the floor. "I know. But why does it have to happen with a guy like you."

"Thanks a lot." He left the bed and grabbed his boxers.

She faced him, placing her hands on his upper arms. "You know what I mean. If you weren't such a commitment-phobe, it'd be different."

"You might be doing the Snoopy Dance, then?"

"Yeah." She dropped her hands. *I don't want to love him. I don't want to like him. But he's an amazing lover.*

"So, you like me against your will?"

"Sort of. Not really, but...well, maybe." She nodded as she plucked her robe from the back of the door.

Whit came up behind her. He wound his arms around her waist and kissed her neck. "Can't we have whatever it is we have? And leave it there?"

"So open-ended?"

"Come on, honey. What we have is special. Let's enjoy it while it's hot."

"And when it fizzles?" She faced him. "What then?"

"We'll cross that bridge when we come to it. Don't throw this away."

Push him away. But the sex was incredible. "I'll bet you say the same thing to all your women."

He stepped back. "Ouch. No. A line? No way. You think so little of me?"

"You're a player. You admit it. What else am I to think?"

"How about maybe I like you? I have the hots for you."

"Every man has the hots for a woman, a dozen women."

"I'm not a man-whore." He reached for his pants.

She turned a jaundiced eye on him. "Aren't you? I see you out with different women all the time."

"I date only two women—now it's down to one, after I accidentally stood Candy up. Only Elsa."

"Oh? I don't share."

"You want exclusive after one trip to the bedroom?"

She nodded. The sting of tears pricked at the back of her eyes. Silence followed. She retreated to the window to avoid his gaze. "Never mind," she said, fastening her robe around her. "I don't care. Date whoever you want. This was a one-time thing. Ain't happening again." A lump in her throat made her stop speaking.

Whit moved closer. He rubbed her arms and softened his voice. "Hey. I didn't say 'no.'"

"I don't want to have to ask. I didn't ask. Forget I said anything. Screw anyone you want, but not me. Not again." The tears burst forth. *I've got my pride.* She turned away from him, making a beeline for the tissue box. Facing the wall, she wiped her eyes. Whit was right behind. "Can't you take a hint? Go home. Go to her...whoever. And don't bother me again. Ever!"

He caressed her shoulders, his touch scorching her skin through her thin robe. She stiffened when he kissed her neck. "Don't be like this. Come on. Give me a chance."

"A chance to do what? Give me Monday Wednesday Friday and her Tuesday Thursday Saturday? Uh uh. No way." Bess shook her head.

"Let me get a word in here, would you?"

A shudder ran through her chest as she took a deep breath. Emotion choked her. *I can't be in love with him. I don't even know him. But I want him. I want him so much.*

Whit turned her by her shoulders until she faced him. She only glanced up, too ashamed to look him in the eye. His brows knitted, his eyes concerned, and his lips were compressed into a thin line. "I'd never do that to you," he whispered. "I'd never hurt you. You're special, Bess. Not like other women."

"Why? Because I cook?"

"Because you're you. I'm done with Elsa. Say you'll be with me. Mine. Alone."

Her heart lurched. *Does he mean it?* She nodded.

"No, say it." His fingers squeezed.

"I'm yours. Yours alone...if you're mine alone."

"Fair enough. Yep. No more dates with Elsa...or anyone else. Only you."

Happiness pushed doubt out of her heart. She grinned at him. Whit took her in his arms for a long kiss. Bess melted against him, letting joy flutter up inside. Inhibitions took a backseat to need. *More. More.*

With one hand, Whit pulled the sash of her robe loose. It opened, and he slipped his hands under the fabric. Closing his fingers around her waist, he slid them up, over her breasts. Her breathing became rapid as he massaged.

"Again?" She peered into his eyes.

"Hell yeah, again. And again and again..." he whispered into her hair. She felt him harden against her belly, and every nerve came alive with expectation. "Do you have a spare toothbrush?"

"I do."

"Good. I'm spending the night."

"You are? I mean, you are. Of course. Fantastic."

"Damn right." He led her to the bed. A sneeze and a yawn came from the pugs on the floor as they rearranged their positions.

"Pups, your walk is coming. But first..." He didn't finish as Bess pushed him down on the mattress. Giggling, she jumped on next to him. He wrestled her underneath him and made mad, passionate love to her.

At eleven, Bess, Whit, and the pugs left the elevator and went out into the night. They strolled down the avenue, taking their time, allowing the dogs to sniff every lamppost.

"What's on your menu for tomorrow?"

"What am I cooking? Nothing new. Looking over ideas for next week. I have the day off."

"Good. You can sleep in. After we're finished, you'll need the rest."

"With a dog, you can never sleep in."

"Go back to bed, then."

"And what are these plans?" She threw him a flirtatious look.

"Making love all night."

Goose flesh broke out on her arm. "How will you get up in the morning and go to work?"

"I don't know. You might get me fired." He grinned.

"I can see the headline on your show now—'Oversexed Newsman Sacked for Too Much Sack Time.'"

"Clever."

"To answer your question, I'll be experimenting with the crockpot tomorrow. Trying to cook fruit in there. Maybe make a fruit compote or applesauce."

"Can I stop by? Maybe take you out to eat afterward?"

"Wonderful! By seven o'clock, I'll be elbow deep in fruit mush and frustrated as hell."

"I can take care of it before dinner," he snickered.

Bess slapped him playfully on the shoulder, making Dumpling bark. Of course, Homer followed. "Let's get these noisemakers home," Whit said. They turned and led the dogs back to the building. Crash raised his eyebrows in a meaningful look at Bess, making color heat her cheeks.

Whit took her hand in the elevator. *He's making a big play for me. Does he mean it? What do I do? Go with it. Pick up the pieces later?* Bess chewed her lip. Both dogs sat in the kitchen for a treat. Dumpling warmed up to Homer, as she let him share her space in the bedroom.

Bess checked her watch and yawned. "Bedtime."

"My favorite word," he said, grinning.

Bess held out her hand, and he joined her. They undressed quickly and slipped between fine, cotton sheets.

Whit pushed up on his elbow. "Do you prefer to be in your own space, or—"

"I prefer 'or,'" she said, putting her hand over his mouth, cutting him off.

Whit lay back and opened his arms. Bess snuggled up to him and turned on her side. He spooned her, resting his arm over her waist. His fingers closed around her breast.

"Do you mind?"

"Stop asking questions. Don't you sleep with a ton of women? Don't you get the drill?"

"Sleep with doesn't mean sleeping."

She faced him. "You don't spend the night?"

"Not usually."

"Oh, no commitment. Right." She nodded. "And now?"

"Like I said before. You're different."

If it's a line, it's a damn good one, because it's working. Bess resumed her position on her side. Whit wrapped himself around her. Peace washed over her, keeping her smile broad.

"You smell good," he whispered, planting a kiss on her neck. Bess reached over and turned out the light. Dumpling took her cue and climbed the stairs at the end of the bed. Homer followed. The two pugs found space at the bottom of the empty side. They curled up and were snoring almost immediately. *How can I feel so safe with the world's most unsafe man?* She shifted, and he moved with her. Her eyelids drooped closed, and sleep took her away.

SATURDAY AFTERNOON, Whit got a call from his brother, Jeff.

"What's up?"

"Just checking in," Jeff said. "What's new, little bro?"

"Met a new girl." Whit sat back on his couch and sucked down some beer.

"Oh?"

Whit smiled. He could practically hear Jeff's eyebrows rise. "Yeah. She's a neighbor."

"Uh oh. Too close for comfort. How're you gonna ditch this one if she gets needy?"

Whit swallowed. This was something he hadn't considered. "Don't know. She's not gonna get needy. We have an understanding."

"I thought you knew women."

"I do."

"They're all cool until you've been dating for a couple months. Then, they get needy, very needy, and the dreaded 'm' word surfaces." Jeff chuckled.

"Gimme a break. Bess knows I'm not into marriage."

"And she's okay knowing you don't want marriage?"

"Well—sort of." Whit sat forward.

"Exactly! She isn't, and you're in denial. A place you seem to live these days."

"Did you call to lecture me?"

"Actually, I called to see if you got in touch with the shrink I gave you."

"I don't need a shrink."

Mirthless laughter followed. "If ever there was a guy who needed a shrink, it's you."

"So, you think I'm crazy?"

"No. I think you need a little help. Hell, Whit. No one comes out of a family like ours whole. Dysfunctional? We wrote the book."

"Including you?"

"I was eleven when Mom left. It wasn't as traumatic for me as for you...and Robbie and Mal. Besides, I've been."

"So you said. But you've never elaborated. Besides, I thought Janice was your shrink."

"You don't tell people what you talk about in therapy. Only with your shrink. Janice came along at the right time. I'd just gotten over my marriage phobia. She was patient and understanding. But without the shrink, it wouldn't have been enough."

"Real men don't need shrinks."

"Real men who are smart admit when they do and go."

Whit snorted. "You never give up, do you?"

"You're thirty-five, Whit. There's still hope for you. I'm happy. Happier than I thought I could ever be. I have the family I always wanted. I know you want the same and I want you to have it too. This is the only way, buddy."

"When and if I decide to have a family, I'll have one."

"Have to get married first."

"So, I will."

"I want to hear you say you'll get married. Use the 'm' word."

"What's it to you, anyway?"

"See? You're avoiding the issue. You know I'm right. You know you want what we didn't have. You want it so bad, you can taste it. You almost had it, once. Without help, you don't stand a chance."

Whit sat back and took a long drink.

"Whit? Whit?"

"I'm here. Thinking."

"Oh. Okay. You scared me. I'm only hounding you like this because I love you. You're like my kid. Hell, I raised you at least as much as Dad did, maybe more."

"I know, Jeff. I trust you. It's just—"

"What? You're scared? No one's going to hurt you in therapy. Go. Trust me. It'll change your life. Tell me you'll consider it."

"I'll think about it. How's Dad?"

"Fading. A little more each day."

"The kids?"

"They're great." Whit could hear his brother's smile over the phone. "You'd be a great father, Whit."

"Hey, I am a father. At least, a foster father. I'm taking care of a homeless pug."

"Great! A step in the right direction."

"He's wonderful...funny. Great dog."

"How's the job?"

"Fine. Pick called. In a couple of weeks, I'll be going to Asia to write for his paper."

"Does your new girlfriend know this?"

"I haven't said anything. It's a little early. Only had our first night together."

"Better tell her."

"I will. I will."

"Gotta go. Soccer games."

"Give my love to Janice. You were lucky to find her."

"Damn straight. Take care of yourself. Call Dr. Sumner."

"Thanks for the advice, Jeff."

"Love you, buddy."

"Love you, too."

Whit put his cell down and pushed to his feet. He stood by the window, staring at the city, building after building of steel, cement, brick, and stone all laid out before him. A chill shot through him for a second. *So many people in this city, and I know so few. Do they all have connections? What about me? Do I want a family, like Jeff says?*

If I did want a family, Bess would be the type of woman I'd want to marry. I'm leaving soon. By then, I'll know. And if she doesn't work out, like everyone else, I'll go to Asia and start a new chapter in my life. Sounds like a plan.

His phone dinged. There was a message.

Special tasting in five. U bring wine.

It was from Bess. He grinned. Homer woofed.

"Okay, boy. Yeah. Time to visit your girlfriend and mine." He picked up a bottle of Bess's favorite Cabernet and plucked a bouquet of pink roses he'd been saving out of the vase. He wrapped the wet stems in a paper towel and strode across the hall. *Don't know what will be. But for now, I'm happy.* A smile spread across his face as he pushed the doorbell, and Homer barked his arrival.

When the door opened, Whit almost dropped the wine. The flowers did hit the floor.

Bess stood in the doorway, wearing only an apron. "Come in, come in. The tasting is about to begin."

Chapter Eight

"WHAT THE FUCK IS GOING on with you?" Sam asked Whit.

He sat, sleeves rolled up to his elbows, pen in hand, by the main computer, marking up copy. "What do you mean?"

"You're smiling all the time. You've stopped being nasty to me. What the hell?"

He chuckled. "Nothing's up, Sam. I've stopped hating you is all."

She narrowed her eyes. "Think I liked it better when you did. Don't know this new guy. Not sure I trust him."

"Remember your motto—never trust anyone. Everyone lies."

"Quoting me to me?" She smiled for a second. "Get your copy done and get your ass in makeup."

"I'm going. Haven't missed a newscast yet."

"There's always a first time," she mumbled.

Whit sat in the chair as the makeup artist did her best to make his shaved face look completely beardless. As she worked, his mind replayed his steamy night with Bess. His fingertips tingled at the recollection of touching her. He could swear he smelled a touch of lilac in the air. She satisfied him in bed like no other woman ever had. Soft, responsive, full figured. He loved having something to hold onto.

Afterward, they had indulged in the most delicious chocolate torte he'd ever eaten. And a glass of *Bailey's* Irish Cream topped it off.

Whit had to admit he slept better. Nights with Bess relaxed him. He'd even become accustomed to Dumpling and Homer snoozing at his feet. Their snoring, annoying at first, was now soothing. Three weeks had passed since he had first bedded her, and he applauded himself every day on his good taste and having the balls to make a move on the luscious woman across the hall.

The minute he walked into her apartment, the aroma of something wonderful in the kitchen made him salivate and brought him peace at the same time. It reminded him of the smells from playmates' houses.

When he was nine, his best friend, Mike, had the nicest family in town. Whit had hung out over there as much as he could. They had taken pity on him and invited him to dinner often. The fragrance of tasty food cooking coupled with the sound of a mom's sweet voice had made him feel part of a normal family, even if only for a few hours.

Days when he would return home to face a meal of lukewarm, canned ravioli and frozen green beans thrown together by his clueless father or big brother, the reality of his situation slapped him in the face. He'd disappear into his room afterward, lie on his bed, and dream he was Mike's long lost brother. He'd picture moving in, sharing a room with Mike, and being cared for by his doting mother. This had been his favorite fantasy, and it had soothed him to sleep more nights than he cared to remember.

Bess's place had the same homey feel, and even more mouth-watering scents emanating from the kitchen. Her easy, unassuming ways made him comfortable. He'd moved a toothbrush and razor into her bathroom. He'd uncork wine, clear the table, and help with the clean-up—a task he had loathed as a child, but didn't mind now.

Whit was too smart to take her warmth and generosity for granted. He took her out to tony restaurants at least once a week, brought flowers, wine, and complimented her on the dishes she prepared.

The makeup lady looked at him. "Excuse me?"

"Nothing," he said waving his hand. Within these few weeks, Whit found himself at Bess's place more than his own. He and Homer had a standing invitation, though Whit always called before showing up.

As a kid, he had developed excellent social skills. He had figured out being anything but totally polite was sure to dry up dinner invitations quickly. The meaning of the word gratitude was something he had learned early. His reward had been the warm welcome he had received from parents' of friends.

"Whit, how nice to see you. You're always welcome at our house."

"Daniel, why can't you be more well-mannered like your friend, Whit?"

As a boy, he had assumed no one knew how bad things were in his house. Thought he'd covered it up well. By high school, he guessed everyone had known, especially the parents. They had taken pity on him. His excellent behavior had only made it easier for them to do "the right thing" and invite one of those "poor Bass boys" to their house for a decent meal.

When he was fourteen and a star on the junior high football team, he had overheard parents of his friends at the game. He had bent down at the water fountain and gotten more than expected when he overheard a conversation.

"Isn't it amazing Whitfield Bass isn't a criminal? Growing up without a proper home. Look at him, quarterback of our team."

"It's a miracle he got so big. We have him to dinner once a week so he can get a square meal. Poor boy with no mama to look after him."

"His dad did the best he could. But traveling all the time, it's a wonder they're fed at all."

Whit's face had flamed. The desire to throw their words in their faces warred with the wish to simply slink away. Whit had done neither. He had stood up and wiped water off his lips with the back of his hand. *Not their fault I had no family. Couldn't be mad at them. Sure appreciated those meals.*

There were no childhood illusions left. No rose-colored memories of his family. He had been a realist from then on. Whit had known he'd have to take care of himself without the help of others if he didn't ever want to hear a repeat of that conversation. So, he had manned up. By then, Jeff had already married and moved to Baltimore. Whit and his brother, Robbie, were still at home.

Jeff had invited him to visit whenever the boy could scrape together the train fare. Jeff had become as important to Whit as their father, and far more accessible. But he had a wife and soon a family. Whit hadn't intruded often, but holidays were hard to resist. One Thanksgiving, at sixteen, he had told Robbie off and deserted his father for Jeff's house.

He had ridden the crowded train, his nerves raw from the emotional battle at home. He had been embarrassed, barging in on Jeff's cozy life. But when he arrived, they had been waiting on the platform—Jeff, Janice, her parents, and her sister carrying a sign. It read "Welcome, Whit." At the time, he had burst into tears. Even now when he recalled the scene, his eyes misted.

When the makeup was finished, he pushed to his feet, tore off the bib, and rolled down his sleeves. He smiled, thanked the artist, and returned to his desk.

Sam rushed over. "This just in. Undercover cop killed in car bombing," she said, thrusting papers into his hands. "It's our lead."

"Who is it?" His pulse kicked up. *Couldn't be.*

"I dunno? It's in there, somewhere. Mc somebody. You've got twenty minutes. Get familiar with this."

"Not McNeil?"

"Yeah! You know him?"

"Terrance McNeil?"

"Yeah, yeah."

Whit sank down into his chair, only half listening to his producer.

"You're the perfect person to do this lead, since you knew him. Make it poignant, Whit."

"You can't...you can't run this. Not yet. I've got to...talk to someone...call someone..."

"Bullshit! Whad'ar you crazy? We haven't had a juicy lead like this in weeks. Of course, we're going with it. Make it good, pretty boy."

Bess! For a moment, Whit didn't know what to do. Bess always watched his broadcast. She turned it on while she was cooking. He opened his cell and dialed.

"Rory! Whit. Get over to Bess' now. Right away. Yeah. Don't let her watch the news. Please. Whatever you do, distract her. But don't let her watch the news. I'll tell her later, in person. Of course, it's bad! Please, please." He closed the phone. *Rory's on her way.*

Whit sweated. The hour grew nearer. He took his seat.

The makeup lady showed up with powder and puff. "What the hell? You're drenched. Who turned up the heat in here?"

CRASH BUZZED THEN LET Rory and her pug, Baxter, into the building.

"Bess, grab Dumpling, and let's go for a walk."

"News is coming on in a few. Can you wait a half hour?"

"Baxter needs to go." Homer greeted Rory and sniffed Baxter.

"I've got Homer, too."

"Whit leaves him here with you every day?"

"Not every day. Most days. Dumpling has grown used to him. They still don't eat together, but otherwise, it's peaceful."

"Come on, let's go." Rory tossed the two harnesses to Bess.

"But Whit. He knows I'm watching. Always asks me for a critique..."

"Tell him you got waylaid this time." Rory tugged on Bess' sleeve.

"I'll record it."

"No!" Rory screamed.

Bess jumped. "Okay. What's going on?"

"I'm afraid Baxter is gonna pee on your floor. Come on."

Bess leashed the dogs and joined her friend. They walked in the park and talked. *Rory seems nervous.* "Everything okay with you and Hack?"

"Great. Why do you ask?"

"You're usually so relaxed, but tonight, you're edgy."

"Oh, yeah. Right. Got some bad news about a friend."

"Want to talk about it?"

"What are your plans for Thanksgiving?"

"Rory, are you okay?" Bess put her hand on her friend's arm.

"Of course. Why do you ask?"

"You're not yourself. You're jumpy and keep changing the subject."

"I've got some things on my mind I'd like to forget."

"Oh, okay. Nothing too Earth-shattering?"

"I hope not," Rory mumbled.

The two women walked and talked for forty minutes.

"I'm cold. Let's go inside." The women guided the dogs back to the building.

"Coffee?" Bess asked.

"You having some?"

"I'm freezing. Yeah."

"Count me in."

Bess turned on the machine and put out two pieces of coffee cake from her new recipe.

"Pistachio coffee cake?"

"Yeah. Not my best idea, but I don't want to throw it out."

Rory laughed. "So, you feed it to me. Makes sense." Rory took a bite. "I actually like it."

"Good. Want to take the rest home to Hack?"

Rory put up her hands in protest as the buzzer sounded.

"Must be Whit. Crap. He'll be upset I missed the news."

"Not this time," Rory muttered. Bess stared at her friend as she went to the door. Dumpling and Homer, barking up a storm, followed her. Rory leashed Baxter.

When Bess opened the door, Whit rushed in. Homer jumped on his leg, trying to reach his master's face. The broadcaster's brow was furrowed. He petted Homer then eased him away, worry gathered in his eyes.

"Sorry, I missed your broadcast." She stretched up to kiss him. "Rory stopped over, and we had to take the dogs out."

He put his hand on her arm. "It's okay."

Rory and Baxter came to the door. "Time for me to go," Rory said.

"Thank you." Whit nodded to Rory.

"No problem."

Before Bess could form a question, her friend and Baxter were gone. Whit closed the door behind him. He went to the liquor cabinet and pulled out a bottle of brandy, took down two glasses, and filled them.

"What's going on?" Her pulse raced.

"Sit down, Bess," Whit said, carrying the drinks to the sofa.

"What happened? Something...something bad happened?" Her breath hitched in her chest.

"Sit." He put one glass on the coffee table and took a swig from the other.

"Oh my God." Chills ran up her arms, and tears clouded her eyes. "It's bad, isn't it?"

"Bess...I..."

"Spit it out," she said, squeezing his arm.

"There was a car bomb, an explosion, today. Someone was killed..."

"Who? Who?"

He held up his hand. "A cop."

She gasped. "No, no, not Terry? Not Terry. Tell me, tell me, Whit, tell me it wasn't Terry."

"I can't."

Through the tears, she saw the pain on his face. "Please, God, tell me it wasn't Terry!"

"It was. It was Terry. He was killed."

"Oh my God! No, no, no, no, no, no..." She got up and paced back and forth in front of the window, shaking her head and repeating the word 'no' over and over again.

Whit cut her off, grabbing her arms with his hands. "Stop, stop. It's true. I'm so sorry, Bess, so sorry." His soft words broke into her consciousness. Emotion erupted through her like lava through a volcano. Adrenaline pumped, and she could hardly breathe. Looking into his eyes, she knew the truth.

Bess fell against his chest, sobbing, her knees buckled. He tightened his arms around her, holding her up, and let her cry. Her throat closed. Tears streamed down her face, onto his suit jacket. Nausea hit her stomach as she gulped air. She pushed away from him and ran to the bathroom, where she threw up twice.

"Are you all right? Bess? Open up."

She hugged the cold, porcelain bowl, propping herself up. She cooled her forehead on the rim. As soon as her breathing became regular, she pushed up on shaky legs.

"Bess! Answer me!"

"I'm okay." She splashed water on her face, brushed her teeth, and rinsed her mouth. Then, she closed the toilet and sank down, waiting for the strength to stand to return to her legs.

"Please, open up."

She looked at the door, her eyes focused on the lock. She leaned forward and clicked it open. Whit entered. She gazed up at him with puffy, swollen eyes.

"Oh, baby," he said softly. He lifted her by her arms and walked her back to the living room. Easing her down on the sofa, he held her and stroked her hair.

Strength had bled out of her body. She could barely lift her arm.

"Drink this." Whit held the snifter to her lips.

She took a sip and choked at first then it went down nice and smooth, warming her inside. "What happened?" she asked.

"It was the lead story. I couldn't get Sam to postpone it until tomorrow."

"So, that's why Rory came?"

"I called her. I wanted to be here when you found out."

She touched his cheek. He held up the brandy, and she took another dose. The alcohol eased the tension in her body. "Please, tell me everything."

Whit went through the details with her. Bess broke down several times. She finished her drink and stretched out on the sofa. He covered her with an afghan. Dumpling jumped up and curled up at Bess's feet. She fell asleep in minutes.

WHIT WALKED THE LENGTH of Bess's apartment several times, trying to figure out what to do. *She's so upset, she must still love him. Right? Then, she won't fall for me. We can go on the way we are without her wanting a commitment. How long can you love a dead man? What am I thinking? This is awful for her. She needs me. I need to do something. Think, think!*

He plopped down on an overstuffed chair. Homer joined him, sitting at his feet. *The dogs!* Whit grabbed both leashes and picked up Dumpling, who seemed glued to Bess's leg. He headed for the elevator. *A nice, long walk. Perfect!*

When he hit the street, he directed the pugs to the park. The weather was cloudy and chilly, but not cold. The brisk exercise warmed him up. As he headed for the Great Lawn, his mind wandered.

She's so close to the perfect woman. But if she's still in love with Terry, there's no room for me. Fine. I'm leaving soon, anyway. Good thing. Get away before I make another mistake. Bess is tempting. He thought about her luscious body and her soft lips. His lips tingled as he remembered their last kiss.

The pull to spend all his spare time at her apartment was strong. Whit could barely resist his desire to be close to her, and when he smelled something delectable in the air, his stomach forced him to ring her bell. She welcomed him. Although Ned had recovered and resumed taster duties, Bess respected Whit's appraisals of her concoctions as well.

He liked feeling important to the accomplished baker. He'd never been part of a woman's working life, except for the few times he'd screwed up and had an affair with one of his producers. *Angie, Beth...what disasters.* He'd quickly learned to resist sleeping with women at the station, no matter how attractive.

Everything about Bess kicked him right out of his comfort zone. He'd never dated a woman who could bake, loved dogs, and showered all around her with kindness. Whatever happened to their friendship pact? He chuckled. *It didn't last long.* Chemistry got in the way. Resisting temptation had never been one of his strong suits, especially when it came to beautiful women.

Why should he? It's not like he treated his women badly. He took them out to nice places, called when he said he would, showed up on time, and offered genuine compliments with his bouquets of roses. So what if his heart remained well guarded and unavailable? It didn't reduce the parade of women willing to warm his bed.

He parked his butt on a bench while Homer zeroed in on one tree. Dumpling joined Whit, curling around in a circle, pressing up against his hip. She snorted once, then shut her eyes. His hand draped over her, idly caressing her soft fur.

Bess is different. Whit had been careful to pursue young, serious, career women, who didn't have marriage and babies in minds. Models were perfect. The only compromise he'd made was in their body type. He preferred women with more meat on their bones. But if these women were safer, he'd forego the pleasure of a bit more to love.

As he approached forty, he worried his appeal to younger women would fade. But being a well-known broadcaster kept him in demand. Life was good. *Great job. All the women I want. Terrific apartment. Perfect dog. Perfect life.* While gazing in the mirror in the morning, Whit reminded himself of his good fortune.

Then, why did he get so depressed at holidays? Why did he linger while walking past a playground, captivated by the joyous shrieks of small children? If he was so happy, why did he have to convince himself of it every God damn day?

Dumpling changed position. Whit's phone rang. *Jeff.* "Hey, how you doin'?" he asked his big brother.

"Great. Have you called the therapist, yet?"

"Not exactly. I've been pretty busy."

Jeff ignored the answer. "You don't have to tell anyone you're going."

"I hadn't thought about it. I have a pretty good life."

"Do you, Whit? You can't commit to a woman, and you stubbornly refuse to even consider creating the family we never had. You call yourself happy?"

"I've lived this long without a traditional family. I'm used to it."

"What's good about being used to being alone?"

"Absence of pain. Besides, I tried it once. Gemma. Remember?"

"Yeah, what a bad choice."

"Thank you for your support." Whit frowned.

"Maybe if you got some therapy, you'd make a better choice and have what you want."

"Thanks, Jeff. I'll think about it."

"Sounds better than I usually get from you."

"Anything to get you off my back."

"Fine. Be an asshole. You used to listen to me. Guess your job's gone to your head."

"Jeff, I—" But his brother had hung up.

Is he right? Whit had always relied on Jeff, the only steady, positive influence in his life. Jeff was rarely wrong. He addressed Dumpling. "Should I believe him? Call the doctor? Am I nuts, Dumpling?"

The pug opened her eyes and shot him a cold stare.

"You're no help," Whit said. A ding from his phone drew his attention.

Here's the number. 212-752-2214
Dr. Richard Sumner. Call him. Now.

Whit chuckled and turned toward the dog nestled next to him. "Okay, okay. He wins."

He dialed. A machine answered. "This is Whitfield Bass. My brother, Jeff Bass, referred me to you. I'd like to set up an appointment." Whit left his number then stowed his cell in his back pocket and pushed to his feet. Dumpling whined. Whit bent down, and she licked his face. "Nice to know you approve."

He picked up the leashes and headed back to The Wellington. A small sense of relief flashed through him for a moment, making him smile. *Maybe Jeff's right.*

"Bess might be awake by now and wondering where you are, Dumpling. Let's go."

The pugs trotted along, leading the way. *They're smart. They know they're going home.* He exchanged a greeting with Crash as they made their way to the elevator.

Once they were in Bess' apartment, Dumpling ran over to the sofa and jumped up. She licked Bess' face until the blonde woke up.

"You're awake?"

"Am now. Thanks, Dumpling." Bess rubbed her eyes and stretched her arms to the ceiling.

"We went to the park. How are you feeling?" He sat on a chair next to the couch.

"I'm a little better."

"Feel like getting up? Going to dinner?"

"I don't know if I could face a restaurant."

"How about we order in? Chinese?"

Bess looked groggy. Her natural sparkle and energy had drained from her like air from a balloon. She moved in slow motion, swinging her legs over the edge and pushing to her feet. A stumble threatened to throw her to the ground, but Whit caught her before she fell.

"Guess my legs aren't quite ready."

"No worries." He guided her to the table. "Coffee?"

"I'll get it," she said, attempting to stand.

Whit gently pushed down on her shoulder. "I'll do it. Sit."

She watched him handle her fancy machine. He brought milk and poured two mugs. Bess sipped the hot brew and slipped her hand over his fingers. He looked at her with a warm smile.

"Thank you so much for being here."

"Of course. Where else would I be? Now, what do you feel like eating?"

"I'm not hungry."

"How about...some egg drop soup and a couple of dumplings."

Dumpling barked at the mention of her name. Bess and Whit chuckled. Homer woofed along. Whit opened his cell and placed their order.

"I want to go to the funeral. Do you know when and where it is?"

"Not yet. I'm sure we'll be covering it. I can give you a lift in the van."

"Are you allowed?"

"Why not? You can't go alone. You're coming with me."

"Thanks." She smiled.

After dinner, Whit tucked her into bed and cleaned up the kitchen. He walked the dogs again then undressed and slipped in next to Bess. *If I leave my boxers on, maybe I can resist making love to her. She needs to sleep.* He cuddled up behind, spooning her. She moaned without waking up. He folded her into his embrace and closed his eyes.

A couple of hours later, he awoke with a start. *The funeral. Will it be safe? Terry was murdered. Is Bess safe? If this was a hit, will she be next?*

Chapter Nine

THE VAN STOPPED ADJACENT to the path to Officer McNeil's grave to let Bess out first. Whit followed. They walked up the grass toward the mound of dirt next to the casket. The funeral had been closed, but the family had opened the burial to friends and the press. Bess wore a midnight blue, shimmery silk dress. She covered it with an elegant, lightweight, cream-colored, wool coat. Even a heavy layer of makeup didn't disguise the pale cast to her skin. Her eyes were slightly swollen and her nose pink, which she discovered when she looked in her pocket mirror.

Whit wore a black suit and dark gold tie. *He looks gorgeous, even dressed for a burial.* She wanted to hold his hand, but knew it was inappropriate. *He's working. I should keep my distance. Don't embarrass him. Be professional. No one knows about Terry and me. Be quiet. Blend in.*

She followed her own advice and trudged up the hill to where some men in uniform stood next to Terry's family and friends. A woman with a tear-streaked face, who looked like she hadn't slept in days, approached.

Whit stepped forward, introduced himself and shook her hand. "Mrs. McNeil?"

"Mona," the woman replied.

"I'm so sorry for your loss," Whit said.

Bess looked for an empty chair. Before she could become part of the crowd, Mona picked her out. She stepped forward. "I'm Mona, Terry's wife. Who are you?" No hand was offered. Instead, Mona rested her fists on her hips.

Bess felt the color drain from her face. "Bess Cooper. You're his wife? I thought he was divorced."

"Almost divorced. Separated. You his girlfriend?" The question in her eyes hardened into hostility, making Bess's blood run cold.

"We were friends."

"Yeah? I'll bet. Friends with benefits?" Mona narrowed her eyes. Her gaze swept over Bess, making her feel naked.

She pulled her coat tighter. "Only friends."

"You never slept with Terry?" Mona arched an eyebrow.

Bess shook her head, avoiding Whit's gaze.

Mona's mouth set into a firm line. "I'll bet. Figured he'd end up with someone like you," she muttered.

"Would you mind if I asked you a few questions?" Whit said, leading Mona away from Bess, who searched for a seat and sank into it heavily.

Married? He said he was divorced. Was he lying? Guess so. Almost divorced? This explains where he was on Saturday nights? She shuddered at the revelation he'd been lying to her all along. *Couldn't be. Even she said they were almost divorced. Isn't it the same thing?*

The cameraman and soundman followed Whit. She couldn't hear the questions and answers, so she turned her attention to the crowd. There were at least thirty people, most in blue police uniforms. A few came up to her and asked her how she knew Terry, and she gave them the line about being friends.

"Glass of water, miss?" An officer handed Bess a paper cup along with a warm smile.

Is he coming on to me...at a funeral? "Thanks." She took it and sipped, moving her gaze away from him.

Before he could continue with the conversation, Mona was on her way back. Whit and the crew trailed behind. The stormy expression on the widow's face warned Bess it was time to leave. She pushed to her feet and turned toward the van. But Mona kept coming. She caught up to the pretty baker and tugged on her arm.

"I know you! You're the chef slut," Mona said in a voice too loud for the occasion. All heads turned to look.

"What?" Bess's eyes grew wide.

"No, no, not chef. Uh...uh...baking! Yeah, right. *Baking with Bess*. You're Bess! You had your claws in my husband, you fucking bitch. And now he's dead." Mona slapped Bess across the face.

Tears of anger clouded her eyes. She sensed the heat in her cheeks. "Get away from me! You're crazy!" Bess screamed. Several policemen pulled Mona, swearing and kicking, away. Another couple of men in blue spoke softly to Bess, who was rubbing her cheek.

"Yeah, that's assault. But she's recently become a widow. You don't want to press charges, do you? I mean, the decent thing to do is to forgive and forget..."

Whit grabbed Bess by the arm and steered her to the van. "Come on. Let's get you out of here." He helped her into the back of the vehicle, got in, and shut the door.

"Did you hear her? Oh my God! She's crazy! Terry was separated, divorced or almost. I'm none of her business. She hit me!" Bess pulled out a mirror and examined her swollen lip.

"Are you all right?"

She burst into tears. "I'm mourning Terry, too. She's not the only one."

"Did you sleep with him?"

"Of course."

"You lied?"

"I wanted to save her the humiliation. Besides, it's nobody's business what Terry and I did behind closed doors."

"You're right, you're right. Let's head back, guys," Whit said.

Bess wiped her eyes with a tissue, but her skin still stung. The soundman handed back a cup with some ice and the remainder of his iced coffee. Bess held it to her face. They drove back in silence. She fell asleep, her head lolling against Whit's shoulder.

They pulled up in front of The Wellington. Bess got out and thanked the men. Crash opened the door, and the van pulled away from the curb.

WHIT WAS ON EDGE WHEN he got to the studio.

"What did ya get? Anything interesting?" Sam asked the three-man crew while she shuffled through some papers attached to a clipboard.

"Not much. Interview with the widow—" Whit began.

"Great stuff!" Alan, the cameraman, cut him off.

"Yeah. Awesome. Cat fight, tears...the whole shitload," Barry, the soundman, added.

"Fantastic! Let's see," Sam ushered them into her office.

Whit grabbed Barry's arm and pulled him aside. "What the hell do you mean?"

"I got the whole thing between the baker-lady and the cop's widow. I even had the sound going for the car ride home."

"You can't use it!" Whit's eyes widened.

"I can and will. Actually, Sam will. Hell, she was in a news van. What did she think? We'd stop recording because she told the truth? How perfect! Her confession in the van."

"It was a private conversation. You can't use it."

"Shoulda warned her, buddy. Sam's gonna love this." He shoved Whit out of the way, entered Sam's office, and closed the door.

Whit burst in. "Some of this was a private conversation. Bess had no idea she was being taped. We can't use this."

Sam shushed him and waved her hand. Alan and Barry got the tape rolling, and Whit's mouth hung open. They had caught the entire fight, including Mona's accusations and Bess' denial. Then, they fast-forwarded to Bess's tearful confession in the van.

Whit's heart raced. *This'll destroy her. She's a public figure.*

"Wow! Great job, boys. And they say nothing ever happens at a funeral. Hah!"

"Sam, you can't run this."

"Oh? And why not?"

"You'll ruin her career."

"She's a baker. Who'll care?"

"Sam, didn't you hear?" Alan asked. "She isn't just a baker. She's the baker on *Baking with Bess.* You know, the show on the shitty cable channel?"

"Oh my God! She's the same Bess?" Sam did a victory dance. "A homerun, a touchdown, a hat trick...way to go! Get it cleaned up and ready to run. I want it on the six o'clock tonight-re-run at eleven."

Alan and Barry pushed by Whit and out the door. He heard them congratulating themselves. Horrified, Whit sweated. "You can't use this, Sam." He paced in her office.

"I can, and I will. Tonight. Be prepared, because you're doing the story."

"No. I refuse. Bess Cooper's a friend of mine."

Sam narrowed her eyes. "She's sleeping with you, too? Interesting. Of course, we'll keep you out of it. This is the news, Whit, not kindergarten. You're doing it."

"I'm not."

"You do the story, or you're fired."

"You can't fire me. I have a contract."

"We'll see what the lawyers say."

"I suddenly feel a bout of the flu coming on." He sneezed then whipped out a handkerchief and blew his nose.

"If you walk out of here..." Sam held up a fist.

"Threatening me? I'd hate to get everyone on the staff sick. I might be contagious. Might be bubonic plague. Better get to the doctor."

"Goddam it, Whit! Get your ass in here."

"Are you going to do the story?"

"Okay, okay, you win."

Whit let out a big breath. "Thank you, Sam. I owe you."

Whit left her office, glancing back, not trusting the look on her face. *This isn't over.* He picked up the news copy for the show and read it over while he sat in makeup. *Bess doesn't need more grief. She's got enough to deal with now.*

Whit smiled at his courage in standing up to his producer, Samantha. As time for his broadcast drew near, the makeup artist gave him a final touch.

The lights were on. Whit slipped into his seat at the news desk, took a sip of water, and cleared his throat. Glancing over the lead stories on his desk, he did a few speaker warm up exercises with his voice, waiting for the cameras to roll.

The teleprompter came on. He focused on the type and opened with his typical greeting then the screen went blank for a fraction of a second before a new story appeared.

"This just in," he read. "Confrontation between slain police officer Terrence McNeil's' widow and the popular cooking show star, Bess Cooper, today at the cemetery..." Whit froze and looked down at the paper in front of him.

"Wait. Taking this out of order." He struggled to keep his hands from shaking. "Excuse me. An elderly man was struck by a car and killed on Queen's Boulevard," he said, glancing up to see Sam jumping up and down, her face turning as red as the flesh of a watermelon. She kept making a slashing gesture across her throat, but Whit ignored her. He kept reading from the sheet, paying no attention to the words scrolling by on the prompter.

Finally, the camera cut from Whit to the film of the day's events at the cemetery and in the van. Now, it was his turn to become purple with rage though he couldn't stop it. Locking eyes with a smug, triumphant Sam, Whit thought he'd bust a gut. The story continued to roll on the screen, cutting to commercial when the tape was over.

Whit knew if he marched out, he'd be violating his contract and fired on the spot. At this point, there was nothing he could do. The tape had run. The truth was out, and he could no longer cover it up or stop it. *Getting fired won't help Bess.* He corralled his emotions and read the next story from the teleprompter.

Who knew a half hour could drag on forever? Breaking for a minute of sports and weather didn't help. He caught his breath and studied the next story. No time to think. No time to calm his racing pulse. He knew Bess would watch the broadcast, especially because he had interviewed Mona. Bess wouldn't miss it, or coverage of Terry's burial, either.

Finally, the program ended. But instead of tearing out of the studio as fast as he could to console Bess, he hung around to speak to Sam. "Sam, this the lowest thing you've ever done."

"It's the news, Whit. Get over it or get another job."

"Is it news? Or private information. What good does it do anyone else outside of the parties concerned to know? Nothing but scandal, titillation."

"Yep. Bet our ratings go up. And I'm gonna re-run the tape tonight, too. So, tell your little chickie to tune in at eleven."

"You have no heart, no soul." Whit shook his head.

"I have a job. Which'll be more than you can say if you ever pull a stunt like this again."

"If I have to take down someone I care about to keep my job, then it's not worth keeping."

"Is this your resignation?" He couldn't tell if she was hopeful or nervous.

"No such luck, Sam. I don't give up easily." He picked up his briefcase.

"Good. Because you have a following, and I'd hate to lose you."

"Really? You have a funny way of showing it."

"Look, Whit. I have a job to do. And because I'm a woman, I have to be tougher than the guys if I want to keep it. This isn't anything against you. It's a juicy story that'll goose up ratings. You don't worry about ratings, but I do. Every day."

"I wouldn't trade places with you for anything," Whit said, heading for the door.

"'Night," she called after him, but he didn't answer.

Thank God, I'll be in Asia soon writing real stories instead of digging up dirt. His mouth tasted foul, so he popped a couple of pieces of gum. *Makes my stomach turn. Bess, please God, I hope you understand.*

BESS TURNED OFF THE television and plopped down on the sofa. She tried to control her breathing. Her cell rang. It was Rory.

"Did you watch the news?"

"Of course."

"Bess, did you say those things?"

"I did. I had no idea I was being recorded. I thought it was a private conversation with Whit...in the van..." She burst into tears before she could continue. Rory said something before she hung up, but Bess didn't hear. *Whit, how could you? How could you betray me for a story? I trusted you. Believed you were sincere. You set me up. Why?*

Her heart hurt. As she was coping with Terry's sudden death, Whit proved to be a traitor. She had feelings for him. Now, he had thrown her to the wolves. *Sure hope my producer wasn't watching. God, what happens if he was?* A small shudder flashed through her. She went to the liquor cabinet and pulled out the brandy bottle. *It's getting low.* She poured a small snifter and took a drink. The smooth liquor warmed her.

She returned to the sofa and stretched out. Dumpling joined her, and Homer curled up on the floor nearby. *You park your dog here then stab me in the back? I love you, Homer, but you have to go.* Bess wanted to be angry with Whit. She wanted to hate him, throw things at him, but the pain of his betrayal stopped her. Too wounded for anger, she kept asking herself why he did it, but she couldn't come up with an answer.

Another sip of brandy, and her eyes closed. The snoring of the pugs lulled her to sleep, but the buzz from the lobby woke her with a start. She pushed up slowly and made her way to the intercom. Her Dinner Club friends had arrived. She heard the voices getting louder as the elevator neared. All talking stopped once they spied Bess waiting in the doorway.

The women and their dogs filed past their hostess. Miranda plopped down a bag of take-out from the Chinese restaurant. Brooke opened it, and they all started talking again. Rory went to the cabinet for plates. Miranda grabbed silverware.

Then, Bess clapped her hands and all activity stopped. "What's going on here?"

"We thought the damn news show would upset you. So, we're here to feed you, and let you know you're not alone," Brooke piped up.

Tears clouded Bess's eyes, but she blinked them back. "You guys are the best."

"So, how are you?" Rory perched on a stool at the breakfast bar.

"I'm confused. I don't know why he did it. When I told Whit I wanted to go to the funeral...he offered..." Bess poured out the story, and the other three listened while they passed around eggrolls, Mu Shu Chicken, and fried Tofu. When she finished laying out the details, the women packed up the empty cartons and placed them in the garbage.

Before discussion could continue, the doorbell sounded, and Homer ran over, barking.

"Must be Whit," Bess whispered. Her heartbeat kicked up, emotion heated her cheeks.

"This is our signal to leave. Come on, ladies." Rory said. The Dinner Club women leashed their dogs and headed for the door.

Whit stepped back to let them out. He nodded a greeting. They avoided his gaze and silently headed for the elevator. He crossed the room in three strides and gripped Bess's arms. "You saw the broadcast?"

"Of course."

"Bess, I...I'm so sorry. I had no idea..."

"You mean to tell me you didn't know they were recording?"

"No, I didn't. I really didn't. It never occurred to me they'd record something so...so...private. Between us. In the van."

"But you knew they were shooting the fight?"

"I didn't think about it. All I thought about was getting you away from her and safely back home. I should've been more aware. I should've told them to cut. I didn't. I'm so sorry. You have no idea."

"You didn't arrange this—or hope for this—to boost your career?"

He stepped back. "Of course not! I'd never do that. I'd never hurt you to advance my career. You must believe me."

"You betrayed me. Sold me down the river. I'm branded. People will think I'm a cheater, an adulterer, and a liar. My little white lie to save Mona's feelings. I'll never live it down."

"It's not a big deal. She's the one who slapped you, even though you said you were only Terry's friend. She was in the wrong."

"So? I'm the single woman. She's the grieving widow. I'll be the bad guy."

"Bess, forget it. The public is fickle. Today's news is gone tomorrow."

"Not this. And you were going to broadcast this, weren't you?"

"Absolutely not! I told my producer. We had a huge fight over it. She said she wasn't going to run the story and then—*blam!*—there it was on the screen, big as life. I stopped in the middle and changed to the story about the old man getting killed in Queens."

"I saw it."

"She cut me off! Then ran the tape. They never do—well, rarely. I was screaming."

"I'll bet." Bess narrowed her eyes.

"You don't believe me?"

"It's hard."

Whit's frustration exploded. "I come here begging forgiveness, telling the truth, and you don't believe me? Damn it!"

"I didn't say I didn't believe you."

"Yes, you did. The way you looked at me. Shit! First, Sam doesn't listen, and now you. Women! Who needs 'em?" He threw up his hands and strode to the window. Homer followed, barking.

"Women? Now, you're lumping me in with your mean-ass producer?"

"I didn't say I put you in with her."

"Then, what did you say?"

"I said-forget it. Come on, Homer." He picked up his dog. "Thanks for taking care of him."

"You're leaving?"

"It's obvious you don't want me here."

"It's obvious you don't want to be here. You got what you wanted from me—some sack time and food. Oh, and Homer. Time to take off, right?"

"What?"

"You heard me. You gave me up to bring a hot story to your producer. Probably sleeping with her, too. I've served my purpose. You're ready to move on."

"I can't believe you're saying this." His eyes widened.

"Why not? It's true, isn't it?"

"Not one word."

"Please, I'm not stupid. You're probably sleeping with every important, publicity-generating woman in Manhattan. The Great Whitfield Bass. Newsman extraordinaire! Ruins reputations at the drop of a hat!

Be sure to spell his name right under those pictures in every newspaper and magazine," she sneered, snapping her fingers.

"You bitch! I never suspected you of...of..." Whit looked flustered, and his face reddened.

"What? Standing up for myself? We women-bitches, all of us."

"Take your nasty attitude and shove it, Bess. Never pictured you like this."

"Only pictured me naked and willing, huh?"

The look of shock on his face told her she'd gone too far. *He sold me down the river. Why am I feeling guilty? He's got this coming. Bastard.* Anger flowed full force.

But he didn't look like a bastard. He didn't wear a nasty, smug, sly grin. His cool gray eyes, once lustful and seductive, registered pain and confusion. "I thought you got it, what we had. Never simply sex."

"Wasn't it?"

He shook his head, tucked Homer under his arm, and proceeded to leave without another word. Whit turned and shot one hurt then angry look at Bess before he slammed the door.

"Good riddance," Bess muttered to herself. Dumpling stretched and yawned. "Right, girl. Time to go out." Bess fastened the leash on her pug, and they went down in the elevator.

Chapter Ten

BESS AWOKE IN THE MORNING feeling worse than the night before. All the righteous indignation from the day before fizzled. She took a tablespoon of regret with her first cup of coffee. *Why did I scream all those things at him? He didn't do the broadcast. It was obvious they cut him off. Yes, he should have told them not to shoot or record, but how did he know they were? What have I done?*

Her appetite went south. Coffee alone would have to do. Bess boarded the elevator. Whit rushed in with Homer a second before the doors closed. They rode to the first floor in silence. A thousand times, Bess wanted to say something, but words wouldn't come. Neither one looked at the other. The uneasy quiet stopped when they landed in the lobby.

Bess decided to walk to work. A heaviness surrounded her heart. *Whit and I are through. After what I said to him, I'm not surprised.* She argued back and forth with herself about Whitfield Bass and his betrayal. Was it or wasn't it? She had expected to feel triumphant, well rid of the heel who had sabotaged her. But she didn't. Their breakup left a big hole in her heart. She cared more than she had admitted.

When she arrived at the cable office building, Ned met her at the elevator.

"What happened to you? You look like you lost your best friend."

"I did. What's up this morning?"

"Carl wants to see you."

"The weekly meeting?"

"No, privately."

Fear spiked through her, releasing adrenaline. Carl never met privately. She only sat with him in group planning meetings. He was the CEO of the network. *Crap! Bet he saw the newscast.* She hadn't considered how it might look to the station. Now, she was convinced the conversation with Mr. Blackstone would not go well. Her hands got clammy, and her mouth dried up like sand in the desert.

Ned walked with her. "What's up? Carl never meets with on-air people."

"Can't be good," she said.

He squeezed her hand and laced his fingers with hers. She shot him a grateful smile as they turned the corner and approached the gigantic office. Ned peeled off as they reached the door. "Good luck," he whispered, blowing her a kiss.

The large man sat behind a big desk cutting across a corner of the massive office. *If it's a good meeting, he'll join me on the couch.* Carl did not get up but swiveled to face her and indicated a chair in front of him with a gesture. With a quiver in her belly, Bess sat down.

"Did you happen to catch the six o'clock news last night?" he asked.

Bess took a breath. "I did."

"Was the stuff about you on the level?"

"It depends on what you mean by 'on the level.' He wasn't married when we were dating."

"Did you lie to the widow about your—uh—relationship with the cop?"

Bess let out the air she'd been keeping in. "I was only trying to save her feelings. Obviously, she was upset, and I figured..."

"You were caught lying on television to a grieving cop widow about your relationship with her husband. Bess, it looks bad. No matter what the facts were, it's not the kind of image we want for the show."

There was a moment of silence.

"We've had a few phone calls from viewers, too. None sympathetic to you."

"Are you firing me, canceling my show, Mr. Blackstone?" She heard her heartbeat in her ears.

"Not canceling, exactly. I was thinking more of taking a hiatus until this thing blows over. And the phone stops ringing."

"Hiatus?"

"We'll run repeats for a couple of weeks until this hoopla dies down."

"Oh, I see."

"Your show has been popular, Bess. I'd hate to lose it."

So hiatus is the nice way of saying I'm finished? "What are the show's chances of going back on the air?"

"Don't know. I don't like to predict these things. If there are no more headlines, I can see lifting the ban...I mean...hiatus, maybe. According to your contract, we'll suspend your salary since you won't be shooting any new episodes. We'll withhold payment until you start shooting again. Your contract comes up for renewal in a month, I believe. Let's wait and see, Bess. I'd hate to give you wrong information."

"I understand, Mr. Blackstone," Her chest constricted, and her heartbeat increased. *I've got to get out of here before I break down.*

"You have a growing fan base, Bess. It's too bad this had to happen. I hope you can get past it." He stood up and shook her hand, signaling the meeting was over. Bess managed a tiny, wan smile and made a beeline for the door.

Once back in her office, she turned to face the window. Tears stung at the backs of her eyes. A knock on her doorjamb made her jump.

"Hey, Bess. Sorry about the hiatus. Go. Take a vacation. Bet you could use one." Woody, her producer, lounged in the doorway.

"Don't tell me to go on vacation. My whole livelihood, my career, is about to get flushed. Last thing I feel like doing is taking a vacation."

"You could be back on the air in a couple of weeks. Fun in the sun time."

Bess cocked an eyebrow at him. "Sure, sure. Like I almost believe you."

"Your contract has a couple of weeks to go."

"Yep. Then, I'll be canceled."

"At least they have to pay you while you're on hiatus, don't they?"

"No, actually, they don't. If I'm not shooting, they can withhold my salary." Tears clouded her eyes.

"I didn't know. I'm sorry. I love your program. It's too bad."

"Thanks."

Ned pushed through before Woody could close it. Bess glanced at him, then turned back to the window. "You can go, Ned. Won't be needing you today, or maybe ever."

At the sound of him sinking into a plush chair, Bess swiveled around to face him.

"So this is it, huh? Tail between the legs and slink out?"

She nodded as a few tears broke through.

"A quitter? You surprise me."

"What do you want me to do? Get nasty? Fight them? I get it. I'm the wrong kind of news right now."

"Go home. Think it through. Re-group."

"I'm going. But I have no clue what I'm going to do."

"Don't assume your contract will be canceled."

"We'll see. But I'm not taking bets. They always go the easiest way for the company. Which means canceling me."

"Don't be so sure, babe."

"No one's irreplaceable."

"You are to me." Ned squeezed her hand.

Bess fished around in her purse, looking for a tissue. Ned slid his handkerchief across the desk. She took it and wiped her eyes.

He leaned over and kissed her on the cheek. "I adore you. Don't give up."

"Feeling's mutual."

As soon as he was gone, she left the building. The heaviness in her heart over the breakup with Whit doubled its weight. Loss of her job left her rootless. *What will I do with my time?* Bess had been working one way or another since she was fourteen. Being unemployed at thirty-two was a new experience, and not a pleasant one. *How can you relax on a vacation when you don't know what's going to happen to you when you get home?*

"Howdy, Miss Bess. You're home early," Crash said, holding the door open for her.

At the sight of his friendly face, the dam burst, and Bess collapsed sobbing into his embrace. He held her close, whipping out a hanky. The roughness of his uniform against her cheek soothed her. Crash had always been friendly, but respectful. He made her feel safe. She was embarrassed to have crossed the line with her outburst. She pushed off him, taking a deep, shuddering breath, trying to control her emotions.

When the elevator door opened, Whitfield Bass sauntered into the lobby with Homer. She met his gaze, and his expression turned stony. Bess tried to hide her tears, but he faced her.

"What happened?" he asked.

"Nothing."

"Clearly not 'nothing.' This couldn't be over me?"

"Don't flatter yourself. I lost my job because of your broadcast."

"Come on. No. Your show was canceled?" Concern filled his eyes.

"I'm on hiatus. My contract is up in a couple of weeks. I'm sure the station has no intention of renewing."

"Did they say they wouldn't renew?"

"Not in so many words. But I got the message."

"Then, you're not outright fired."

"Look, Mr. Wise Ass, when they say you're on hiatus for a convenient few weeks, then your contract is up...duh. You don't have to be a rocket scientist to know what they mean."

"Suppose you're right."

"Thank you, Mr. Know-it-all."

"You don't have to get snippy."

"Snippy? Snippy?" Her voice rose. "I've been ruined, dragged through the mud, and fired because of your double-dealing, and you don't think I have the right to be snippy?" She slapped him across the face.

Crash was as surprised as Whit, whose face turned red.

Bess sucked in air. Her hand flew to cover her mouth. "I'm sorry, Whit, so sorry," she muttered, her eyes wide.

"Yeah. I'll bet." He rubbed his skin. She tried to cup his cheek, but he captured her wrist. "Oh, no. One shot is all you get."

"I didn't mean it."

"Yes, you did."

"I'm upset about the job..."

"And I'm responsible. I get the drill. I'm sorry you lost the show. I wish I could change everything, but I can't." He took out his card. "Here's my office number. If I can do something to help you find a new gig, call me."

She wanted him to take her in his arms and hold her. She wanted to disappear into him, bask in his love, and be soothed by kind words. She already suspected he had told her the truth about the news team, it probably wasn't his fault. Instead, she'd slapped him, assaulted him. And in front of Crash, too. *I humiliated him. How stupid am I? Now, he's gone forever.*

Crash opened the big door, and Whit and Homer made a prompt exit. She stared after him, but he didn't look back. She did spy him rub his cheek once more and shame filled her.

"I'm so sorry, Crash."

"Don't apologize to me, miss."

"I embarrassed you, Whit, myself. I'm not having a good day." She moved toward the elevator.

A big greeting from Dumpling with slurpy kisses made Bess smile. She checked her watch then opened her cell.

"Miranda. Hi. What are you doing tomorrow?"

IT TOOK A COUPLE OF days to gather the women together, but by the end of the week, they rallied around Bess. On Friday, the Dinner Club women marched into The Wellington. Bess greeted them at the door.

"I'm sorry I don't have dinner for you guys tonight. It's been a horrible day..."

"Get a jacket. We're taking you out," Miranda said.

"Yep. You need food." Brooke leaned against the doorjamb.

"And a good Cosmo."

"You noticed?" Bess raised her eyebrows.

"Hell, yeah. La Mer Bleu. Our treat," Rory said.

"It's too expensive. I couldn't..."

Brooke picked up a blazer lying across the arm of the sofa, Miranda petted Dumpling, and Rory pressed the button for the elevator.

"I guess there's no arguing."

"Right." Brooke held the garment while Bess slipped it on.

The meal was rich, with creamy sauces and sinful desserts. The Cosmos were followed by a bottle of wine, compliments of the chef.

"I think he's got a crush on you," Miranda whispered in Bess's ear.

"He's a sweetie—just professional courtesy." A little heat rose in her cheeks.

"Chef's got the hots for Bess," Rory teased.

"Wish Whit still did," Bess sighed.

"I wouldn't be so sure it's over," Brooke said.

"I slapped him. Across the face. In front of the doorman." Bess put her hands over her eyes. "He'll never forgive me."

"He will, if he cares for you. And I'm sure he does." Miranda said, signaling for the check.

When the taxi pulled to the curb, Crash was there to help Bess out. She teetered a bit. Leaning heavily on him, she raised her hand and waved at her friends as the cab merged into traffic, taking them to their homes.

"Are you okay, miss?" Crash propped her up and headed inside. Bess giggled and eased into the doorman's strong grip. "I'd take you upstairs, Miss Bess, but there's no one to man the door. Wayne hasn't arrived yet."

"It's okay. I'm fine. I can make it." She eased away from him and smoothed her jacket. Her mind wandered back to dinner. Pierre, the chef, had come to their table to present the wine. He had kissed Bess's hand and wiggled his eyebrows. She had flirted back blushing and laughing at his double-entendres. Her friends watched, wide-eyed, as Bess, emboldened by Cosmos, led him on.

She chuckled to herself. *I've still got it.* The doors opened, and she proceeded to her place. Before she could grab the knob, she noticed the door was already open. And Dumpling wasn't there, barking and scratching to get out. She took in a breath and sobered up quickly.

Fear spiked in her veins. *Someone broke in? Are they still there? Where's Dumpling?*

She nudged the door with her foot. Peeking inside, she saw her belongings scattered everywhere. *Someone's been here. Might still be here!* She screamed and backed up. *Dumpling!*

Whit flung his door open at her second scream. His hair was tousled, his feet bare, and he was tying his terry robe at the waist. "What the hell is going on? If you're having wild sex...could you keep it down? It's midnight."

Bess trembled. "My apartment...someone's broken in. They took Dumpling, or she's...she's..." Emotion choked her, and words wouldn't pass.

"What the..." He padded out to join her.

"Look," Bess said.

Whit took a gander, moving slowly until he saw the destruction. "Holy shit. Your place has been trashed."

"Where's Dumpling?" Tears cascaded down Bess's cheeks. She pushed past Whit and called for her dog. At first, there was silence then a faint whimper and a scratch.

"She's alive!" Bess ran in, repeating the pug's name then listening.

"I'm calling the police. Bess, come out of there. It's dangerous."

"Not until I find Dumpling."

"Give me your cell."

Bess dug her phone from her bag and handed it to Whit. When she threw open the closet, the small pug bolted out, barking. Bess picked her up, cuddling the frightened dog. Whit spoke into the cell, but Bess wasn't listening. She was cooing to her pooch.

"Police are on their way. They said for us to get out and not to touch anything."

Bess looked at him. He looked gorgeous, hair hanging in his eyes, robe askew, revealing his bare chest. And the cool expression in his eyes. She followed him out the door then slid down into a cross-legged position on the floor.

"What the hell? Get up, Bess." Whit took her by the arm.

"Where am I gonna go?"

"My place. I told the police we'd be there. Come on." He guided her inside. She petted Dumpling's head and spoke softly to the creature. Homer barked. Whit parked Bess on his sofa and headed for the liquor cabinet.

"No more," Bess said, shaking her head. "I think I've had enough."

"Been drinking?" Whit cocked an eyebrow.

"Out with the Club. We celebrated my getting canned."

"Celebrated?"

The fog lifted. "Oh my God! My apartment! It's totally trashed!" Fear and panic welled up in her chest. Dumpling responded by barking. When Bess touched the dog's side, the pug whimpered.

"They've hurt Dumpling! Probably kicked her." Tears poured forth.

"We'll take her to the vet tomorrow."

But Bess couldn't stop crying. Whit sat down next to her and put his arm around her shoulders. She turned her face into his chest and sobbed. He enclosed her in his embrace and kissed her hair.

"It's gonna be all right, honey. It's gonna be all right," he whispered.

"I can't go back there. My home! It's wrecked."

"Stay with me."

She eased back and raised her gaze to meet his. "Really?"

"Of course."

"In the guest room?"

"In my bed, but only if you want to."

She nodded. "Thank you."

A knock interrupted them. "Police!"

Whit opened the door. Both pugs barked, and the officer stepped back.

"Miss Cooper?"

Bess came forward. "I'm Miss Cooper." She picked up Dumpling, who eyed the man with suspicion.

"Does your dog bite?" he asked.

"She won't hurt you, as long as you don't hurt me."

"Say, I know who you are!"

From the news or my show? She sensed heat traveling to her face.

"You're the baker-lady. McNeil's girlfriend, right?"

Bess nodded, not wishing to continue the conversation.

His brow knitted. "This may not be a simple break-in." He turned and called to his partner, who was in Bess's apartment. "Joe, this lady is McNeil's girl. Maybe the break-in has something to do with what he was working on?"

Joe's brows shot up. "Could be. Miss, could you come in here and see if there's anything missing? Please don't touch anything."

She handed her pug to Whit. Dumpling squirmed, but he had a firm grip, so she settled down. Bess wrapped one arm around her waist and rested her other hand on her chest. *I don't want to see what they've broken. Is grandma's watch missing? The vase from China?*

Bess picked her way around items on the floor. The intruder had scattered her sofa cushions, upended every container, opened all her cabinets, and pulled out everything but dishes. The apartment had been ransacked, leaving hardly any room to walk.

The bedrooms had been torn apart as well. Bess checked her jewelry case, which was intact. Everything of value was still in her apartment. Even spare change in a jar hadn't been touched.

"I think my partner's right. This wasn't a robbery. The perp was looking for something."

"I have no idea what."

The first officer had finished interviewing Whit and joined them.

"Hank, I don't think this was a robbery. This guy was looking for something."

"Yeah." Hank nodded. "Wonder if he found it."

"Doesn't look like it."

"Could be. Miss, you can't stay here. We need a forensics team in here."

"Can't stay in my own apartment?"

"Sorry. This is a crime scene. We'll try to get it processed quickly, but I make no promises."

"Can I have your cell number, so we can reach you?"

Bess wrote it down. Whit came up behind her and rested his hand on her shoulder. "She'll be staying with me, if you need to reach her."

The officers exchanged a look then nodded. "Fine, Mr. Bass."

"Is she in any danger?" he asked.

"Can't say, sir. Possibly. Fortunate she wasn't home tonight. We'll interview the doorman and find out who came in."

"Can I come with you?" Bess asked.

"Of course."

Whit took the dogs and retreated to his apartment while the policemen and Bess went to the lobby.

"He was dressed as a cop. Said he was Officer McNeil's partner and needed to pick up something McNeil had left behind. So, I let him up," Crash told them.

Bess gasped. "Terry didn't leave anything behind."

"Nothing you're aware of, Miss Cooper," Hank said.

Joe got on the radio and called for a team. "What did this man look like?" he asked Crash.

The doorman gave a good description, which didn't match Terry's partner. They looked at the security footage, noticing the man had averted his face from the camera. But he was a foot shorter than Terrence McNeil's real sidekick, so the officers knew he was a fake.

"I'm afraid you're in real danger, Miss Cooper. Do you have somewhere you can go for a few days?"

Bess burst into tears. She picked up her cell and dialed Rory.

"I'm on my way," Rory said.

Crash gave Bess his handkerchief. The two huddled together while the cops conferred with another officer outside. When Rory and Hack arrived at The Wellington, a police car with lights flashing was parked at the curb. Joe and Hank were standing on the sidewalk, talking. Another officer was on his radio. When Crash saw Rory, he opened the front door.

"What happened?"

"Miss Rory, so glad you're here. It's been a three-ring circus."

Bess stepped forward. Rory hugged her friend. Hack stood behind Rory. Before Bess got out more than one sentence of explanation, Whit, dressed in jeans and a T-shirt, joined them.

"Let's go up to my place." He told Crash to send the police up if they needed Bess, took her hand, and ushered them into the elevator. Once safely inside his apartment, he locked the doors and offered everyone drinks. Bess opted for coffee, as did Hack and Rory. After he flicked the switch on the coffeemaker, Whit poured himself a brandy.

Bess recounted the story of the break-in.

"A guy disguised as a cop broke in here?" Hack asked.

"The police think Terry left something in my apartment and that the guy might be back. They don't know if he found what he was looking for or not."

"You can stay at my place, Bess. I'm living at Hack's, but still have my digs."

"She can stay here with me as long as she likes," Whit offered.

Rory shot Hack a smile. "Duh, can't guess which one she'd choose."

"Wait!" Whit shot up from the seat. "Better idea. I've got a house in Rye. She can stay there. No one will ever find her there. She'll be completely safe."

"A house in Rye?"

"Rye's only about twenty-five miles away. Yeah. A small, stone cottage right near the beach."

"How come you never told me about this?" Bess asked.

Hack nudged Rory and shot his gaze at the door.

"Seems to me you're well cared for, Bess." Rory pushed to her feet. Hack followed.

"We'll be going," Hack said, heading out.

"Thank you both for coming. I know it's late."

Rory hugged her friend, took Hack's hand, and pushed the button for the elevator. The forensics team was already in the apartment, taking samples and dusting for fingerprints. The two pugs had curled up together and were snoring away on Whit's sectional sofa.

He stretched out and patted the cushion. "This way we're here if the police need you."

Bess smiled a sleepy yawn and lay down next to him. Whit turned on his side, closed his arms around her, and sighed. Bess cuddled into his embrace, folded one arm under the pillow and the other over his. As heat from his body warmed her, a small sound of contentment passed her lips. Peace surrounded her. *Whit's here. I'm safe.*

They slept for an hour before the officers knocked. The dogs gave short, half-hearted barks before shutting their eyes again. Bess answered questions, drank more coffee, and then returned to snooze alongside Whit until eight o'clock.

Chapter Eleven

THE NEXT MORNING, WHILE Bess was conferring with the forensics team, Whit called the real estate agent and took the stone house off the market. Then, he sat back, sipping coffee, his feet resting on an ottoman, and stared out the window. He replayed in his head his recent conversation with his therapist, Dr. Sumner, and thought about the question left unanswered when the session ended.

"Why should I keep the house? I'm never going to use it."

"Leaving the country, selling a house you love. Sounds like you've given up. Like you don't think you'll ever have the life you want."

"I've already given it up. I told you. It isn't my dream anymore. Not since I was a kid."

"You can tell me a hundred times, Whit, but it's you you have to convince."

"I am convinced. I've got the job in Asia coming up. I'll be living a different kind of life."

"The life you want?"

Silence. Then, "I think so."

"If you didn't want a wife and family, why'd you buy the house?"

"I told you, for Gemma."

"Why didn't you sell it when you and Gemma broke up?"

Whit opened his mouth then closed it without uttering a word. The verbal sparring ended. Dr. Sumner had won. Whit had no answer. "I fell in love with the house."

"Yet, you've never lived in it. Never even finished furnishing it. But never sold it. How come?"

"Good question. I don't know."

"Our time is up for today. Why don't you think about it, and we can discuss it next time."

Whit had thought about the question repeatedly for days. His reaction to the stone house was out of character. It disturbed him. He was a man who knew what he wanted, went after it, got it, and was satisfied. There was nothing wishy-washy about Whitfield Bass. Yet, here was this house, hanging around, doing nothing except eating up money. And he hadn't sold it. *A rational man would have dumped it long ago. Why didn't I?*

Now, he was glad he'd hesitated to unload the place. He needed it. Letting Bess live there would help make up for his horrible blunder of allowing the crew to record her. He had felt responsible from the get-go, but he couldn't find a way to fix his error. Now, he had one. *Let her stay there until it's safe to come home.* He smiled. *Good thing I didn't sell it. But I still don't have an answer for Dr. Sumner.*

He'd be a bit embarrassed to bring her to a house that didn't even have a kitchen table. *If I gave her some money, would she furnish it for me? Why do I need to furnish it, if I'm going to sell it when she leaves? Guess I'm not. Not while Bess needs it.* He took a deep breath. A sense of satisfaction filled him. Atonement was a wonderful thing.

Bess would stay with him in New York for a couple of days. She'd sleep with him. He drooled at the idea. And at the house! The mattress there was still wrapped in plastic. He and Gemma had broken up before he could get her onto it. It didn't even have sheets. Now, he'd christen it with Bess. His groin tightened at the picture in his mind's eye. Bess naked in bed in the stone house. A fire in the bedroom fireplace? He chuckled.

As his thoughts drifted to a more explicit scene, the door burst open. Bess looked frazzled. Her hair was askew, her lipstick chewed off. "How's Dumpling?"

"Fine. Sleeping. When do you want to go out to my house?"

"I have to spend a couple of days here, taking care of things. They said they'd be finished in the apartment later tonight. I need to get everything straightened up before I go anywhere."

"You shouldn't be there alone."

"I won't. Dumpling'll be there with me."

"No offense, but she wasn't much help the first time."

"It'll be daytime. I'll be safe." She patted his chest.

"But you'll be here with me at night?" Whit snaked his arm around her waist.

"Of course." She shot him a flirtatious glance. "I need a shower."

Whit rounded up a fresh towel, his terry robe, and a washcloth. As she turned on the water, he put up a second pot of coffee.

BESS'S MIND WHIRLED. She cranked up the hot water to wash away cold fear. *Someone disguised as a policeman. Terry, what did you do? Why is this happening? This is my life. No job. In danger. Everything shot to hell.* A tremor snaked up her spine.

Whit was there. When I needed him, he was there. He's taking me in. The warmth of his affection and protection swam through her. She turned down the water temperature. *Can I rely on him? What about this house? Is it nice? Habitable? Do I have a choice?* A quick shudder at the consequences of not leaving town shot through her. She turned off the spray.

Stepping into his thick robe, being surrounded by his masculine scent, made her needy and comforted at the same time. She rubbed the lapels against her cheeks. *Thank God, he doesn't hate me for slapping him.* Gratitude mixed with lust in her veins. She used his hairbrush and brushed her teeth with her finger before joining him in the living room.

She grabbed a mug of coffee then wrapped the robe tighter against a cool, October breeze.

"Should I close the window?"

"I'm okay."

Whit came up behind her and wrapped his arms around her. "How about I keep you warm this way?"

The touch of his hands and the pressure of him against her sparked desire. "I was thinking of something else. When do you have to be at work?"

"Noon." His breath teased her neck, followed by gentle pressure from his lips as he kissed his way down from her earlobe to her shoulder. Bess closed her eyes. His fingers curled around the lapels of the robe, slowly easing it open. His fingertips skimmed over her skin. "You're so soft," he murmured, his lips almost touching her ear.

His hand closed around her breast, squeezing gently. Bess leaned back against him, stretching her chin up, opening her neck. He dove on it like a hungry vampire. His kisses combined with his massage started her motor. Need grew between her legs. She wanted him.

"Bess, I..." he murmured.

"Don't talk. Love me," she whispered, pulling her sash loose.

He took her hand and led her into his bedroom. She looked around with curious eyes. It was masculine, like the living room, but stark—not much furniture. A queen-sized bed dominated the space. There were two low, ebony dressers and two matching end tables. A chrome lamp arced high to rest over one side of the mattress.

The walls were bright white, and the floor polished wood with a plush area rug in a modern black and white design. *This room is cold. Not passionate like Whit. Who did this?* One large black and white etching was mounted to face the bed.

A chill made her close her robe. "Who decorated this?"

"I hired someone. It's serviceable. It works."

"Serviceable is about all it is. Brrr. It's freezing in here."

Whit ripped down the black comforter and the white sheet underneath. "I'll warm you up. Slide in." He stood back and made a little bow.

Bess shed her covering, draping it over the bottom of the bed, and climbed in. Whit ripped his T-shirt over his head and unbuttoned his jeans.

The bedclothes were icy, giving her gooseflesh. Bess rubbed her arms. The gaze from Whit's gray eyes warmed her. He stared at her, looking her over before placing a knee on the mattress.

"You're incredibly beautiful."

"If you say so."

"Are you kidding?" He climbed up.

"I'm a little hippy. Could easily lose ten pounds...fifteen."

"Don't lose an ounce."

She shot a skeptical look at him.

"I like women with meat on their bones."

"Couldn't tell by your dating history."

"Best way to stay single. Date women who aren't marriage-minded and who don't want to ruin their stick-thin figures with pregnancies."

He's not single. He's professionally single. What am I doing here? Why do I find him irresistible?

"Enough talking," he said, bringing his mouth down on hers.

Bess's mind shut off. Her senses ruled. Whit tasted good. His tongue danced with hers, possessing her mouth as his body pressed her down. The hair on his chest tickled her breasts, making her nipples hard. They flattened against his muscles as he lowered himself.

Bess raised her hips until they met his. His erection grew pressed between them. She reached for him, running her fingers along the silky skin. He groaned, burying his face in her neck.

Whit shifted his weight, rolling to the side, and ran his hand down her chest and over her hip, resting it on her thigh. He gripped her hard for a moment then loosened his fingers to slide them to the front. Her body ignited when he touched her core. Heat ratcheted up quickly as he explored. She smoothed her hands down his back, pushing her fingertips into his muscles. A whiff of pine aftershave mixed with his masculine scent teased her nose. Unable to resist, she closed her lips over his skin, tasting him with her tongue. The slightly salty flavor pleased her.

His fingers zeroed in on a sensitive spot. Need spiraled through her body, coiling tension in her center. Bess bucked her hips. A low chuckle escaped Whit's lips as he lifted them from her shoulder. He eased a finger inside her. Bess thought she'd explode. She searched for him, but he had moved his erection away.

"Uh, uh, uh...naughty, naughty," he whispered, lowering his lips to her breast, and slipping a second finger into her.

"Oh, God, Whit. What are you waiting for?"

"You," he muttered.

"No, no, don't. I want you, now."

"But—"

"Now!" She dug her nails into his back.

"Ow! I see."

"I'm ready to—" But he cut off her words with his mouth. After removing his fingers, he glided them over her slippery flesh. Her hips moved rhythmically. He pushed up on his knees and positioned her legs, resting one on his shoulder. Then, he plunged into her all the way.

She gasped, clutching his shoulders, her eyes closing. The pleasure was so intense she was afraid she'd burst into tears. "Whit," she mumbled, unable to move.

Passion surged through her, growing more urgent, with every thrust. The heat increased as he pumped harder and faster. She bit down on his shoulder, moving her hips with his.

"Baby, baby, baby," he muttered.

Sweat broke out on his back and forehead. Bess gripped him as the coiling of tension prepared to snap. A powerful orgasm shot through her like a rocket, stiffening her muscles hard and long before relaxing them, sending pleasure to every part of her body. She cried out his name as her hips undulated.

He upped his speed before uttering a low groan. Her name flew from his lips as he pounded into her one last time. Then, his head went limp. He rested his forehead against her neck as he ground to a halt. His tongue snaked out to lick her for a second before he pushed up on his hands.

Bess could hardly speak. She'd never had a climax of such intensity before. He raised his head, and she saw a warm glow in his eyes. He planted a soft kiss on her lips then her eyelids and each cheek. "Bess, honey."

She put her thumb on his lips. She wanted the glow to last, the spell to be unbroken. She combed his hair off his forehead with her fingers and arched her back. She kissed him with all the love in her heart.

Whit rolled off to the side. He stared at her body, making her shy. She pulled up the sheet.

"Must you?" He pushed it down just enough to reveal her breasts.

"You're staring."

"Why not? You're a work of art."

Sensing heat in her cheeks, she lowered her lids, her eyelashes fanning out on her cheeks.

"The blush is very becoming."

"You mean the blush becomes Bess?" She fluttered her lashes and giggled.

Whit laughed. "Joke all you want. It was Earth-shaking."

She nodded, running her finger down his smooth cheek.

"Like it better shaved?"

"Like it both ways." *I like you any way I can have you.*

Whit propped himself up on his elbows, freeing his hands. He closed his fingers around her breast. "A good fit. Just right."

"Bigger than a model's?"

"Oh hell yes. Perfect." He explored her, rubbing gently against the soft flesh then following with his lips. "I could stay like this forever," he said.

Bess ran her fingers through his hair and cupped his head. She leaned forward and kissed the dark, shiny locks, sliding her hand down his neck to his back. "Hold me," she whispered, sliding down under the covers.

Whit scooped her into his embrace. "With pleasure." He covered them with the sheet and comforter before tightening his grip.

Bess wound her arms around him, snuggling her face into his neck and shoulder. The touch of his bare skin warmed up hers, which had begun to cool. She took a deep breath, inhaling his masculine scent.

"Happy?" he asked.

"Delirious."

He stroked her hair. Her heartbeat slowed and peace flowed in her veins while a gentle smile settled on her face. She felt Whit relax against her. When she closed her eyes, sleep overtook her.

BESS AWOKE TWO HOURS later. She saw Whit's arm slung over her waist. He shifted, pulling her closer. The heat from his body kept the bed a perfect temperature. Comfort enveloped her. She had no desire to leave. Whit opened his eyes.

"What time is it?" He rolled over to face the clock. "Shit. It's eleven." He threw down the covers and swung his legs over the side. "Sorry, but I've got to get to work."

"I understand. I'd better check on my apartment." Bess pushed to her feet. Whit handed her his robe and padded into the bathroom. She heard the shower running. *Wish I could get in there with him. No time.*

When they were both dressed, they left the pugs at Whit's, stopped at her apartment door, and knocked. Officer Joe answered.

"Hey, Ms. Cooper. We'll be done in here sooner than I thought. Come on in. Don't touch anything. You, too, Mr. Bass."

The place was still a God-awful mess. Bess glanced around. "What a disaster," she said, shaking her head. Her eye picked up a new detail. "Will you look at this?"

Both men looked at her. "What?" Whit asked.

"The guy didn't bother with Dumpling's bed. It's untouched."

"Guess he figured whatever he was looking for wouldn't be there. Besides, can't hide anything in it."

"Can I pick up a toothbrush and some clothes?"

"I think the team is finished with the bedroom. I'll check."

"What a mess! It'll take you days to get this straightened out."

"I'm going to throw it together and leave. The whole thing creeps me out."

Whit put his arm around her shoulders. "You stay with me until you're comfortable."

"Thanks." She beamed a smile up at him, and he kissed her.

"Hey, hey, no PDA," Officer Joe joked. "Okay, Ms. Cooper. You can have the bedroom and bathroom back."

"Is it safe for her to clean up in here?" Whit asked the policeman.

"She shouldn't be in here alone. Even with the doggie, it's not safe. Maybe in two weeks. Give us a chance to figure out what happened."

When Bess's suitcase was packed, a couple of reporters stopped them at the door. They fired questions at Bess. Whit's station had interviewed her right after the police had arrived. By this time, she figured publicity couldn't hurt. *Maybe it will keep the robber away.*

Bess unpacked at Whit's, and he went off to work. Then, she thumbed through cookbooks looking for ideas for new recipes. She found peace burying her nose in a cookbook.

Her cell buzzed. It was Ned.

"Are you okay?"

Bess explained everything.

"I'm glad you weren't there."

"So, are they missing me terribly and ready to put me back on?" She was only half kidding.

The silence was uncomfortable.

"Ned?"

"Not exactly."

"Oh? What do you mean?"

"They work fast. They've hired some chick named Jenny. They're giving her your show."

"*Baking with Jenny*?"

"No, *In the Kitchen with Jenny*."

Her chest tightened. She could hardly breathe.

"Bess?"

"I'm here," she coughed out.

"I'm sorry."

"This is why you called me?"

"I didn't think it'd be fair to have you hanging on, hoping, ya know?"

"Did they tell you to?"

"Of course not. If they found out, I'd get my head handed to me. Didn't want you waiting—hoping."

"Thanks, Ned."

"Maybe you can find something else?"

"Yeah, maybe. If I don't get murdered by a robber first." She snorted.

"Don't say that. Hey, if you do, by some miracle, get something, will you call me?"

"Still want to work with *Scandal Woman*?"

"Hell, yeah. You're the best."

"So are you."

Despair descended on her like a thick fog. She wouldn't have admitted, even if Ned, or anyone else, had asked her directly, but she had been hoping this would blow over. She'd been praying the station would forgive and forget and put her back on the air. But Ned had squashed her hopes with the truth.

Bess became restless. She pushed up from the sofa and paced. *Time to walk the dogs.* She leashed the pugs, donned a jacket, and headed for Central Park.

She did her best thinking while walking in the park, usually with Dumpling. The dogs trotted along, stopping to sniff lampposts from time to time, allowing her to get lost in thought.

What am I doing with Whit? He said he's never getting married, and I'm falling for him. Stupid, stupid girl. Don't do it. He's nice, he's kind, he's handsome, he's a great lover, best ever, but not a good reason to get my heart broken. Do I think I can change him? Can I make an elephant fly? Listen to what he's saying. He doesn't want to get married. He doesn't want children. Believe him and move on. Find someone else. Or cry your eyes out for months.

Back at Whit's place, Bess consoled herself the way she always did, by preparing a fabulous meal. She swiped a few cooking tools from her kitchen and played country music. She chopped, sautéed, sliced, and browned all afternoon. When Whit returned to the apartment, the enticing aromas in the hall would come from his place, not hers.

At the rush of cool air, she looked up. Whit had arrived.

"Something smells great. What is it?" He poked his head into the kitchen.

"Something new. My own pasta concoction. Lots of fresh veggies, some sausage, over penne. You like?" She offered him a sample.

"Wow, almost as delicious as you," he said, after swallowing. Bess put the wooden spoon down, allowing him to pull her close for a kiss.

"How was your day?" she asked, leaving his embrace to retrieve some dishes from the cabinet.

"Full of murder, robbery, assault, and theft. The usual. Except for coming home to you."

THE NEXT MORNING, WHIT eased his *Bentley* off the Thruway and turned left on Midland Avenue, heading for Rye's beach area. "Remember, there's no furniture."

"None?"

"Well...hmm. A bed, and a sofa."

"A bed? I should have known." She snickered.

Whit pulled off the road into the Midland School parking lot and put the car in park. "Okay. You wanted to return the favor?"

"Yeah?"

"Here's the deal. The house needs furniture. You can stay as long as you like if you furnish it for me."

"Furnish it?"

"I'll give you the money. You buy whatever you want."

"I thought you wanted to sell the house?"

"I'm not sure what I'm going to do. No one can live there unless it has furniture."

"Deal. Let's drop off the bags, check out the house, and go to a local furniture store."

Whit eased back onto the road and stepped on the gas. "Sounds like a plan."

They were silent in the car the rest of the drive. Whit steered into a short driveway and put the car in park. Bess was out in a flash. A deep breath of fresh, salty air from Long Island Sound energized her. She stood on the flagstone walk splitting the shallow front yard in two and stared at the building. It was two stories of mixed stone, with several windows, sporting small panes of glass cut into the front. Two were almost hidden by the small front porch. *Big enough for a couple of rockers.*

The front door was a worn, weathered wood with its white paint flaking off, and sported wrought iron hinges. The brass handle needed polishing. Small hedges fenced in the property while a bit of ivy attempted to climb one wall.

Whit joined her. There was sweat on his upper lip. "The house needs work. In the back are sliding glass—" The words rushed out of his mouth until Bess put her finger on his lips.

"It's charming. One-of-a-kind. Wow, it's great. Let's go in."

He smiled, fished in his pocket for the keys, and unlocked the front door. Bess passed into a small entryway. Through an arch was the living room with a vaulted ceiling. Bedrooms on the second floor opened onto a gangway spanning the length of the house, ending at a wooden staircase. A large, stone fireplace looked especially grand in the near-empty room. The walls were grimy beige. A closed door to the right invited curiosity. Bess's gaze went to a beige, suede sofa, sitting at an awkward angle in front of the hearth.

Gotta check out the kitchen. She ignored the room on the right and turned left. *Perfect place for a big table.* French doors opened onto a flagstone patio. She moved through another archway into the kitchen.

"Looks like it hasn't been updated since the 50's." She swiped a finger through the thick dust on the Formica counter. Her mind worked, ideas, colors, and textures spun through her brain. When Whit spoke, she didn't hear him.

"I said—what do you think?" He hiked his jeans up and shifted his weight.

"Oh. Sorry. Thinking. What do I think? I think it's grand."

"Grand? It's too small to be grand." His brow furrowed.

"It's great, beautiful. Has a lot of potential. All the right details. I love the French doors."

"The kitchen is tiny, compared to yours."

"Every kitchen is tiny compared to mine. It can be opened up. It'll be great once you renovate it."

"Ouch. How much will it cost?"

"Depends on what you want to spend. Since you're going to dump the place, you probably don't want to renovate the kitchen."

"Dump the place sounds pretty harsh."

"It's what you're doing, isn't it?"

"I'm not sure. I might keep it."

"I'd never sell a place like this unless I had no money."

"Why?"

"Because you can never replace this. There's no other house like it on Earth."

"I suppose."

"You're not very sentimental, are you?"

He simply looked at her.

"Figures." She walked back into the living room and headed for the closed door.

He followed. "Why?"

"Don't want to get married. No kids. No attachments. Dump the house. Keep it lean. No sentiment. Come and go as you please... Isn't this a charming room?" The space wasn't large, but it had a bay window with a window seat, plus another large window with lots of glass panes.

"Let's go upstairs."

They climbed to the second floor. There were two good-sized bedrooms and one smaller one, like a maid's room. In the master bedroom, she gasped when she saw the old fireplace.

"A fireplace in the bedroom?" She glanced his way. "Perfect for seduction." She wiggled her eyebrows.

Whit tinkered with the flue. "It looks like it hasn't been used in fifty years."

"It can be fixed."

"And you're going to seduce me in this room?" he asked, grinning.

"I think the fireplace is going to seduce us both." She chuckled.

"Also a practical way to cut down on the expense of heating this place," he said.

"Mood killer." She laughed.

She went to the window, her eyes drawn to the view of the Long Island Sound lapping at the beach a few hundred yards away.

"A view of the water." She drew in a breath. "It's fabulous. This place has such potential... A backyard!" She bounded down the stairs.

"The gardener hasn't done much. I've only got a basic plan with him."

She stopped short and turned to face him. "Stop explaining. It's fine. I love the house. You're lucky to have found such a special place. No more excuses."

The backdoor was between the dining area and the kitchen. Whit unlocked the bolt, and they went outside. The small yard was neatly trimmed. About three times the size of the front lawn, it had dirt beds for flowers and almost no landscaping.

"It needs planting," he said.

"Part of the fix-up plan...if you intend to keep it."

They returned inside. Bess guesstimated the length of the table she'd need and a few other items. "Let's go shopping."

"Let's eat. I'm hungry."

They drove into town. A hamburger joint on Purchase Street was open, so they slid into a booth and ordered.

"You have your stuff with you, don't you?" he asked, taking a bite of his cheeseburger.

"Yep."

"Good. I'll give you the keys to the car and the credit card. I'll take the train back."

"Leave me here?"

"Yep. You need to be safe. You will be, here. No one'll find you."

She sighed. "True. I'll have to cancel the Dinner Club."

"For a little while." He took her hand. "Please? Don't take any chances."

She stared at him for a moment before plucking a pickle off the plate and popping it in her mouth. *He looks worried. Maybe I should be more worried.* "As we agreed. I thought you'd be staying here, too."

"I can't. I have to work. Besides, if you're decorating, I'll be in the way."

She nodded. "Okay. A couple of days."

They finished eating, Whit paid the bill, and they strolled to the train station. After a passionate goodbye, she drove back to the house. Without Whit, the place looked sadder and more dilapidated. *I love this house. But it's his. Will I ever have one of my own? Not as long as I'm unemployed.* She sighed and pulled out paper and pen to make a list.

Chapter Twelve

WHIT SHOWED UP EARLY for his appointment with Dr. Sumner. He paced until the doctor opened the door. Then, he strode in and sat down.

Dr. Sumner took his time settling in the chair opposite Whit and smiled. "You seem anxious to see me."

"Yes."

"Do you have an answer to the question about the house?"

"No. But I think I was meant to keep it, at least until now, to keep Bess safe."

"Oh? How so?"

Whit went on to explain about Bess and the break-in. "Then, she said, 'you're going to dump the house,' and I cringed."

"Why? You do plan to sell it, don't you?"

"But she said dump. Like I was dumping a girlfriend. And it hurt. I don't want to dump the house. It needs work, a lot of work. I was embarrassed to bring her there."

"Did she mind?"

"Not at all. But suddenly, my dream house, my beautiful house, looked like a piece of old junk. The door is worn, paint is chipping off. The windows are so dirty you almost can't see out. And the worst!" Whit put his head in his hands.

"The worst?"

"The kitchen looked like it hadn't been updated since the Civil War. 1950's style. Ugly. Old-fashioned. And I wondered what she thought."

"What did she say?"

"It could be fixed."

"And you said..."

"I didn't say anything. Something else in my life to be fixed. I wanted to take a match to the whole place."

"Did she hate it?"

"No." He looked up and made eye contact with the doctor. "She loved it. Said it had potential, could be nice."

"That's good, isn't it?"

"To renovate the kitchen'll cost a fortune."

"But if you intend to keep the house, it'll last for years."

"If. The question remains. If."

"You still don't know why you haven't sold the house?"

He shook his head. "The question echoed in my head a hundred times on the train ride back. It's a dump, and yet, I still own it—and even spend money on a gardener. What an idiot."

"An idiot? Maybe you love the house, too. Maybe is represents something to you."

"You mean the family I never had?"

"Perhaps."

"I suppose it does. I mean, in case I find someone. If I change my mind about my whole life." He chuckled.

"You'd have a place to put a family."

"Yeah. Don't you have to have the family first, doc?"

"Different people do things in different ways. Whatever works for you, Whit."

"Double talk." He scowled.

"You want me to give you the answer."

"Seems the fastest way."

"I can't."

"Why? Because we'll be done then?"

"Hey, don't be insulting. No, because the one with the answer is you, not me."

"I knew you were going to say that."

"So, give yourself the answer. Give yourself permission to see inside."

"Maybe if I go away for a few months, I'll find it then."

"I hope so. Time's up for today."

"What happens here when I go to Asia?"

"We go on hiatus until you return."

"I'll miss it."

"You can always come back."

"Do you think I'm ready to go out on my own?"

"Do you?"

"Guess so. I've been on my own forever, anyway."

"Maybe that's the problem."

"Maybe it is."

Whit followed the doctor to the door. They shook hands, and he left the building. He walked the thirty blocks back to the studio instead of taking a cab or the subway. He wanted time to think. Seeing the house through Bess's eyes changed everything. His palace had morphed into a dump. The creepy unease of embarrassment slid up his back. *She knew it wasn't a palace. She was being polite. How could I fall in love with it? What a hellhole. I'll never be able to sell it.*

When he arrived, the place was abuzz with news. Sam was yelling at the copy boy, the weather girl was complaining about her computer, and the sound guy yelled at everyone to shut up. *Business as usual.* Lost in his own thoughts, Whit went to his office. He shuffled papers, barely glancing at the top stories. *The new job can't come soon enough. I need to get away.*

Sam exploded into his space, waving her arms and perching on the arm of a chair. "Where the hell have you been? There's a new scandal about the mayor's deputy. Seems his wife is growing pot in their backyard and selling it. We've got another rape in Central Park, though I don't know what these chickies are doing there alone at three in the morning. And people came to blows outside the mayor's office over some dumbass off-leash law."

Whit narrowed his eyes. "Earth-shattering, isn't it? Isn't there any national news?"

"Yeah. All bad. Here. Read these. Top stories, unless there's news from the Mid-east."

As quickly as she blew into his office, she blew out again. He smiled. *Sam loves the drama. Scandal, her favorite food.* Whit picked up the papers, sat back in his chair, and read.

BESS WOKE UP AT SIX. After shopping for linens, basic kitchen items, and ordering furniture, she'd collapsed early last night. The new coffee maker sent a tantalizing aroma through the house. She poured a mug, donned her jacket, leashed Dumpling, and headed for the beach.

The breeze from the gray, November sky cooled the air even lower than the reported temperature. The deserted shore was quiet and calm. Bess released the dog to run free. The waves were small compared to the ocean. She walked along, heading toward Playland, an amusement park closed for the season.

Dumpling followed, sticking to the firm, damp sand. The tide was going out, leaving a sprinkling of broken shells in white and various shades of periwinkle blue and gray. The task of furnishing Whit's house loomed large. Bess had never done anything like it for someone else. She'd furnished her own apartment with no problem as she was the only one she had to please. Bess chewed a lip as she second-guessed her choices.

Deliveries would begin arriving in the afternoon. She needed to go back to the hardware store and supplement the rudimentary kitchen supplies she had bought there the day before. The wind picked up. Bess pulled the zipper of her jacket higher, her mind occupied with details and decisions. Dumpling barked at a lone seagull and chased it along the shore. Bess almost didn't hear her phone ring.

On the screen was a number she didn't recognize. She grimaced. *Is this a damn sales pitch? On my cell?* She was about to turn it off when it stopped. She shrugged and went back to making a mental shopping list when it went off again. The same number. *Salespeople don't usually call back.*

"Hello?"

"Bess, don't hang up."

She stopped. "Terry?" A chill shot up her spine. *It can't be.*

"Yeah. Don't hang up. Please, Bess. Listen."

She sank down hard on the sand, her eyes wide. The mug fell beside her, spilling the remaining coffee. Dumpling joined her. "Terry? Is it really you? You're not dead?" Tears gathered in the corners of her eyes.

"I don't have much time. I'm not supposed to be calling you."

"What the hell?" Anger pushed sadness out of her heart.

"I'm not surprised you're pissed. Give me a minute."

"Start talking." Her lips compressed into a frown.

"The undercover work I did got dangerous. I got made. I had to get out of town."

"Oh?"

"This is a burner phone. Not traceable. Still, it's dangerous for me to talk to anyone I've known from before. But I had to call you."

"Why? To explain about your wife?"

"I'm sorry. We were practically divorced. When they arranged for me to leave town, Mona came with me. Had to. It wasn't safe for her, either. We've reconciled. She understands about you now. She's sorry for causing trouble."

"Lovely, but I've lost my job."

"I'm sorry, babe."

"Don't 'babe' me! I cried my eyes out when I heard you were dead."

"It couldn't be helped. I'm sorry. Listen. I don't have much time. You're in danger. I figured it out when I read about the break-in at your place."

"Ya think?"

"I didn't know you'd go to my funeral. The press and all. They know about you, figured out where I hid it. Now you're not safe."

"Are you going to help *me* leave town?"

"Got one better. I know what they were looking for."

"What?"

"A notebook. I kept all my names and stuff in a small notebook."

"The stuff this case is about?"

"It's a police corruption with the Mafia case. In my notebook, I have the names of the officers and Mafia guys involved. The creep who broke into your place was looking for it."

"Why would he look there?"

"Because I hid it there."

"Oh my God!" She pushed to her feet and paced.

"Yeah. I'm sorry. There wasn't any other safe place. I didn't think they'd find you. Then, you hit the news, and your connection with me came out..."

"They destroyed my house looking for it."

"I'm so sorry, baby. Maybe they didn't find it."

"The police think they did."

"I'll tell you where it is then you have to promise me something."

"What?"

"You'll take it to the nosy news bastard who lives across the hall."

"Whit?"

"Yeah. Him."

"Why?"

"He'll give it to the police chief and brag about it on the air. Then, they'll leave you alone. So, you gotta promise, if I tell you where it is, you'll do what I ask."

"I promise. But why can't I take it to the police myself?"

"The chief won't see you. And the bad cops'll make sure you have a fatal accident before you get to him. Besides, the bastard'll put it on the air. Then, the bad cops and the Mafia guys'll know you don't have it. They won't come around again looking."

"Okay, okay. You make sense. Where is it?"

"In the one place they didn't look..."

"Dumpling's bed?"

"On the nose, babe." He chuckled. "The one near the kitchen. I taped it to the bottom."

Bess laughed in spite of the situation. "You're too much."

"Look, I'll get in trouble if I stay on much longer. You promise to do as I said, right?"

"Right. I will."

"You were great, babe. We had something special. Sorry it had to end this way."

"Me, too. Be safe."

"You, too. I'll be watching when I can."

"Thanks." She closed her cell.

The wind picked up. The only sound was the occasional cry of a hungry seagull. Bess retrieved her mug, brushing off the sand, leashed her pug, and headed back to the house. *He's not dead.* She smiled. Anger dissipated, and happiness flowed. *Glad he's alive.*

After dropping Dumpling off, she picked up the car keys and headed outside. *Have to get this furnished a bit before I can go back and clean this up.* She planned to stay the night to receive deliveries then return to get the notebook and remove the danger from her life.

Bess spent the day moving furniture, setting up the kitchen, and picking paint colors. By nine o'clock, she was exhausted. Dumpling had already crashed on the bed. Bess crawled between the new sheets and huddled under the down comforter. She wished Whit was there to warm her and hold her close during the night.

THE KNOCK ON WHIT'S door at ten startled him. Fresh from the shower, he fastened the sash on his robe and stowed his coffee mug in the kitchen.

"Bess? What are you doing here?"

"Come, I need you." She tugged on his sleeve and headed toward her apartment.

"What's going on? Let me finish my coffee first." He turned her around, and they ended up at his kitchen table. He poured her a cup.

She explained everything, except where she got the information. "I can't tell you."

"Why not?"

"I can't. I promised. It's a safety thing."

Whit waved his hand in the air. "Okay, okay. Continue."

"I want you to come with me...in case."

"Let me get dressed."

"Can I watch?"

He laughed. Bess followed him into the bedroom. Whit threw on jeans and a long-sleeved T-shirt. Then, together they approached the door to Bess's apartment with caution, as if it were wired to explode. Once they opened the door with no bomb going off, they padded straight toward the kitchen. A small, green, fuzzy oval lay on the floor.

"It's in her bed?"

"Yep." Bess turned it over, and there it was. Fastened with duct tape to the rubbery matting on the bottom was a small, black notebook. She detached the tape and stood up.

"We'd better get outta here. Let's look at it over at my place," Whit said, taking her hand.

They hurried out of the empty apartment and across the hall. Whit locked all three locks on the door. Bess's heart pounded.

"Wow. That was scary."

"Yeah. In a funny way, it was."

She handed the notebook to Whit. He opened it, paged through, stopping to glance at a page or two from time to time. "There's a ton of information in here. I don't know how much will be helpful, but there's plenty."

"Take it away. If I never see it again..."

"I know. Time for me to get to work." Whit changed into a suit and tie, kissed Bess, waved to the dogs, and headed out.

At the studio, he stopped in Sam's office and shut the door.

"What's up?" Sam sat slumped over a report. A half-filled cup of coffee took up the last smidgeon of space on her messy desk.

"I've got a great lead for a fantastic story."

"Yeah?" She straightened and narrowed her eyes.

He explained about the notebook, now resting safely in his breast pocket. He smiled to himself as he watched Sam salivate.

"This could be my *Pulitzer*," she muttered.

"Our *Pulitzer*."

"Gimme, gimme. Where is it?"

"Nope. It goes to the cops right after we look it over. We gotta call the police chief and arrange its safe delivery. But first...I want to make a deal." Whit took a chair.

"A deal? You have the story of the century, and you want to make a deal? What kind of a newsman are you?"

"One with a conscience. Here's the deal. Get Bess Cooper's show, *Baking with Bess*, back on the air."

She made a face. "I have no pull with the rinky-dink cable station."

"I know. But you do here. In fact, you're the most powerful producer at Eagle Broadcasting."

"You flatter me." But Whit saw her puff up.

"It's true. Get her a five-year contract. I want it done, or I send the notebook to the police chief, anonymously, by courier." He sat back, propping his feet up on the trash can.

"Why, I can't...Where would I put the show?"

"Rumor has it you're canceling the gardening program, anyway. Too many pesticides, his ratings are manure..."

"Ha ha, very funny."

"It's true, though, isn't it?"

"Maybe...I don't have the power..."

"Stop lying. If you say so, it'll be done. Especially when you tell them you have an informant with *Pulitzer*-level information." Whit studied her face.

"I suppose I can at least ask."

Whit pushed to his feet. "Let me know when the contract is ready to sign."

"I can't work that fast." She took a sip from her mug.

"Bullshit. I've seen you work faster. Remember the Mahoney case?"

"It was an unusual situation."

"So is this. You have twenty-four hours before I send it."

"What? You're joking?" She slammed her mug on the desk, splashing coffee on her report.

"Never been more serious. Twenty-four hours." He moved toward the door.

"Where's the info? How do I know it's safe?"

"You'll have to trust me." He heard her snort as he turned.

Using all his willpower, he kept a smug smile at bay until he was alone in his office. He looked over the papers on his desk, trying to concentrate. Happiness filled his veins. *Making it up to Bess.* When his phone rang, he answered it with cheer.

"Pickford Williams."

"Hey, Pick. How the hell are ya?"

"You're in a good mood."

"Yeah, well, did a good deed today."

"A boy scout? Is this Whitfield Bass?"

Whit chuckled. "Present and accounted for. What's up?"

"The job. You've got two weeks to say goodbye and pack your bag, buddy."

"Contract?"

"Six months."

"Excellent."

"Meet me for a drink at nine at the Shelton Arms hotel. We'll sign the contract, go over travel budgets, and that kinda shit."

"You're on." The phone clicked off. Whit sat back and rested his feet on a chair. *Perfect. I get Bess situated then I start on my new life. She can use the house while I'm away. No rush to sell it if I'm gone. Perfect timing.* He called to tell her he'd be late and sauntered toward makeup.

Sam grabbed his arm. "Contract will be on your desk at nine o'clock tomorrow morning."

"Good. You can have the info when it's signed."

"It'll be signed by Montgomery."

"Fine. When Miss Cooper signs it, you'll get the information."

"Hardass."

"Takes one to know one."

Whit breezed through the newscast. His confidence had never been higher. *Nothing like tying up all the loose ends of one's life. Dr. Sumner was a stroke of genius. I'm cool with keeping the house and moving to Asia.*

He arrived at the Shelton Arms early, ordered a scotch on the rocks, and dialed his brother.

"Hey, Jeff. Wanted you to know I'm going to Asia for about six months. Maybe longer."

"Asia? How come?"

"Taking a job there for *New York News Review.*"

"A promotion?"

"More of a lateral move."

"You're running away."

"Nope, clearing the field for a new start."

"I'm sorry."

"By the way, thanks for referring me to Dr. Sumner."

"You're seeing him?"

"Yeah. He's been very helpful."

"Has he? And you're still running away?"

Whit sighed. "I told you. I'm not running away. I'm starting something new."

"So you say. I'll miss you. Are you coming to see Dad before you go?"

"I will if I have time."

"Translation—no. Hey, it's your life."

"Even with this shit you're dumping on me, you're a great brother, Jeff. You've always looked out for me. I never said 'thank you.' Want you to know I appreciate it."

Silence. Then, "You're my kid brother. Someone's gotta keep an eye on you."

"You have. You're one of the good guys."

"Thanks. Stay out of trouble. Get married. You won't regret it."

"Hey, you found the only good one in the bunch, Jeff. What can I do?" The minute he said it, a wave of guilt washed over him. *Thank God, Bess didn't hear.*

"I thought you had someone." A hint of suspicion broke through Jeff's voice.

"She's sort of a friend." *You never used to be a liar.* Sweat broke out on his forehead.

"Friend with benefits."

"More or less."

"Can't pin you down. Always slippery. You haven't changed. Hell, your personal life is your own business."

"Right."

"I was hoping this might be the one."

"What happened to my personal life is my own business?"

"I still can't talk to you, can I? Good luck in Asia, Whit."

"Thanks."

Whit didn't breathe a sigh of relief when the conversation was over. He wanted to keep talking but didn't know what to say. *Jeff always misunderstands. He's sort of like talking to Dr. Sumner. Why can't I make him see I'm okay? He worries too much.*

"Hey, Bass, what's eating you?"

Whit looked up into the chubby face of Pickford Williams. "Hey, Pick, sit down, sit down."

"Look like you've got the weight of the world on your shoulders."

"Nah. Talking to my brother."

"Let's talk about Asia."

"Okay, shoot."

The waitress returned, and Pick ordered a scotch for himself and one for Whit. "You're not my boss's first choice. Sorry."

Whit cocked an eyebrow. "Oh?"

"Yeah. He wanted Jamison Keller."

"From *Business News Today*?"

"Yeah. But Keller's got some book commitment or other. At least for the next few months."

"So, I'm on trial?"

The server put down their drinks and a bowl of pretzels.

"If you love it there and want to stay, fine. But if you want to return, Keller could fill in."

"Why are you doing this?"

"Because I know you."

"What the hell do you mean?" Whit finished his second drink and signaled for another.

"I don't think you're serious about Asia."

"I've never been more serious. As soon as I sign the contract, I'm giving notice."

"Come on, Whit. I know you. Known you for years."

"And?"

A fresh scotch arrived. Pick ordered nachos. "Something's up with you."

"What do you mean?"

"Only a feeling. You're a stick-with-it kind of guy."

"Yeah? So? I've been with the station for three years."

"Three years is nothing. You've got a good thing going there. Making a ton of dough."

"So? I want something different."

"We'll see." Pick raised his glass. "Here's to...uh...happiness."

"Okay. Happiness." They clinked glasses and drank. "How's Annie?"

"Good. Pregnant."

"Again?"

"We've only got one, Whit."

"Congratulations."

"You should try it."

"Marriage? Kids? Me?" He laughed. "Got the wrong guy."

Two drinks became four. Whit and Pick rehashed college days. Whit signed the contract and stumbled into a taxi at midnight.

Bess must be asleep by now. Whit fumbled with the lock on his front door. The pugs barked. *Damn! They'll wake her up. Shit. Open up, you fucking door.* Tempted to kick it, he got it open before he lost even more of his temper. *She's up by now. And I'm drunk. Shit. Not good.*

When he entered, she raised a rolling pin to strike, but he hollered, "Bess! It's me!"

She blinked, rubbed her eyes, and put the wooden weapon on the counter. The dogs jumped on him, trying to lick his face. Whit slid down to the floor and giggled like a schoolboy when the dogs attacked him with affection.

"Drunk?" Bess asked, hand on her hip.

"Had a few with an old friend."

"I see. It's after midnight. Pardon me if I go back to bed."

"Don't go without me." He pushed up and teetered after her. Her diaphanous robe barely concealed her form. He eyed her with lust. *Drunk and horny.* He snickered.

"What's funny?"

"Men are supposed to be impotent when they're drunk. Not me. I could do you all night."

"Really?"

"Yeah. Come here." He reached for her.

"You reek." She moved away.

Whit went into the bathroom. He splashed cold water on his face, brushed his teeth, and used mouthwash. More sober, he entered the bedroom, yanking his tie loose. "Let me try again." He draped the silk length over a chair and unbuttoned his shirt. "You are the most beautiful woman on Earth." He unbuckled his pants and folded them up. Within a minute, he was naked, crawling up the bed toward Bess.

She sat up and giggled. "You look like a lion."

"I am a lion, coming for his mate." When he reached her, he cupped the back of her head and drew her to him. "I need you," he whispered.

"I'm here."

He eased her back and covered her mouth with his, gently seducing her. "Beautiful Bess," he muttered into her mouth. His hands pushed the sheet back, putting them skin to skin. He kissed his way to her neck then down. Bess ran her hands over his back then up his chest.

"Ummm, love your body," she whispered.

"Love you, honey," he said, running his hands up to her breasts. He closed his fingers over the warm flesh. "Perfect," he said.

He raised his head to gaze into her eyes, where love shone through. Love and desire. It set him off. Lust flew through his veins. "Oh, baby, baby, baby," he said, sliding his hands up and down her body then between her legs. She was wet. He couldn't remember when he'd been as hard. Whit couldn't wait. He parted her legs, mounted her, and thrust. She gasped and arched.

A sober thought penetrated his brain. *Did I hurt her?* He stared into her eyes. "Are you all right?"

"God, yes. Don't stop."

He let go, withdrew, and plunged in again and again. He slammed into her, harder and harder, wanting to own her, to possess her, body and soul. *She belongs to me.* "Mine," he repeated, over and over, in rhythm with the movement of his hips. He kissed her roughly, tore at her lips. His hands gripped her arms and squeezed tight.

"Ow, let go," she said, squirming under his grasp.

"Sorry, sorry." *Take her, make love to her, but don't hurt her, you moron.* He uncurled his fingers and rubbed her arms.

"I'm okay." Her mouth was dark pink, inviting him. He kissed her, his tongue seeking hers. She raised it to meet him. As he increased the pace, Bess moved with him, her hips undulating with each thrust.

She cried out his name, making her heat surrounding him hotter and wetter. Whit lost all control as an orgasm claimed him, sending pleasure shooting through his veins. He buried his face in her neck as the hard tips of her breasts pushed into his chest.

"Oh, God," he said, spent and exhausted.

"Holy crap. You were...an animal."

Whit lifted his head. "Are you okay? Was it too much?"

"It was incredible. It's like you were unconscious or something. On automatic pilot."

"A lion..."

"Yeah. Except for the roaring and biting me on the back of the neck, yeah. You were."

Whit gave a poor imitation of a lion's roar. Startled, the pugs barked. Homer had been in the living room. He ran in and jumped up on the bed.

Bess was warm and soft beneath Whit, and he didn't want to move. "Homer, get down!" But the pug forged ahead, licking Whit's face and shoulder. Bess laughed when Dumpling put her cold, wet nose between their bellies. Whit jumped.

"No privacy," he muttered, moving back on his haunches. His hot stare covered her body. "I could look at you all night."

After a quick wash-up, they cuddled together under the covers. Bess backed into his embrace. Whit folded his arms around her.

"I love you, too," she said.

His eyelids drooped. "Hmm?"

"Answering you."

"What?" He jerked to attention.

"You told me you loved me, so I thought I'd respond."

"I didn't." *Never tell them you love them. Whit's rule number one.*

"But you did. Are you denying it?" She moved away and rolled over to face him.

"I couldn't have. I never...never say the 'L' word."

"You did tonight. To me. I heard it perfectly."

Silence followed. *Could I? Do I? Bess is so different. But the "L" word?*

"It's okay if you want to deny it. I get it." She curled up alone at the far end of the bed. He heard the hurt in her voice.

Her separation affected him physically and emotionally. The cool air chilling his skin in her absence doubled the effect. *Do I love Bess? Maybe I do. Shit. But it feels good. Feels damn good.*

He inched nearer to her. "I didn't mean it."

"Yes, you did. You meant to take it back or call me a liar." She kept her back to him.

He got closer. "I'd never call you a liar. It's just..." He hesitated.

Bess faced him. "Just what? You said it only to manipulate me? Only to make me think you cared?"

"You're twisting my words. If I said it to you, I meant it. I haven't said the "l" word to anyone in a long time. Since I bought the house."

"So, you *do* love me?" She rested her hand on his cheek.

He kissed her palm. "I did. I do."

"You love me?"

He nodded as he stroked her hair.

"Then say it."

His heart squeezed, and his chest tightened. "I love you, Bess. I love you very much." He brushed his lips over hers. Relief surged through him. A door in his heart opened.

She snuggled up to him. "Now, tell me about the house."

"It's late, can't it wait until morning?" He pulled her close and rested his hand on her breast.

"Give me the short version. It's been bugging me. What does a man who has sworn off marriage and kids want a house for? And why does he keep it, practically empty, for years, paying for upkeep? Why didn't he sell it?"

"Good question. I'll give you the answer for it when I figure it out."

"Not a clue?"

"It started with a woman named Gemma..."

"Do I want to hear this?"

"You asked." He chuckled. "How about the short version?"

"Fine."

Whit pulled the covers over their shoulders against the nippy air, planted two kisses on her neck, cuddled her into his embrace, and began the tale.

Chapter Thirteen

"I LOVE SURPRISES," Bess said, strolling down Central Park West, holding Whit's hand.

"This is...well, you'll see." He smiled at her, excited anticipation rushing through his veins. *Wait until she sees the contract. Eagle Broadcasting is much bigger than her old cable network. More money. More respect. She'll be great, too. I bet she pushes the ratings through the roof.* Pride in Bess swelled his chest. He beamed at her, and she shot him a quizzical look.

"You're awfully...full of yourself this morning. I expected you to be a bit hung over."

"Not one iota. I'm fine. And can't wait to see the look on your face." He chuckled.

He hummed the tune "Gone Gone Gone" by Philip Phillips as they rode up the elevator in his building. With a tight grip on her hand, he wove his way through the chaos in the studio. People yelling with ears to cell phones, producers arguing with on-air people...another typical day at Eagle. He noticed Sam narrow her eyes as he strolled by.

He walked into his office, and there it was on his desk. *The contract.* He maneuvered Bess around, pulled out his chair, and gestured for her to sit down. Then, he picked up the papers. "This is for you."

She took it and held it close to read. "What the hell? This is a contract."

"Exactly. For a new show. *In The Bakery with Bess.*"

"For me?" She raised her eyebrows.

"Right."

"How? Where? How did you get this for me?"

"Your reputation as a top chef and baker in New York..."

"Bullshit. Come on. Fess up."

"Okay. I traded the information in the notebook from Terry for a contract for you."

She rose out of the chair. "You what?"

"Sit down. Relax. This kind of thing is done all the time. I'm sure Terry'd approve."

"What exactly did you do?"

"I offered to give her the exclusive on this story before I take the info to the cops in exchange."

"But they don't want me here."

"When I pointed out what publicity you'd generate after all the scandal, her beady little eyes lit up. She's going to blast you all over the air. You'll be a big success here, Bess. You were too big for the rinky-dink network, anyway."

"So, you want me in the big-time?"

"Damn right. It's where you belong, baby. Nobody cooks like you."

Her eyes filled with tears.

"More money, too, right?" he asked.

"A ton more," she said.

"Good. Eagle can afford it. You'll attract all the big, packaged goods companies. There'll be plenty of revenue."

"You did all this for me?"

"I'm responsible for you losing your job. I had to do something to make it right."

"So, this is payback?"

His eyes widened. "You make it sound bad. I wanted to help."

She pushed to her feet, cozied up to him, and kissed him. "It's the sweetest thing. But it's blackmail, isn't it?'

"I prefer to think of it as deal-making. Happens all the time in this business. *Quid pro quo*. An exchange of goods or services."

"Is it real?"

"Of course. As soon as you sign the contract, I'll give her the notebook." He glanced up to see Sam lurking outside his door.

Bess fished a pen out of her purse and signed on the dotted line. She put one copy in her handbag and handed the other to Whit. He delivered it to Sam, who was waiting in the doorway.

"Gimme," she said, gesturing.

Whit pulled the notebook out of his breast pocket. "I've contacted the police chief. He's waiting for this. It's gotta go on tonight."

"Why?"

"So the men looking for it know Bess doesn't have it anymore. Or she's in danger."

"Deal. Take a crew," Sam said. She started to walk away then turned and raised her hand to wave at Bess. "Welcome to the station. Be in my office tomorrow, eight sharp. We'll meet with your producer. Bring ideas for four shows." She disappeared into the hallway.

"That's Sam. Nothing pretentious or phony about her. Right down to business."

Sam poked her head in again. "By the way, no sex in the office, you two."

Whit laughed while Bess blushed. She stood up.

"I've got a ton of work to do to prepare for tomorrow. I don't know how I can thank you."

"Forget it. It's the least I could do."

She headed out. Whit followed. He entered Sam's domain and closed the door.

"Closed door? Must be something big. What could be bigger than this scandal in the police department?"

"Me."

"You?"

Whit sat on the chair across from her. "I'm quitting."

Sam bolted out of her seat. "What?"

"Yep. I'm taking a newspaper job in Asia." He pulled the folded copy of his resignation from his breast pocket.

"You can't quit." A smug look washed across her face. "I've got your contract."

"I can. Read the fine print. Two weeks' notice."

"I don't believe it." Sitting, Sam scrolled through documents on her computer. "Here it is."

"Read it, Sam."

He watched her study the screen, her expression changing to one of disbelief.

"Who the fuck ever agreed to this?" She pushed to her feet.

"You did."

"Thanks a pant-load for pointing it out."

"I'm sorry. I love it here, but this is a special opportunity."

"To go to Asia? Hell, eat at the Chinese restaurant every day, same thing." She paced.

Whit laughed.

"This is your story. It's big. *Pulitzer* stuff. You can't leave now."

"I'll be here for two weeks. I can still work on it."

"Come on. You've got a following. Our ratings'll be in the toilet if you leave."

"This is something I've got to do."

Her face brightened. "Hey! How about this? You take a hiatus—get this newspaper shit out of your system then come back. Say we give you two months? Three?"

Whit was silent. *Would I want to come back? What if I hate it there?*

Her smug look returned and she sat. "Gotcha, didn't I?"

"I didn't expect this...especially from you."

"Don't think I've gone all sentimental. You bring in ratings. Those sexy eyes and your haircut. You could be reading the phonebook and women would watch."

"Thanks for your vote of confidence in my journalistic skills."

"You know me. No bullshit. Yeah, we need you. You'll be back." She tilted back in her chair a satisfied smile plastered across her face. "Don't sublet your apartment."

"Two months?'

Pressing her advantage, Sam shot up, leaning forward. "Yeah. A case of *Chivas* says you'll be back in two months."

"*Chivas Regal*?"

"Yep." She nodded.

"You're on."

He stood. "I've got to get to the police station."

Sam handed him the notebook. "Here. Chrissy made a copy."

As he opened the front door, he heard Sam's shrill voice scream for her assistant. "Chrissy! Chrissy! Get Montgomery on the phone." He smiled, shook his head, and headed for the elevator.

Sam poked her head out. "Take Barry and Alan with you."

"Those assholes," Whit muttered.

"Yeah. Go."

Thought she'd toss me out like old shoes. At least I can get a case of scotch out of it. He hit the sidewalk. Barry and Alan were waiting in the van with the motor running. They were quiet on the ride downtown, giving Whit a chance to think.

Everything's a go. Two more hurdles. Telling Bess and Dr. Sumner. His face clouded. Telling Bess wasn't going to be easy. Of course, he'd gotten her a great job, and he'd leave the house in her hands. *Perfect place for weekends away from the city. She knew I don't commit. Should be fine.* Something else troubled him. *She'll have the freedom to find a man who will.* His brow furrowed. *Shit!*

BESS PRACTICALLY RAN home. She called Ned then texted the Dinner Club for an emergency celebration at her place. With a mug of fresh coffee, she sat down and opened her idea folder. She plucked out favorites then made a list of possible recipes to go with each one. After polishing off a scone, she dug into her recipe box and consulted some cookbooks.

Ned stopped by on his lunch hour.

"I can't believe you're taking the show to Eagle. What a coup."

"Don't tell anyone. Wait until the show airs."

"Feeling insecure?"

"You never know."

"Okay. No leaks here. Can you hire me?"

"I'm going to ask tomorrow."

"I can't wait to get out of the rat trap. Jenny is such a bitch!"

"Hang in there. I'll see what I can do. In the meantime, tell me what you think of these meal and dessert ideas."

Bess laid out cards and pictures. When he left, Bess had four show concepts she hoped would please Sam.

She leashed the pugs and headed for the park. As a precaution, she donned a down jacket and decided on a short walk. The biting wind whipping up Central Park West confirmed her choices. Dumpling and Homer turned their faces away and followed along.

Excitement bubbled up in her veins. A show on a major network and the love of her life by her side. *I am in love with him, right? No.* She hadn't finished decorating the stone house, but was sure Whit wanted her to continue. As her work on the place progressed, her affection for it grew. Every new piece of furniture made it seem like hers. *I've always wanted my own home. This isn't mine, but it feels like it.*

Her uncertain life had taken a sharp turn. From idle to beyond busy. Her mind skipped from one pleasurable pastime to another—working hard, furnishing the most charming house on the East Coast, and making love with the most wonderful man in the world. She laughed and spoke to Dumpling and Homer. "How did I get so lucky?"

The female barked.

"I know, girl. I'm lucky to have you, too." Bess's face hurt from smiling. Although the sky was overcast and the scent of snow was in the air, it was a sunny spring day for her.

She steered the dogs back home. The Dinner Club was due to arrive in time for Whit's broadcast. Bess played pop music and danced while she prepared *hors d'oeuvres* and dinner. She finished off the remnants of a bottle of Cabernet as she moved from the counter to the stove and back.

At six thirty, her buzzer sounded. The Dinner Club ladies had arrived. Mugs of hot buttered rum were passed around. Dogs circled and played before finding warm spots to plop down and sleep.

Brooke took down plates, Miranda got the silverware, and Rory corralled wine glasses.

Bess turned on the television and set out a buffet on the stove. The hearty meal of meatloaf, mashed potatoes, and Brussels sprouts was consumed while the women watched Whit turn the evidence over to the police on the news. He kept her confidence when asked where he got the book. He asked the police chief some hard questions.

Pride filled Bess's heart. *He's incredible. What a story. Delivered it all perfectly.*

As the women were cleaning up, they asked about Terry.

"So, he left you in danger, but then you found the notebook, and now you're safe?" Brooke raised an eyebrow.

"Sort of." Bess covered the leftover meatloaf.

"And you decided, right now, to give it to Whit?" Miranda stopped and looked at her.

"Okay, okay. It sounds fishy. I can't talk about what happened. I'm grateful the notebook is with the police and not in my apartment anymore."

"Whit looked like a hero," Rory said.

"He is. He's my hero."

The women froze. They stared at Bess. Heat rose to her cheeks.

"What?"

"Whit belongs to you? I thought he'd never belong to any woman?" Brooke asked.

Bess didn't answer. She tucked the containers of leftovers in the refrigerator.

"Whit, Mr. No Commit, is the love of your life?" Miranda cocked an eyebrow at Bess.

"Bess, you didn't fall for him, did you?" Rory chimed in.

Unable to avoid their questions, she turned to face them. "Well, maybe. A little. I mean when someone's done what he's done for me..."

"He got you a job, after losing you yours in the first place," Miranda said.

"It's the house. It's—it's more."

"It's sex, right?" Brooke stared at Bess.

Bess sensed an increase in the heat in her cheeks. "And other things."

"Are you going to get hurt? Please, Bess. I don't want you to get hurt," Rory said.

"You said it was fun and games with him. Nothing more," Brooke said.

"I know I'm probably in trouble, but I can't help it. He's amazing. And it's too late. I'm already in love."

Joy seeped out of the celebration as each friend expressed her doubts about Whit. Bess defended him until she couldn't. *They're right. I'm probably on the road to disaster, but I can't stop. I love him.*

The knock on her door at eleven pulled her from her bed. Yawning, she opened the door to a triumphant Whit. He held a bottle of champagne and wore a wicked grin. "Did you see it? Did you see the broadcast?"

She nodded, rubbing her eyes.

"The whole city is talking about it. I had several phone interviews with newspapers. They made me late. You were in bed?"

"Been a long day."

"Damn. I wanted to celebrate." Whit put the bubbly in the fridge. "We can wait until tomorrow." He kissed her. "And it's all due to you. How can I ever thank you?"

"You've saved me from those bad guys. No thanks necessary. I'm going back to bed. Care to join me?"

Whit pulled on his tie and followed her. Once in bed, they snuggled together.

"I want to take you out to a fancy dinner tomorrow. We can celebrate my story and your new job."

"Sounds good," Bess said, the warmth of his body lulling her to sleep.

"I have something else to tell you, too," he whispered.

"Fine," she muttered. *Oh my God. He's going to propose!* She smiled once before she was asleep.

BESS TORE HER CLOSET apart, looking for the perfect outfit. *What does someone wear when a marriage proposal is on the menu?* She was so excited she couldn't keep still.

The early morning meeting had gone well. Sam had been curt to the point of rude, but she had approved Bess's ideas. *I'll have to get used to her style.* Her new producer didn't know much about cooking, but he knew about ratings and advertising. They had given her the green light to hire Ned, who had been thrilled at the news.

Whit's marriage proposal would be the whipped cream, the hot fudge sauce, and the cherry on the sundae of her life. She paced, trying to calm herself. She spied a teal blue, scoop-necked dress. *Perfect!*

After selecting gold jewelry, she ran a bubble bath. *Grandma's gold watch. Aunt Delia's earrings and matching necklace.* By seven thirty, she was ready. She called down to Crash to hail a cab for her. She was meeting Whit at Belle Culottes, a pricey French restaurant on West 55th Street, at eight o'clock, and she didn't want to be late.

Wine! She poured a half-glass of wine and downed it quickly, hoping it would settle her nerves. *It's not every day a woman receives a marriage proposal from the man of her dreams. I've got a right to be nervous.*

She slipped into the waiting taxi. Always careful with money, Bess had been dying to try the food at Belle Culottes but didn't because it was expensive. Her mind raced, wondering what was on the menu. Her stomach growled. She'd been too jumpy for lunch. *Something delicious and French. Hmm, lamb? Whit? Food, girl.* She giggled in the backseat as the vehicle cut through the late, rush-hour traffic.

The doorman at the restaurant opened the door and gave a short bow. She mentioned Whit's name to the Maître d' and was shown to a table in a quiet corner. Whit was waiting. A bottle of Moet et Chandan was chilling in a silver ice bucket. Butterflies invaded her stomach.

"You look gorgeous," he said.

She smiled, too excited to speak.

"Champagne?"

She nodded, watching the waiter fill two flutes.

Whit raised his in a toast. "To a wonderful life."

Bess cocked her head slightly. *Not exactly the toast I was expecting.*

"This is the perfect time for both of us. You're starting a new career in the big-time at Eagle, and I'm following a new path, myself."

Marriage. Got it. Right. She grinned at him.

He looked down before making eye contact with her. Something in his expression made her appetite go south. He took both her hands in his. "I've been searching for a way to say this..."

A tightness gathered in her chest. *Ask me! Ask me!*

"I suppose there's no easy way. Kinda like ripping a bandage off. Gotta pull and it only stings for a second."

Sweat gathered under her arms. The constriction in her throat choked back words. *No easy way? Bandage? Sting? Can proposing be so difficult?*

"Bess..." he started then hesitated.

"Yes?" All she could hear was the thumping of her heart.

"I don't know how to say this."

"Spit it out." Her heartbeat doubled.

"I got an opportunity...I mean...I'm taking a new job."

"New job?" Her heartbeat tripled.

"I'm going to Asia to write for *New York News Review*."

Her heart ran into a brick wall. Her throat dried up like a worm on the pavement in the hot August sun. Her mind went blank.

"I'm leaving in two weeks. It's sort of a dream of mine. To get away. Do something different. Leave the usual behind."

She stared at him with wide eyes.

"I'll miss you. We're so great together. But you know I don't commit. I've always been upfront about it. You've probably got some terrific guy in your back pocket, waiting for me to move over and give him some space. If not, I hope you'll still want to see me when I get back." His words sounded brave, but his eyes looked worried.

Bess thought she'd gone deaf. All she heard was blah, blah, blah..."going to Asia" and, blah, blah..."miss you." Emotion pushed up against the wall of her chest, but she shoved it down. Her hands twisted the cloth napkin, and her breathing came in short spurts. She stared into space, feeling the blood drain from her face.

"Bess?"

She rolled her gaze back to his. *He looks pale.*

"Are you all right?" He peered into her eyes. "Do you want some water?"

As quickly as it shut off, her mind flipped back on. *Get out of here. Now. Leave.* She put her hands on the table and braced herself. "I don't feel good. I'm going home."

"What? Bess? Are you okay?"

"No, I'm not." She felt his hand at her elbow. His eyebrows were knitted. "I'm going home." Uncertain if her knees would hold her, she stood, her fingers gripping the chair back.

"Let me settle up for the champagne, and I'll take you."

She touched his forearm. "I'd rather go alone." The wall in her chest cracked bit by bit. *Get out now, while you're still holding it together.* Emotion seeped through the cracks and oozed its way up her body, landing first in her stomach then continuing north.

"I can't let you go like this. Are you sick?"

"I'm fine. I'm going." She moved in slow motion, picking up her coat. "Goodbye, Whit."

He rose from the table, still holding her elbow. She ripped her arm from him, took a huge, shuddering breath, and headed for the door.

"Wait! Bess! I'll only be a moment." But she kept going.

The doorman smiled. "Taxi, miss?"

She nodded. Her mind blanked out as she rode home. Once inside the house, she was greeted by the pugs. Bess went into the bedroom, peeled off her fancy outfit, and slipped naked into bed. *I'm a stupid fool.* Tears pushed through. She buried her face in her pillow.

Sometime later, the dogs barked. She raised her head and heard the pounding and her name being called. After donning a robe, she padded to the kitchen. She attached Homer's leash and took him to the front of the apartment.

"Bess! Open up! Come on. Please?"

She opened the door and put Homer in Whit's arms. As she closed it, he put his foot in the way.

"Wait! Please. Can we talk?"

"There's nothing to talk about. You're going to Asia. It's a done deal. Here's your dog. I wish you luck." She concentrated on keeping her breathing even.

"Wait! I don't want to part like this."

"Oh? And the dinner was to let me down easy? I've saved you a big tab. You've let me down without the dinner. Let's call it over, okay?"

"Not okay. I don't want to never see you again."

"You're going to be pretty far away for a quick dinner out, Whit."

"Look, I thought we were on the same page. A terrific affair, but one with no future."

"You made it very clear from the beginning. So, now it's over. Goodbye."

She slammed the door and locked it. Her heart hurt. Every part of her body ached. She threw on sweats and leashed Dumpling. When Whit left the hall, she tiptoed to the elevator and walked her pug through the bitter cold to the edge of the park. It was dark by the playground. She sank down on a bench and let out the emotion she could no longer contain. She sobbed, causing Dumpling to bark.

As soon as she could stop, she hurried back to the building, hiding her tear-stained face from Crash. The heat of his concerned expression penetrated her.

"Did the asshole break your heart, Miss Bess?"

She couldn't look at him and didn't answer. Dumpling stopped to be petted. Bess jerked on the leash. "Come on, girl." When she raised her gaze, Crash met hers. The knowing look on his face sent shame through her. She picked up her dog and headed for the elevator.

Once the pug had received her treat and was unleashed, Bess broke down again. She cried so hard she threw up, running into the bathroom. She hung over the toilet bowl, like a drunk, sobbing and puking. Dumpling curled up outside the door.

After fifteen minutes, she stood up, washed, and went to bed. Her mind shut down, welcoming sleep. Bess was out cold until morning.

Chapter Fourteen

EVEN WITH PICK'S HELP, Whit had a ton to do. There were Visa's to worry about, travel and living expenses to hash out with the publisher, and his broadcast to continue, especially the police corruption investigation.

Even so, the next morning as he leashed Homer for a walk before work, he thought of Bess. Their paths had not crossed yet that day, but Whit made a mental note to send flowers. *Roses. A dozen. Red. Maybe pink.*

On the way out the door, Crash grabbed him by the lapels.

"You broke her heart. You piece a shit. I'd like to mess up your pretty face."

"What? What are you talking about?"

"Don't give me any crap. You know damn well. You broke Miss Bess's heart. Asshole." Crash let go and opened the door to admit another resident.

Whit straightened out his jacket and hurried out the door before the doorman could make good on his threat.

Did I break her heart? She wasn't in love with me. Oh, yeah, so maybe we each said it once, but in the heat between the sheets, hey, we say things. What did she think was going to happen at dinner?

The next day, he found the keys to the stone house in an envelope, taped to his door. *Shit!* He tried calling, texting, emailing, but didn't get a response from Bess. Finally, he wrote a note and taped it, and the keys, to her door.

Bess,

Please take these back. You told me you were going to furnish the house for me. I'm counting on it. I'm sorry if I hurt you. I didn't mean to. I'll miss you. But I'm not going forever. I hope when I get back we can share some weekends at the stone house. You're special to me. I thought we had an understanding. I see I was wrong. I guess I was stupid. I hope you'll forgive me.

Whit

P.S. Please use the house as your own.

Not signing "love". Don't commit again. I'm gonna drop the word from my vocabulary.

The same night, he found a note under his door.

I don't go back on a promise. I'll furnish the house because I said I would. As for weekends there together, don't count on it. A lot can happen between now and whenever you get back.

Bess

P.S. Though you didn't ask, yes, I'll keep Homer while you're away.

Whit let out a breath. *She agreed to furnish the house. So I can probably see her again. I hope so. I didn't mean for us to be over.* This relationship was like riding a roller coaster, and he wasn't sure he was ready for the hills and steep drops.

He sent Bess an email invitation to have dinner with him before he left, but she declined. His heart was heavy. Instead, he managed to squeeze in one last appointment with Dr. Sumner. He eased into the chair opposite the doctor, uncertain as to what he'd be talking about.

"I have to ask. Did you find the answer to the question?" The doctor sat back.

"Why I haven't sold the house? No. No answer. But I'm furnishing it."

"Oh?"

"My girlfriend, Bess...wait. She's not my girlfriend anymore. She said she'd finish doing the house while I'm away."

"Why isn't she your girlfriend?"

"I don't know. I took her to a fancy restaurant to tell her I was leaving. When I told her, she freaked out. Got up and left before even ordering."

"Why do you think she did?"

"I have no idea. And she wouldn't tell me. And now, she's not speaking to me."

"What did you tell her?'

"I was taking this job..."

"No, I mean before. Before you got to the restaurant. Did you say anything special?"

"I had something to tell her."

"Oh?"

"Yeah. So?"

"You said you had something to tell her, and you wanted to take her to a fancy restaurant to do it?"

He nodded.

"What do you think a woman might suspect? Would a guy take her to an expensive restaurant to break up with her? Unlikely. What might he want to say to her in a fancy place?"

The light bulb went on in Whit's head. He buried his face in his hands. "Oh my God. I never thought."

The doctor sat quietly.

"You think she was expecting me to propose?"

"Would explain her reaction, wouldn't it?"

"Poor Bess. Oh my God, I had no idea. I never thought she'd. I told her I don't commit. She was fine with it."

"Do you think she'd be upset if she planned to turn you down?"

"She'd be relieved, right? She got so pale. Her hands shook. I thought she was going to fall down. She wouldn't wait for me. Wouldn't let me take her home. Now, she won't speak to me."

"Do you blame her?"

"Oh, God. I went to her house. Banged on the door, demanded to know what happened. What an insensitive asshole." He shook his head.

"She's in love with you."

"Why didn't I see it?"

"I don't know, Whit. Why didn't you?"

Pain shot through him at the thought of the anguish he'd caused Bess. He'd never wanted to hurt her. Now, he had. Seriously. And he was leaving in a few days.

"I guess it was easier to move on if I didn't think she was in love with me."

"Bingo."

"I'm an idiot."

Silence.

"She's wonderful."

"Do you love her?" The doctor crossed his legs.

"Guess I do."

"Don't you know?"

"Okay, okay. Yeah. I do." Whit crossed his legs.

"Still not gonna commit?"

"Can't. I'm on my way. I have to do this. She's in love with me, but she won't speak to me. Exactly what I expected. Love doesn't mean anything. A woman'll still run out on you, even if she loves you. Bess is a perfect example."

Dr. Sumner uncrossed his legs and sat forward. "Wait a minute. Who ran out on who?"

Whit cocked an eyebrow. "What do you mean?"

"You ran out on her, Whit. At least be honest with yourself. You told her you were leaving. She didn't leave you. You thrust her aside."

"I did?" He paused. "Guess I did."

"And she's still willing to furnish the house for you?"

"Said a deal's a deal. But she won't spend a weekend there with me."

"Can you blame her? Think of how she must have felt. Furnishing the house with the idea she'd live there with you as husband and wife."

"Thanks for making it worse, doc." Whit looked down at his hands.

"I'm not doing anything. I'm only holding up a mirror so you can see the truth. If you don't like what you see, it's because of what you've done. Your behavior. Has nothing to do with me."

"I don't like what I see. I've broken her heart, and I never meant to. Now, she's going to break mine."

"If you don't like what you see, change the picture."

"You mean look at something else?"

"No, do something different with your life. It's not too late to make amends."

"She's not speaking to me."

"Smart man like you can find a way. You don't have to get your heart broken."

"I don't know what to do."

"What did you do to win her?"

"I don't know. Be myself?"

"Works for me. Don't give up, Whit. This woman seems like a keeper."

"It's what I wanted. I wanted her to wait for me."

"Did you ask her to?"

"Sort of. I assumed..."

"Ah, ah, big mistake. Never assume. Communicate."

"I don't know if I'm going to like it there. I want her here for me when I get back. I won't be staying there forever."

"When you first decided to go, it was to be a permanent change."

"Now, I'm not so sure."

"What's changed?"

"I don't know. Bess? The stone house?"

"Only you can answer, Whit."

"Another one. A question you won't answer." He shifted in his seat.

"I don't have the answer. The answer's in here." The doctor gestured toward his chest.

"I have the answer?"

"Exactly. To both questions."

"Of course, you're right."

"You'll figure it out, Whit. I have confidence in you."

"I'm glad you think so. Geez, I've fucked up everything. So sure I had all the answers. Now the only thing I'm sure of is I don't have any answers at all."

"That's the first step toward finding happiness," the doctor said.

"It's a helluva first step."

The doctor glanced at the clock. "Time's up for today."

Whit stood up. "I don't know when I'll be back."

"You have my number if you need me."

"I'm a little uncertain about leaving you, doc."

"You're ready. Ready for the next step."

"Whatever the hell it is?"

"Right. You'll figure it out. You're on the right path."

Whit stuck his hand out, and the doctor shook it.

"We can continue when you return to the States."

"Okay. Good. You're sure I'm ready?"

"Sink or swim. It's time."

Whit left, choosing to walk home in the cold to think. The idea Bess might have been expecting a marriage proposal made him cringe. *Why didn't I see it? How can I be such a fucking idiot?* The memory of banging on her door, demanding an explanation, shamed him. *She must have felt humiliated.*

Bess, if ever I was going to propose to someone, it would be you. Will she ever forgive me? Will she ever speak to me again? His thoughts hung heavy on his heart, pushing out excitement about his adventure in Asia.

BESS FOUND OUT FROM Crash Whit planned to leave on a Monday. *Perfect. The Dinner Club will be here to help me.* She wanted to talk to him. To kiss him goodbye, to find out why he didn't want to marry her, why he chose to leave instead. But she chickened out. *How do you ask a man why he won't marry you and have any self-respect left? Because he doesn't love me. I've gotta face the truth, like it or not.*

She cuddled on the sofa with Dumpling and Homer. The wind rattled the panes of glass in her windows. She pulled the afghan Rory had made for her tighter around her legs. Thursday was Thanksgiving, and she dreaded the holiday. *Nowhere to go. Nothing to do.* She'd hoped to make a spectacular Thanksgiving dinner for Whit and her friends in the stone house, but now it wouldn't happen.

There were a ton of chores awaiting her in the place. Walls to be painted, rugs, linens, and dishes to be purchased. She'd put on music and break out the roller and can of paint on Thanksgiving. At least it had a chance to be ready for Christmas. *Christmas without Whit.* The idea brought tears to her eyes. *I'm going to have Christmas there, Whit or no Whit.*

Crash was to buzz her when the car arrived for Whit. She pushed the blanket off her legs and paced. According to the clock, it was due in ten minutes. She leashed Homer so he could give Whit a farewell lick. Three buzzes gave her the signal, and she headed for the elevator.

In the lobby, Crash was loading luggage in the trunk. Bess stood inside, by the small space heater. Whit rushed by, not seeing her. Homer's bark drew his attention.

"Bess!"

"I thought you'd like to say goodbye to Homer."

He bent down to pet the pug. "I'm going to miss you, Homes. You'll be in good hands 'til I get back." He turned toward Bess. "I'd like to say goodbye to you."

She gasped.

"Wait! Wait. That didn't come out right. I don't want to say goodbye, maybe farewell for now. Damn it, I want to kiss you." He surprised her with a passionate kiss.

Homer jumped on Whit's leg, but it didn't break them up. The softness of his lips and the insistence of his tongue lured her. She melted against him, yearning for more. She snaked her arms around his waist, tightening her grip.

"S'cuse me," Crash said.

The lovers parted.

"Sorry. Sorry."

"It's all packed up, Mr. Bass."

"Fine, thanks, Crash." He slipped the doorman a twenty-dollar bill.

Whit turned his gaze to her, his eyes melancholy. "There's so much I want to say to you."

She stared at him.

"Please say you'll write to me." He combed her hair back from her face with his fingers.

"Email?"

"Perfect." He bent down to pet Homer again. The pug licked his face. "Hey, buddy. Hang on, okay? Be good to Dumpling. Don't steal her bones. Take care of Bess." He scratched the dog behind the ears then straightened. "Can I call you?"

She gave one nod. Tears choked her. *He's leaving, really leaving, and I never told him how I felt. Never asked him to stay. I shut him out and hid away. Stupid, stupid girl.*

He stepped closer and hugged her. "You mean...everything to me," he whispered. Then, he let go and was out of the building, in the limousine, and on his way. Bess ran to the curb. Tears poured down her face. The car stopped at the light. Whit turned. He put his palm on the glass. She raised her hand.

Then, the light changed, and the vehicle got lost in the uptown traffic on Central Park West. Bess shivered in the wind on the Avenue. Homer did, too. They returned to her apartment. She mixed up hot chocolate and sat by the window. Another gray, November day. The leaves were almost gone on the trees in the park. People starting their Thanksgiving holidays drove past, scurrying along to their families.

Four o'clock, almost dark. *Will I forget him? Will he email me? Call me? If I meant everything to him, why did he leave me? I have the keys to his house, so I can see him again, if I want to. Will I meet someone else? No one can compare to Whitfield Bass.*

Exhausted, Bess fell asleep on the sofa, with a pug cuddled up at each end. The buzz from the lobby at six o'clock woke her. The dogs jumped up, barking, and raced to the door. In a few minutes, there was a scratching. Bess pushed to her feet, rubbing her eyes. "Coming ."

It burst open before she got there. Three women, all talking at once, and five dogs barking and wiggling, blew into the room like a tornado. Bess laughed in spite of her headache.

"Chinese tonight." Miranda opened a brown paper bag.

"Did Whit leave?" Brooke asked.

Bess nodded, grabbing a bottle of Ibuprofen from the cabinet. The room grew silent.

Rory walked over to her and slipped an arm around her shoulders. "I'm sorry."

BESS PACKED UP THE pugs and drove out to Rye on Tuesday. *No sense moping around the city when there's work to do.* She set out beds for the dogs then trekked into Port Chester to a huge hardware store. She loaded up the car with painting supplies, wallpaper, and a few lamps and kitchen tools.

She had created a playlist before going to bed the night before. *Got to get started while it's still light outside.* She outlined with blue tape, opened the primer, and rolled it on the wall. She hoped to cover the dirty color that had been there for years.

Unable to wait until morning, Bess applied the soft, creamy white paint to the living room wall after the primer dried. The clean, bright warmth of the color brought the room to life. Stubbornly determined to have the house in shape for Christmas, Bess worked on. By dinnertime, all the living room walls had been painted.

She ate leftovers from home, fed the dogs, and blue-taped the walls of the little room on the first floor. *This would make a good office for Whit.* By ten o'clock, she was ready for sleep. One final walk along the windy beach with the pugs, and they all settled into the big bed for the night. Bess opened her computer, wondering if she had an email from Whit. Sure enough. There it was.

> *Flight delays. Language barriers. Lousy food. Wish I'd stayed home. Missing you already. What are you up to?*
>
> *Whit*

She replied—

> *Working on the house. Will be painting on Thanksgiving. Can you even get turkey in Hong Kong? Dogs fine. All is well.*
>
> *Bess*

Keep it light. Don't let him know how much he hurt you. Start to disengage. I've got to save myself.

Bess found Thanksgiving Day was like any other day if you spent it listening to music, painting and putting up wallpaper. By Friday, the entire downstairs had a fresh coat and the powder room was complete. The soft cream of the living room and dining room gave way to a soothing, light bluish green in the study. The kitchen was a bright coral, with a small table, in a bright white that contrasted with the colorful walls.

The dark entryway was the cream color, but one shade warmer.

By the end of the weekend, the upstairs was finished, too. The master bedroom was a subtle, slightly grayish blue with silver trim. The other bedrooms were bright yellow with sky blue trim and soft taupe with white trim.

The linens for the queen bed were silver and white stripes. Accent pillows in light pink and rose brought warmth to the room. Bess was pleased with her work. By Sunday, she was ready to return to the city and get back to cooking for television.

Each weekend, Bess schlepped Dumpling and Homer to Rye. Soon the house was filled with pine furniture in simple, Early American lines. Cushions, pillows, and artwork kept the rooms warm and inviting. Lighting was soft, but efficient, from floor and table lamps. The wood fragrance from the furnishings and the logs by the fireplace freshened the air.

Bess shopped every antique store in New York City for candlesticks. She placed them on the dining room table, the mantle, on the stair risers, on the dressers in the master bedroom. She bought electric candles as well and placed one in each window. She left them lit when she returned to her city life. Those candles, shining in the windows when she returned welcomed her into the beautiful cozy home she'd created.

Comfortable, cheerful, and inviting, the house was everything she'd always wanted. She tried not to think about turning it over to Whit when he returned. She'd created a living space she loved and went out there at every opportunity.

Every night as she crawled into bed exhausted and in the company of only Dumpling and Homer, she'd check her email. There was always one from Whit. He'd complain about some inconvenience or tell her about something beautiful. He described the people he was dealing with and the places he'd traveled.

She enjoyed his correspondence. As much as she wanted to break away, she opened each message with happy anticipation. The women in the Dinner Club fixed her up with a blind date from time to time. She'd mention these to Whit to tease him, and he always rose to the bait, finding fault with each man. Bess wanted to like someone new more than Whit, but never did.

As Christmas approached, Bess planned a party for the Dinner Club at the stone house. She'd drive them out, have everyone stay over, and return them to the city the next day.

"A Christmas sleepover!" Miranda said.

"Let's do a Secret Santa," Brooke said.

They piled into Whit's car, cramming the pugs in with them, and headed out. The air was crisp and clear. No snow in the forecast. Once they settled in, the women took the dogs for a romp on the deserted beach. The canines stuck their noses in the sand, chased each other and barked at the occasional winter seagull.

Bess needed the gathering of her friends. She hadn't had an email from Whit in two weeks. Fear the relationship was over—perhaps he'd met someone—made her sad. She didn't admit anything to her friends, not wanting to ruin their holidays.

After the fresh air, the ladies divided up tasks. Bess manned the kitchen, Brooke made a fire, Miranda set the table, and Rory tended bar.

The pugs were exhausted. After their dinner, each found a cozy place and curled up to sleep. The women sat cross-legged in front of the fireplace. They shared a bottle of Moscato.

"I have a confession." Tears pricked the backs of her eyes. She glanced at her friends, who waited for her to go on. "It's been weeks since I got an email from Whit."

"Weeks? How many?" Brooke asked.

"Two. At first, it was an email every night. Then, nothing."

The silence was interrupted only by the crack of a twig in the fire.

"There could be a thousand explanations," Rory said.

"Or only one. It's over. This is my first and last Christmas in this wonderful house."

"I love it here," Miranda said. "I didn't see it before you refurbished it, but you've made it so cozy, warm, and beautiful."

The other women agreed. Bess got they wanted to change the subject, so she let it go. "Let's exchange our Secret Santa gifts," she said. Amidst a squeal of laughter, and exclamations, small packages changed hands.

As they finished their final clean-up before going to sleep, Bess sighed and opened her computer. "One more time," she muttered. And there it was. An email from Whit. The subject line had one word—"Christmas."

Chapter Fifteen

WHIT HAD BEEN PREPARED for anything. He'd packed a raincoat, three umbrellas, a down jacket, and a couple of wife-beaters. He had dictionaries for three different languages, as well as translation apps for his phone. He got money changed into the currency of the countries he'd be passing through. He had even packed a spare battery for his computer. Every eventuality was covered. Whitfield Bass was an organized man. Nothing was going to take him by surprise.

The foreign atmosphere had thrown him. Nothing was the same as New York. The smells, the food, the people, even the scenery. At first, he'd been fascinated. He'd met so many people the first week, he knew he'd never remember them all. But by the second week, loneliness had seeped into his heart. The exotic surroundings lost their luster when there was no one to share them with. His first impressions, quirky things he noticed...were all about him, and only him. Was he homesick?

He'd planned for every possible scenario.

The one thing he hadn't planned on was the giant hole in his life left by the absence of Bess Cooper. Bess, Dumpling, and Homer had become his family. They had bounced back and forth from her apartment to his from her bed to his. Dinners had been shared. Dogs had been walked together. Homer had stayed with Bess while Whit was working. Whit had taken Dumpling when Bess had to be at the studio early. They had been a team.

Unwittingly, he had created a small family then deserted them. He missed his old life, Bess, and the dogs. *Damn it, how did it happen? I was supposed to be free.*

He had tried cutting himself off from her. No emailing, no phoning. Did it make him miss her less? The opposite. He missed her more. The torture of checking emails a thousand times a day to find none from Bess was almost more than he could bear. He needed her in his life.

The empty, double bed he had in the small sublet seemed enormous. No Bess. No dogs. He missed the sex, he missed the affection, the camaraderie, the laughing, talking, joking. Someone to wonder if he was okay when he was late. Dinner being saved to be re-heated when he got home. He even missed the snoring of the pugs.

The finely-constructed, emotionally sterile world of Whitfield Bass came crashing down.

Sitting in a bar where the chatter was in a language he didn't recognize, he drank his scotch and thought about Dr. Sumner. After the second drink, he finally understood what the doctor was saying. And he knew the answer to the question.

Why had he not sold the house? Of course. It all made sense, once he discarded his own words. If he forgot all his nonsense about not committing and not wanting the family he never had, he saw he was saving the house for the family he'd always wanted. The family he'd have some day. The family he needed to feel whole.

Something in him didn't believe all his malarkey. His heart knew life could be at least some of what he had imagined growing up. He needed it. He deserved it. And it fit perfectly into the stone house. So, he kept it, a place he loved, to house the people he would love.

A smile crossed his lips. It made perfect sense. *Why didn't I see it before?* He knew the answer. Until he found Bess, the woman to be the core of his family, the stone house was only a symbol. With her, it could become a reality. Satisfaction at having the answer warmed him.

The part of Whit wanting a family had put Bess in charge of making the house a home. Who better for the job than the woman he adored and couldn't live without? *Perfect.*

"So, what the hell am I doing in Hong Kong, alone?" Through the haze of his second drink, he saw clearly what he had to do.

"I have a home. A real home. And a woman who loves me, who should be my wife."

In the morning, he called Pick and the airlines and packed his bag. He sent this email to Bess—

Am coming home. Let's have an old-fashioned Christmas at the stone house. Only you and me. Okay? I'm on a flight due in Dec. 25.

I'll take a limousine from the airport right to Rye. Can't wait to see you.

Love,

Whit

While he waited to board his flight, he got an email from Pick.

Not surprised. Didn't expect you to last. Merry Christmas. Jamison is on the way. Expect to be invited to the wedding.

He sent one to Sam.

Returning to NYC at Christmas. Back permanently. Hope you haven't given away my job. Will report for duty on January 2.

Whit

He made one leg of the trip, but his plane was delayed due to weather. Then, it was canceled. He never got a response from Bess. But then, he only had spotty Internet access. He had to have faith she'd be there. *Me, have faith in a woman? I'll try.*

One delay became two. He managed to re-book, only to have the flight canceled. Slowly the hours ticked away. Christmas was disappearing. Still no word from Bess. Now, no Internet and no cell reception. He was in the mountains and would have to believe she'd be there.

He managed to beg a seat on the last plane out in the middle of the night. He prayed everything would go all right, it would land safely and Bess would be there. *I wouldn't blame her. Hasn't heard from me. Then this. Who am I fooling? She's probably got someone else by now.* He brooded for a moment. *Not Bess. Please, God.*

Kennedy airport was insane with people from flights delayed all over because of blizzards and fog in the United States. He couldn't believe his eyes when he saw a limo driver holding a sign with the name "Bass" on it. *It's gotta be Pick. Bless him.* Whit grabbed the man and led him over to the baggage claim area. They schlepped his luggage to the car, and Whit got in.

He'd been traveling for over twenty-four hours. He rubbed his cheek. *Need a shave. Bess likes scruff. Need a shower.*

The driver did his best to weave his way through snarled traffic. They finally reached the New England Thruway, which was almost bumper-to-bumper. They crawled. Whit thought he'd lose his mind. He turned on his phone to check his email. There were ten messages from Bess. They all said the same thing—"Yes."

After two hours, the limo pulled up in front of the stone house. Whit tipped the man twenty bucks, grabbed his bags, and headed for the front door. He stopped cold. It had been sanded down and painted white. A shiny brass knocker graced the top, two inches below the tiny window. Whit used it.

Bess opened the door. They stood still, staring at each other.

"You look beautiful," he said.

She grabbed his arm and pulled him inside. The warmth of the house embraced him like a loving hug. The scent of a baking ham mixed with the smell of burning wood from the fireplace.

Whit scooped Bess into his arms and kissed her. She wiped tears from her cheek then stepped back.

"God you feel good," he whispered, holding her close.

"So do you."

"I love you, Bess. Love you so much."

"Me, too." She stepped back.

"Well, what do you think?" She chewed her lip and sniffled.

His gaze zeroed in on the six-foot Christmas tree. Voices from the past echoed in his head.

"Christmas tree? Damn, filthy thing! I've got better things to do than waste good money on something to be tossed out in two weeks. And who's gonna clean up those pine needles and shit? You? I doubt it. I've got no time to clean up after a damn Christmas tree," his father had said, when Whit was five.

"Don't touch! It's Anna's job, Whit. She decorates the tree every year. I hope you understand, dear. Tell your father you want your own tree," said his Aunt Ida, the year he had spent Christmas at her house.

"I'm so sorry, Whit. We don't have money to buy a tree. It's all we can do to feed you kids. We're older. We live on a fixed income. Do you understand? You will when you grow up. Put on your coat. Let's go see the tree in town," said his grandmother, the year he had stayed with her.

There was a half-empty box of ornaments on the floor beside the tree. With a tremble in his hand, he picked up a glass ball and hung it on a branch. Emotion gagged him. He felt a sting at the back of his eyes. Whit fingered the needles, fresh and fragrant. A deep inhale brought the sweet smell of pine rushing to his nostrils. He blinked back tears and smiled.

His gaze passed over the room drawn to a garland, with tiny, twinkling, lights, wound around the staircase. Another graced the big window next to the dining room table. The table was set for two, with white plates sitting proudly on placemats of Christmas plaid fabric. A spiral cut ham rested regally on a silver platter, flanked by side dishes of creamed spinach and roasted potatoes.

The sofa had an antique wood coffee table, sporting a hammered copper bowl overflowing with red apples, oranges, and walnuts. Two end tables with large, white, milk glass lamps flanked the couch. Candles burned in brass holders.

Whit's mouth hung open. "It's beautiful. Perfect." *This is it. The home I always wanted. It's mine. Now. Finally.*

"Come see the kitchen and the bedroom!" She took his arm and led him into the kitchen. A faint sweet and spicy aroma of gingerbread teased his nose, and his stomach groaned. He spied a small platter piled high with gingerbread men, dressed with white icing. Cooking utensils and brightly colored dishtowels lay scattered about. *This room is her. She belongs here.*

They trudged up the stairs to the bedroom. Whit took off his coat and laid it over a black, lacquered rocking chair. He sat on the bed and bounced.

Bess held out her hands to him. "What do you think?"

He took them in his, grinning so wide his cheeks hurt. "It's the most incredible house...I can't believe it's the same place." *It's everything I've dreamed of.*

"It needed a little TLC."

I need a little TLC. And you and this house are the prescription to cure the ailment. "Thank you. You've made my dream come true."

Each room was more stunning than the one before.

"You did all this?" He raised his eyebrows. "Amazing."

She nodded, her eyes filling. "Come on, dinner's ready. Of course, it was ready yesterday, but hey, delays are delays." She wiped her eyes with the back of her hand.

When they reached the dining area, Bess handed him a mug of warm mulled wine then joined him at the table. A sense of peace, totally new, drifted through Whit's veins.

"What made you come back so soon, and why didn't I hear from you for so long?"

"I came back for you. I missed you. I tried not to. I'm ashamed to say, I thought not emailing or calling would make me forget you. But it didn't work. I only wanted you more."

"You came back to be with me? Mr. No Commit?" There was a tiny tremble in her voice.

"I've been stupid. Not anymore. I get it. I get you're the best thing that's ever happened to me. I love you. I want to be with you always. Will you marry me?" He pulled out a small box, opening it to reveal a large, round, diamond ring.

Bess gasped.

"Will you? Do I need to get down on one knee?" Whit pushed up from the table and knelt in front of her.

Tears flowed down her cheeks.

"Don't tell me there's someone else?" He frowned.

She shook her head.

"Thank God! Talk to me. Say yes, nod, something!" He grew panicky.

"Yes. I will. Yes."

Whit jumped up and pulled her into his arms. Then, he placed the ring on her finger.

"I thought you were gone for good," she said, burying her face in his chest.

"I couldn't leave you. I love you too much. You're my dream come true." He stroked her hair.

"I promise I'll never leave you," she said, cupping his cheek and wiping her eyes.

"I'm counting on you."

She smiled. "You're my dream, too. I didn't think you were ever coming back." A timer went off. "Oh! The mocha magic cake is done." Bess sprang into action.

"Everything looks good. I'm starved." He tucked into the food like he hadn't eaten in years.

After dinner, he sat back, sipping his coffee.

"Okay. Give. Why the change of heart?" Bess narrowed her eyes.

"You've made it clear you want what I want. Those emails about the house. When I found out what you were doing, I couldn't wait to see it. It hit me one night, after a few scotches, that I had what I've always wanted, right here, with you."

"You don't think I'm going to run away? Leave you?"

"A doctor once told me life has no guarantees. I can't be certain, but I can try to make you happy. He also said by living my version of "safe," I was missing out on life. Messy life with the ups and downs, joys and sorrows. Real living. Which is not what I've been doing."

"A wise doctor." Bess took a taste of her hot drink.

"It's you, Bess. You make the difference. You make me believe I can live my dream."

He walked over to his suitcase and opened it, drawing out two packages. He put them on the table and sat down. "Merry Christmas."

"Like the engagement ring wasn't enough?" She splayed her fingers and held her hand to the light.

"That's different. Go on. Open them."

She ripped off the wrapping to reveal a carrying case. She snapped it open. Inside were a *Nikon D800* camera and two special lenses. She gasped. "Oh my God! A *Nikon*? This costs a fortune, thousands of dollars."

"You said you used to take pictures. Bet you were damn good. Now, you have the equipment to do it again."

Tears filled her eyes. "Dad would be so proud." She kissed Whit.

"This one isn't nearly as grand."

She pulled off the paper. Inside was a large, red leather photo album. "For my pictures?"

"And for the ones you'll take of our family."

"Our family," she repeated, stroking the cover.

"If I don't have pictures, Jeff'll never believe I've done it." He laughed.

"Oh! Wait a minute. This came for you." She pulled an envelope out of her pocket.

Whit looked at the return address. Emotion closed his throat. As he slipped his finger under the flap, he muttered, "Robbie."

While Whit read his Christmas card from his brother, Bess examined her new camera and read the instruction booklet. They finished the bottle of wine. Whit immediately sat down and replied to Robbie with a heartfelt email. He brushed aside two tears as he hit "send."

"Come on. I've waited too long already." He held out his hand as he moved toward the stairs. Whit took a quick shower then made love to Bess. They fell asleep curled together.

The couple stayed in the stone house through New Year's, making plans for their life together. Then they fought the traffic back to the city.

CRASH FLAGGED A TAXI for Whit. He gave the address of Dr. Sumner's office. When the cab stopped, he tipped generously and waited in the waiting room. It wasn't long before Dr. Sumner appeared. They shook hands. Whit preceded the doctor and sank down in the comfortable, leather chair he always occupied.

"I didn't expect you back so soon. What happened?" The doctor eased into his chair and crossed his legs.

"I got it."

"Got what?"

"The answer. The answer to the question."

The doctor smiled. "Glad to hear it."

"I kept the house because I wanted to put my family there."

"Sounds about right."

"I've asked Bess to marry me."

"And what did she say?"

"She accepted." Whit beamed.

"Congratulations." A smile broke through the doctor's usually placid expression.

"She said she loves me and promised never to leave."

"I hope you know..."

Whit held up his hand. "I got it. There are no guarantees. I accept that. I'm going to try everything I can to make her happy, so she'll stay."

"Sounds like you two have a good chance for success."

"We're gonna have kids, too."

"It'll change things."

"I know. I'll take it as it comes. I need the whole package, doc."

Dr. Sumner smiled again. "I understand. I think you'll make a fine father."

"Think so?"

"I do."

"Jeff agrees with you."

"You can count on him for support."

"I know. I'm lucky to have him."

"I think you're ready to go it on your own. You don't need to come anymore."

Panic seized Whit. "But what if everything fails?"

"You can come back. Maybe every three months or so? Like getting your car tuned up?"

"A life tune-up, eh? Sounds like a plan."

"I'm proud of you, Whit. You've worked hard in therapy. Now, you're going to have what you want." The doctor stood up.

"Yeah, doc, I get it. Time's up." The two men shook hands. "Thank you, Dr. Sumner. For helping me get my life back."

"A pleasure."

Whit took a deep breath and hit the street. The sun was shining, cutting the cold a little, so he walked home, thinking about his life.

After a pow-wow with Bess, he put his apartment on the market and moved into her place. A week later, they decided to have a small wedding ceremony at the stone house in July. Bess formed a planning team with the Dinner Club women. Whit needed a best man and two ushers. Jeff and Pick agreed, happily, to stand up for him. Now, there was only one left to call.

While the women were fussing over food during their weekly meeting, he retreated to the bedroom. He stretched out on the bed. It had been five years since he'd heard his brother's voice. *Will I still recognize him? Will he talk to me?*

Sweat gathered on his palms and butterflies invaded his stomach. When he picked up the phone, his mouth was dry. Before he could chicken out, Whit dialed.

"Robbie?"

"Yeah. Who's this?"

"Whit."

A moment of silence seemed like a year.

"Whit? My brother, Whit?"

"Yeah."

"How the hell are you?"

"Fine, Robbie. Just fine. How are you?"

"I'm hangin' in."

"I'm calling because...well...I have a favor to ask."

For a moment, he thought he'd lost the connection. *Robbie's trying to take it all in.*

"Shoot."

"Would you be an usher at my wedding?"

"You're getting married? Mr. Confirmed Bachelor?"

Whit chuckled at the surprise in his brother's voice. "Finally got around to it."

"Fantastic. Sure. I'll be there. Is Jeff coming?"

"Hell, yeah! He's been bugging me for years."

"And Dad?"

"I saw him a few days ago. When I told him, he said he'd step up his physical therapy so he could be here for the big event."

"The last Bass left to fall."

"You're married?"

"Yep. Three years now."

"Bring her. Damn. Gotta meet this chick."

"I'm sorry, Whit," Robbie blurted out.

Emotion closed Whit's throat for a moment. "It's okay, Robbie. I understand."

"I don't know. I was angry."

"I get it. It's in the past. Let's forget it."

"I hope you can."

"We'll start over when you come to the wedding."

"Thanks."

"Gotta go. Bess wants me," Whit lied. The call ended.

He pushed his thumbs into his eyes to stay the tears. A deep, shuddering breath opened his chest a little so he could breathe.

Bess burst into the room, chattering away, but stopped when she saw him. She sank down on the bed and cupped his cheek. "What's wrong?"

He shook his head.

"Can't talk?"

He chuckled, removing his hand from his eyes to look at her. "I'm okay. Talked to Robbie."

"Everything all right?"

"Better than I ever expected."

"You've been through hell. You deserve the best, honey," she said.

Whit stroked her hand and brushed his lips over hers. "I have the best. I have you."

The next morning, Whit bounced into the station. He grabbed the papers on his desk and paced, reading the stories aloud for practice. Happiness flowing through his veins like adrenaline kept him moving. He strode from one end of the studio, to the other. He stopped to gaze out the big windows overlooking Columbus Avenue. When he turned, he trained an eye on Sam.

She sat in her office, typing, until the receptionist entered.

Whit stopped to listen in.

"Delivery for you. From West Side Liquors. What do you want me to do with it?"

"Have them roll it in here."

"Do you know what it is?"

"Yeah. A case of *Chivas Regal*." Sam's gaze locked with Whit's. She smiled, and he laughed.

Best bet I ever lost.

Epilogue

TEN BLOCKS UP ON THE Upper West Side, Miranda put down her book and picked up her cell.

"You've got to help me. They're carrying my furniture out and dumping it on the sidewalk!"

"Brooke? Is that you?" Miranda stood up.

"It's me. I don't know what I'm going to do."

"Slow down."

"I'm being evicted! The effing landlord is taking my stuff and putting it outside. I need help!"

"Oh my God! I'm calling the Club. We'll be right there."

Miranda dialed Bess.

"Damn landlord is throwing Brooke's stuff out on the sidewalk."

"Holy Hell!"

"I told her not to ignore the sign on her door," Miranda said.

"I didn't think you could evict someone so fast," Bess said.

"Brooke had thirty days."

"What can we do?"

"Can you bring Rory, Hack, and Whit? I'll rent a van and meet you at her place."

"But where's she going to go?" Bess asked.

"There's only one place," Miranda said.

"Oh, no."

"She doesn't have anywhere else to go."

"She's a little old for this," Bess replied.

"I'm hanging up. Get the troops. I'm heading to the rental place now."

As she turned the corner onto Broadway, Miranda phoned Brooke. "We're on our way. I'm getting a van, and Bess is bringing Rory, Hack, and Whit."

"I don't have any place to go."

"You do. You don't want to, but you do."

"I can't. She's..."

"Suck it up, Brooke. You can't live on the sidewalk."

There was a pause on the line.

"Thanks, Miranda."

"You're welcome. See you soon."

She closed her phone and opened the door of the car rental office.

The End

Brooke's story continues in the next Manhattan Dinner Club book, Shine Your Love on Me. Want to read it now? Here's the first chapter:

SHINE YOUR LOVE ON ME

Jean C. Joachim

Chapter One

LLOYD SIMMONS, BROOKE Felson's boss, summoned her to his office. He popped a bottle of champagne and filled two flutes. All smiles, Lloyd handed one to her before he closed the door. He took Brooke in his arms for a passionate kiss.

"We did it. We got the account." He nuzzled her neck and slid his hand up her blouse.

Brooke freed herself from his grasp.

"Not here. There are people in the office. "

"So what? We're dating. We're both single. Besides, no one knows except you and me."

"We shouldn't. What if someone walks in?"

"I know you're always looking out for me, but don't be such a wimp."

"I'm not. You're my boss. You could get a lot of sexual harassment heat if anyone knew."

"Can I help it if I'm charming and irresistible?"

Brooke laughed. "Maybe you are. But Simon Walters might not find it a good excuse."

"Just because he's head of the agency? He may be running things, for now, but we just won the Lady Gray gourmet food account, the biggest in the agency. So who's top dog now?"

"You're amazing. It was an incredible win."

Lloyd drained his glass. "We did it together. And you're going to be the Account Supervisor."

She took another sip. Glee bubbled up in her chest, she couldn't stop smiling.

She took a gulp of champagne. "Thank you, Lloyd."

"Your payback for all those late nights...the ones where you were actually working!" He laughed.

Brooke pulled at the knotted scarf around her neck, left it hanging loose, and fanned herself. *Hot in here.* Lloyd came up behind her and cupped her breast with one hand and unbuttoned her blouse with the other. He kissed her neck this time, slipping the silky fabric open.

Brooke faced him and clasped his arms. "Not here. Wait. Come to my place..." she said, nipping at his earlobe.

"It's a tiny hole-in-the-wall. We're alone here. Let me sit down, and you can—"

Before he could finish, there was a sharp knock on the door. Brooke jumped, pushing off from his chest and madly pushing buttons through holes. Too late.

Without waiting for permission, Evelyn Meriwether, Lady Gray herself, swung the door open and stood, staring. The president of the company frowned, her browed creased. She cocked an eyebrow as she cast her gaze at Lloyd, then Brooke, then back to Lloyd again. "What's going on? Trying to seduce the boss? What a pitiful way to get a raise. Improve your work instead."

Lloyd raised his hand to Brooke before she could respond. "What can I do for you, Ms. Meriwether?"

"First, you can call me Evelyn since we'll be working so...closely...together. Second, there's something I wanted to discuss with you. Can you let your secretary go?"

Heat traveling slowly up Brooke's neck burst into her face. "I'm not—"

Again, Lloyd silenced her. "Brooke's the supervisor on your account."

Evelyn made an ugly face. "Bother. I don't want a girl working on my business." She shot a cold look at Brooke, who had buttoned up.

"We can make a change. I'm sure we have another account supervisor who would meet with your approval. Brooke can handle other business. We have many which would benefit from her expertise."

Evelyn raised an eyebrow again. "Expertise? Really? Seems like her expertise can be found on any street corner in Hell's Kitchen."

"How dare—" Brooke's anger was ready to explode, but Lloyd grabbed her, sliding his hand over her mouth.

"Come, come, Evelyn. Appearances can be deceiving. Brooke is very capable, mature, and experienced in dealing with clients."

Brooke picked up on his pointed references and tamped her outrage down. She sucked two deep breaths in through her nose and relaxed. Lloyd removed his hand. She picked up her purse, snatched her jacket from the back of his chair, and moved toward the door, leaving without a word.

Once in the hall, she strode to the elevator, anxious to make her escape before her temper blew. The car she ordered to take her home took forever to arrive. The tops of her ears were hot and indignation burned in her chest. When she hit the street, she whipped out her cell, waiting for her hand to stop shaking before she dialed. The driver opened the door for her. She got in and he closed it.

Miranda answered. "What's up?"

The story poured out of Brooke's mouth as fast as a runaway train.

"Slow down, slow down. I can't understand you."

"Can you come over?"

"Sure. Let me leash Romeo and Juliet, and we're on our way."

Anger seeped out of Brooke little by little. Knowing her friend Miranda would listen and sympathize helped. The support of the Monday Night Dinner Club women soothed away any hurt and always left her feeling stronger.

Every Monday, Brooke joined her friends—Bess, Rory, and Miranda—at Bess's house for dinner. Bess, a baker with her own television cooking show, brought home the leftovers from rehearsal for the women's feast. All pug owners, they had met originally in Central Park, introduced to each other by their dogs. They had become Brooke's best friends. She confided in them and trusted their advice.

The car headed north to her studio apartment in a brownstone on 74th Street. Arriving before her friend, she opened a bottle of wine, poured two glasses, and peeled off her work clothes—white silk blouse, turquoise linen skirt, and matching jacket. She brushed her long, brown hair and peeked into the mirror.

Her green eyes were bloodshot from too much champagne. *So what if I get drunk? It's Friday. I have tomorrow off. What a bitch! And after I worked so hard to win her account. Lloyd better make this good. I don't want to be shunted off onto some unimportant account.* She pulled a shift over her head.

Brooke had been with Gibbon & Walters Advertising for four years. Her first job out of grad school, it demanded a ton of overtime. Proud of her accomplishment, she had worked hard to get the promotion to Account Supervisor.

A sardonic smile curled her lips when she thought about her parents' reaction. *They'd probably say—good, time to leave the corporate prison and get a worthwhile job.* They had been killed in a car accident when she was ten. She'd been raised by her maternal grandmother, Ruth Quincy. She called her "Nan," short for Nana, which Brooke felt too old to call anyone. *I'm twenty-eight, not five.*

Brooke's parents had been counter-culture types, aging hippies, leftover from the 70's. They had believed in legalizing marijuana, were vegetarians, and recycled everything they could lay their hands on. Her father, Jim Felson, had been a teacher. Her mom, Mary Lou, a social worker. Brooke was their only child–their way of not contributing to over-population.

When the police had found pot in their car, they surmised the drug had caused the accident. The levels in her dad's blood had confirmed their finding. Since the information had been leaked to Brooke, she'd become enraged, venting her frustration on her memories of them.

Because she missed them so much, she resented her parents for what she perceived as their careless attitude, their laissez-faire outlook on life. She'd guessed more responsible behavior would mean they'd be alive today. She ended up hating everything they had stood for.

When she was young, she'd adored her kind, loving parents with every fiber of her being. After they were taken away, she'd been nonresponsive almost to the point of comatose. When she found out it might have been their fault, her overwhelming sadness had turned to rage. She resented what she called their "irresponsible attitude" and strove to be their opposite—a mature, responsible, corporate success story.

The buzzer sounded the arrival of Miranda and her pugs, Romeo and Juliet. Brooke handed her friend a glass of Cabernet. The pugs drank from the water bowl Brooke kept filled for guest dogs then curled up on the area rug. The two women got comfy on the sofa.

After explaining what had happened—slower this time—Brooke settled back into the cushions. "It's not like Lloyd didn't try."

"Did he? Are you sure about him?"

"What do you mean 'sure'?"

"How long have you been dating him?"

"Six months."

"And yet, he doesn't stick up for you?"

"It's a client. You have to do what they want."

"Do you? What about love? Devotion? Support?"

"Lloyd has other strengths."

"Like what?" Miranda took a sip.

"He's good in bed." Brooke blushed at her own admission.

"It's not enough. Now, what's going to happen?"

"I don't know." Brooke moved her wine glass from hand to hand.

"You won't get fired, will you?"

"Of course not! God. What a disaster. No way. Lloyd would never fire me."

"Never say never. No one's indispensable."

Tears filled Brooke's eyes. "Would he do that to me? After everything we've shared?"

Miranda put her hand on Brooke's arm. "I didn't mean to get you upset. But sometimes, life sucks. All I'm saying is it might not be a bad idea for you to think about finding a new job."

Brooke bent down and petted Romeo, who was lying at her feet. "You're probably right."

Miranda picked up the television remote. "Let's see what's on. Maybe a movie. Do you have any popcorn?"

"I think so. And I bought chocolate yesterday." The two women found *The Holiday*. Brooke put the popcorn in the microwave, and Miranda opened the box of candy.

"Chocolate caramels, my favorite!" Miranda took one out.

"Me, too. God, they'll cure anything."

"It's not like everything is perfect in my life, Brooke. I don't want you to be where I am."

"You look like you're doing okay."

"Some days, maybe. Let's not get into it. The movie's coming on," Miranda said, turning her attention back to the television. Brooke put the popcorn in a bowl, popped open a couple of Cokes, and propped her feet up on the coffee table.

DESPITE THE COOL, MAY air, Preston Carpenter unzipped his light-weight jacket. Overheated from running in Central Park with three pugs, the man needed to cool off. The sun shone down on the daffodils and tulips, making their yellows, reds, purples, and pinks blaze.

Pres parked his butt on a bench and doled out treats to the waiting dogs.

Two of them, Fred and Ginger, belonged to Ruth Quincy. Pres walked the pair every Sunday morning and often during the week when he took his own pug, Buddy. The three played well together and amused Pres with their antics. Ruth tried to pay him, but he protested. He didn't tell her being near her granddaughter, Brooke, was payment enough.

Pres had developed a huge crush on Brooke. She visited Ruth every Sunday for brunch. Pres timed his pick-up and delivery of Freddy and Ginger to coincide with Brooke's visits, hoping to talk to her, maybe ask her out. But when he did see her, he got tongue-tied, and she brushed him off as the help, the dog walker, and nothing more.

Her presence reduced him to a lovesick thirteen-year-old, tripping over his own feet to open the door for the woman of his dreams. He was frustrated. *I'm thirty, experienced with women. Why does she affect me this way?*

He checked his watch. *Only ten. She never arrives before eleven.*

"Okay, guys. We've got to kill another forty minutes." He pushed to his feet and led the dogs to a field adjacent to the Great Lawn. He threw a *Cuz* ball, and they ran around like crazy, chasing the oddly bouncing toy. After half an hour, they stretched out on the grass, panting, to cool off.

"Okay, okay. I get it. Playtime's over." Pres took hold of the leashes and led the pooches out of the park. They arrived at Ruth's building, The Huntington, a posh high-rise on Central Park West.

Rocky, the doorman, greeted Pres and petted the animals. When they got off the elevator, Ruth opened the door, and Pres unhooked the pugs. They congregated immediately at the water bowls in the kitchen.

"Coffee?" asked the attractive woman with stylish white hair. Dressed in khaki slacks, she wore a grass-green T-shirt that brought out the green in her eyes—the same shade as her granddaughter's.

He narrowed his eyes. "What's up?"

"She's not here yet. So I thought..."

"I see. You know, don't you?" He sensed color gathering in his cheeks.

"Why do you think I hired you to walk the dogs on Sunday? You're perfect for her."

"You know, and I know, but somebody forgot to tell Brooke."

"Come." Ruth took his arm and escorted him to her dining room. The table displayed a glamorous brunch with Limoges china and sterling silver flatware. A silver tea service awaited. She showed him to a chair then poured two cups of coffee.

"Scone?" she asked, offering him a plate piled high.

"Breaking bread with the help? What'll Brooke say?" He took one and broke off a piece.

"She *is* a bit of a snob, isn't she?"

He raised his eyebrows in response.

"Her mother wasn't. Brooke needs to grow up. Stop this silliness and get back to her roots." Ruth shook her head then lightened her beverage with real cream.

"What was her mother like?"

"Mary Lou was sweet. Gentle. A social worker with the softest heart. She'd cry at the drop of a hat. Or laugh. She loved calico cotton dresses, country, and folk music, cooking, and sewing. And Brooke. She took after me." Ruth's face glowed with pride.

"What happened to Brooke?"

"She was ten when they died. It nearly destroyed her. She idolized her mother and father. They were a close family. A fever kept her from being in the car with them. I thank God." Ruth's voice shook. She turned her gaze from the window and stared into her cup.

The sound of a key in the lock interrupted their private conversation. Brooke entered, wearing a pink calico, short-sleeved dress, and a beige leather jacket. Her brow was furrowed, and she appeared distracted.

She's beautiful. Pres's stare traveled slowly from her glossy, dark brown hair down to her pink flats. His groin tightened slightly, and his mouth went dry.

She looked up, and their gazes met. But the heat he'd hoped to see wasn't there. "Hi, Pres. Didn't expect you." She put a bag of bagels and smoked salmon on the table.

"Dear, dear. Put it on a platter. You're ruining the look of the table."

"Sorry, Nan. I wasn't thinking." She marched into the kitchen.

"You can stop drooling, Pres," Ruth whispered.

"She looks—today-oh my God."

"Your day'll come. Have faith." Ruth poured a cup for the young woman and refreshed the other two. Brooke joined them, carrying a silver platter with the salmon, cream cheese, and bagels artfully presented. "Better, dear."

"Looks beautiful," Pres said. His blue eyes tried to make contact with her green ones, but she kept her gaze on her coffee.

"Yeah. Thanks."

"How was your week?" Ruth asked.

"Shitty. Oops, sorry, Nan."

" It's fine. I'm no prig."

"Well, then. Shitty. Double shitty. Triple shitty."

"What happened?"

"I don't want to talk about it."

Of course, she doesn't want to talk about her shitty week in front of me. I should leave. I don't belong here. He stood up. "Time to go. Buddy," he called. The pug responded, trotting into the dining room.

"Must you? You just got here." Ruth's brows knitted.

"I'm sure he has other dogs to walk, Nan. We shouldn't keep him," Brooke said, spreading cream cheese on half a bagel.

"Actually, Ruth's are the only dogs I walk."

"Hope your business picks up."

He shrugged and sighed. *She's not listening. Why do I bother? She'll never notice me.* A heaviness lodged in his legs, but he forced them to move. Ruth accompanied him to the door. He stopped for a second to watch Brooke. She was standing at the window, munching on her food. His gaze roamed over her body. At six two, he preferred taller women, like Brooke. He guessed her to be about five foot seven or eight. Short girls made him feel like he was dating a little kid.

Her dress bunched slightly around her breasts. His fingertips tingled when he looked at them. He gauged they'd be a good fit in his hands. The neckline revealed a little cleavage, making his groin tighten even more. She leaned slightly, raising her hem. *Long, lean legs. Perfect.* And a rear end neither too small nor too big. He sighed. Making love to her would be a dream come true.

As if she sensed his stare, she turned and shot a small smile his way. He could feel a blush steal into his cheeks. *Being caught gawking at her like a teenager with a boner. Smooth, Preston, real smooth.* He lifted his hand to wave before he headed for the elevator with Buddy in tow.

BROOKE BIT INTO HER bagel slathered with cream cheese and topped with salmon. Finishing her story to Nan raised her appetite. She'd had to edit carefully, so as not to shock her grandmother. Still, she'd got the gist across.

"Caught fooling around in the office by a client? Wow, Brooke," Nan said.

Brooke choked on a small bite, coughing it up, her face heated.

"Thought you could fool me with your story. your round-about explanation? Honey, I'm no stranger to sex. How do you think your mother got here?"

"TMI, Nan." Brooke took a sip of coffee.

"Don't give me any bullshit. Tell it straight. I'm too old for nicey-nicey garbage. Nothing but the facts."

"Okay. Yeah. Lloyd was getting...frisky."

"Why should your client care? It was after hours. You're both single. You two are dating—unless, she's got a thing for him." Nan cut her half bagel in half again.

"No editorializing. I know you don't like Lloyd. Okay. But I do."

"Such poor taste for a Quincy," Nan muttered.

"He's so...so..."

"So what? So not good enough for you. And you turn your nose up at Pres Carpenter."

"He's nice. He's cute. But he's a dog walker, Nan. Lloyd has ambition, a future."

"So does Pres. He's not a dog walker. He just does it for me. He's a writer. And he made a significant sale on a movie script."

"Did he? Then when's the movie coming out?"

"He didn't say. But it was a six figure sale."

"Lloyd makes six figures every year. He's a management supervisor and maybe, someday, president of the agency."

"Well, la-di-da! President of a company doing crap with no value in this world—create advertising! What a waste of time, Brooke. At least Pres is creative. He writes. Lloyd is a bloodsucker, like all advertising people."

"Like me? I'm in advertising."

"Not like you. Your career in advertising is simply a temporary lapse in judgment."

"Temporary? I've been at it for four years."

"Temporary, yes. You'll come to your senses."

"Will I? I intend to make a success of it. Not like my parents, who could barely scrape together the money for rent and food."

"At least they did something worth doing. They helped people."

"Yeah? They were real responsible. They smoked pot. Smoked pot and drove. Real responsible."

"It happened a long time ago. Brooke, you have to forgive them."

"Forgive them? They're not here when I need them. They haven't been here for eighteen years. You think it's been easy, having no parents?"

"You had me."

"I know. I don't mean to put you down. But when everyone else had a mom and dad, I didn't. I needed them. And they were selfish and careless, so they died. I miss them every day." As her voice rose, tears clouded Brooke's eyes. She pushed away from the table. Freddy and Ginger barked. Brooke went into the bathroom to splash cold water on her face.

When she returned, Ruth was finishing her coffee. Brooke took a deep breath and sat down. "I'm sorry, Nan."

Ruth squeezed Brooke's hand. "Don't apologize. I understand. They made a mistake. But you must forgive them. Look at what they're missing—all these wonderful years with you. At least you're still here. You can make a difference in the world. Do the things they didn't have time to do."

"I'm going to. I'm going to be responsible and earn a bucket of money. I'm going to be a success in the corporate world."

"Ack! No, no."

"I'm going to take after Grandpa."

"Grandpa wasn't a very nice person, Brooke. He squeezed people, made money at the expense of his humanity."

"And look at this place. What he provided for you. You should be grateful."

"I am. I love my home. But I wish he could've done it by being a nicer person. I think he could have. He got sucked into the power thing."

"You married him, Nan."

"He wasn't power-hungry when we first started dating. He was the most idealistic man." She sighed as a small smile played on her lips.

"So what happened?"

"He was going to run for office, make a difference. After deciding he'd raise the money himself so he wouldn't be beholden to backers, he got carried away with the money-making part and forgot about the politics."

"Why haven't you told me this before?"

"I didn't want to trash him to you, sweetie. He was good to me, but not to others."

"I'm not going to be mean. Smart, instead. I'm going to be so good at what I do, no one can afford to fire me."

Ruth smiled at her granddaughter. "I only want you to be happy."

"I will be." Brooke fingered the cotton fabric of her skirt. "I love this dress. I think it's my favorite of Mom's."

"It's perfect on you. You look like her." Ruth cupped her cheek.

"Except for the Felson nose."

Ruth laughed. "I know you dress like this for me. It does make me happy to see you wear Mary Lou's things."

"They remind me of Mom, too."

"You're a beautiful girl, Brooke. You don't need sleazy Lloyd."

"He's okay. You'll see."

Ruth sighed. "Go your own way, then. I wish you luck."

They finished their meal. Brooke stowed the leftover food in the fridge and leashed the dogs "Shall I take them for a walk?"

Ruth checked her watch. "Perfect. Mary's coming over to watch *Mr. Lucky* with me. They never watch Cary Grant movies at the senior center, and her roommate is napping. Thank you, dear."

Brooke kissed Nan's cheek and headed for the lobby. The sun had warmed the day, so she opened her jacket and took a deep breath.

"You had a long walk this morning with Buddy, so I'm not going to take you to The Great Lawn again, okay?" The pugs turned to look at her with raised brows. She steered them toward the park as she plotted a route in her head.

Suddenly, Freddy bolted, yanking the leash out of her hand. He went tearing around behind a huge boulder. Brooke called his name, but the dog paid no attention. She tightened her hold on Ginger and ran after him.

As she rounded the corner, she ran smack into something hard and bounced off, landing on her rear end on the grass. Ginger screeched to a halt and barked, jumping up on the leg of the person who had blocked Brooke. She looked up into the sky blue eyes of a tall, brown-haired man in tight jeans and T-shirt.

To keep reading, click here to find the ebook and paperback on Amazon.com:

AMAZON
https://www.amazon.com/dp/B014X9QHMS
AMAZON U.K.
https://www.amazon.co.uk/dp/B014X9QHMS
AMAZON CANADA
https://www.amazon.ca/dp/B014X9QHMS
AMAZON AUSTRALIA
https://www.amazon.com.au/dp/B014X9QHMS

About the Author

Jean Joachim is an award-winning, USA Today best-selling romance author whose books have hit the Amazon Top 100 list in the U.S. and abroad since 2012. She writes sports romance, small town romance, big city romance, and romantic suspense.

Jean has over 60 books in ebook, print and audio. She writes fulltime, never far from her secret stash of black licorice. An avid bird and dog fan, she has a fondness for chickadees and pugs. A music lover, especially classical, she's married, has two grown sons and lives in New York City. She'd love to hear from you, email her at: sunnydaysbook@gmail.com Find her books on her website: http://www.jeanjoachimbooks.com

THERE ARE PUG RESCUES run by volunteers all across the United States. Anything you can do to help, from making calls, to fostering, from transporting to helping with fund-raising would be appreciated. Donations, even small ones, are most welcome. The money pays for veterinary care for abused or neglected pugs.

The mission of these rescues is to find loving forever homes for pugs who have lost theirs. If you want to help, Google "pug rescue", there's sure to be one near you.

Books by Jean C. Joachim

ECHOES OF THE HEART

HEATHER & MIKE: THE ONE THAT GOT AWAY

SANDY & RAFE: SECOND PLACE HEART

LIZ & NICK: NO REGRETS

PAIGE & BILL: ONE FINE DAY

ANTHOLOGY

HOCKEY

THE FINAL SLAPSHOT

BOTTOM OF THE NINTH

DAN ALEXANDER, PITCHER

MATT JACKSON, CATCHER

JAKE LAWRENCE, THIRD BASEMAN

NAT OWEN, FIRST BASE

BOBBY HERNANDEZ, SECOND BASE

SKIP QUINCY, SHORT STOP

EXTRA INNINGS

FIRST & TEN SERIES

GRIFF MONTGOMERY, QUARTERBACK

BUDDY CARRUTHERS, WIDE RECEIVER

PETE SEBASTIAN, COACH

DEVON DRAKE, CORNERBACK

SLY "BULLHORN" BRODSKY, OFFENSIVE LINE

AL "TRUNK" MAHONEY, DEFENSIVE LINE

HARLEY BRENNAN, RUNNING BACK

OVERTIME, THE FINAL TOUCHDOWN

A KING'S CHRISTMAS

THE MANHATTAN DINNER CLUB

RESCUE MY HEART

SEDUCING HIS HEART
SHINE YOUR LOVE ON ME
TO LOVE OR NOT TO LOVE

HOLLYWOOD HEARTS SERIES

IF I LOVED YOU
RED CARPET ROMANCE
MEMORIES OF LOVE
MOVIE LOVERS
LOVE'S LAST CHANCE
LOVERS & LIARS
His Leading Lady (Series Starter)

NOW AND FOREVER SERIES

NOW AND FOREVER 1, A LOVE STORY
NOW AND FOREVER 2, THE BOOK OF DANNY
NOW AND FOREVER 3, BLIND LOVE
NOW AND FOREVER 4, THE RENOVATED HEART
NOW AND FOREVER 5, LOVE'S JOURNEY
NOW AND FOREVER, CALLIE'S STORY (prequel)

MOONLIGHT SERIES

SUNNY DAYS, MOONLIT NIGHTS
APRIL'S KISS IN THE MOONLIGHT
UNDER THE MIDNIGHT MOON
MOONLIGHT & ROSES (prequel)

LOST & FOUND SERIES

LOVE, LOST AND FOUND
DANGEROUS LOVE, LOST AND FOUND

NEW YORK NIGHTS NOVELS

THE MARRIAGE LIST
THE LOVE LIST
THE DATING LIST

PINE GROVE SERIES

UNPREDICTABLE LOVE
BREAK MY HEART
RENOVATING THE BILLIONAIRE
YOU BELONG TO ME
JUST ONE KISS
REWRITE THE STARS

SHORT STORIES

SWEET LOVE REMEMBERED

HOLIDAY HEARTS

CHAMPAGNE FOR CHRISTMAS
CHRISTMAS DUET
HANUKKAH HEARTS
SANTA'S SURPRISE
THE FINAL SLAPSHOT
THE HOUSE-SITTER'S CHRISTMAS
THE HOUSE-SITTER'S COUNTRY CHRISTMAS
TUFFER'S CHRISTMAS WISH

Don't miss out!

Visit the website below and you can sign up to receive emails whenever Jean C. Joachim publishes a new book. There's no charge and no obligation.

https://books2read.com/r/B-A-MDPF-HUVG

BOOKS 2 READ

Connecting independent readers to independent writers.